THE
ARTHURIAN
⊙MEN

MYSTERY NOVELS BY G. G. VANDAGRIFF

Cankered Roots
Of Deadly Descent
Tangled Roots

THE
ARTHURIAN
OMEN

A Novel of Suspense

G. G. VANDAGRIFF

SHADOW
MOUNTAIN

All characters in this book are fictitious, and any resemblance to actual persons, living or dead, is purely coincidental.

Library of Congress Cataloging-in-Publication Data

Vandagriff, G. G.
  The Arthurian omen / G. G. Vandagriff.
    p. cm.
  ISBN 978-1-59038-863-1 (pbk.)
  1. Manuscripts—Fiction.   2. Wales—Fiction.   I. Title.
  PS3572.A427A89 2008
  813'.54—dc22   2007046633

Printed in the United States of America
Malloy Lithographing Incorporated, Ann Arbor, MI

10   9   8   7   6   5   4   3   2   1

To David
for thirty-five years
of more than magic

acknowledgments

To Sandra Whitaker, for her delight and encouragement in this project.

To my sister, Buffy Haglund, for her humor and loyalty.

To Anna Stone, for her selfless reading and editing.

To Kathleen Petty, for encouragement through the storms.

To Suzanne Brady, for her bravery in telling me what needed to be done.

To Jana Erickson, for her unbounded enthusiasm and support.

To scholar Dr. Geoffrey Ashe, for his valuable research on King Arthur.

And, lastly, to David, for his stunning poetry.

A NOTE TO THE READER

Americans generally suppose the terms *England* and *Britain* to be interchangeable, but in fact, the country now known as England was called Britain and its inhabitants Britons until the invasion of the Anglo-Saxons after the fall of Rome. Britons were Romanized, Christianized Celts—fierce, loyal, and determined to preserve their civilization from the barbaric invaders. The Anglo-Saxon "infidels" drove the Britons west to Wales (*Cymru* in the old tongue).

In Arthurian legend, King Arthur rose to power in Wales and succeeded in uniting the island once more under British rule during the Camelot years of the fifth century. The Welsh, modern descendants of the ancient Celts, have nurtured the legend that one day this Once and Future King will return to rule his kingdom again, not from Windsor Castle but from a resurrected Celtic Camelot.

PROLOGUE

WALES
MARCH 1409

Brother Gruffyd's old heart trembled with excitement. He sat staring at his find. At last. The omen they had all been awaiting—a confirmation that the magic of the Once and Future King was abroad in the land, that his hand was at work in the present rebellion.

With thick, shaking hands, Brother Gruffyd caressed the old parchment documents. Written in Latin in the round Breton script, they were embellished in gold Celtic knotting with maps in colors still brilliant. The details of Arthur's Gallic campaigns. He was actually holding them in his ordinary, mortal hands—hands that had done nothing more than pray, carve, and tend sheep during all that he remembered of his life. Never, even in a boyhood spent in heroic dreams, had he imagined that he, Gruffyd ab Blydn, would be an Instrument. Only the strongest of Arthurian magic could account for the manuscript's being here, waiting for this moment, just behind the wall in his cell.

Believers had been seeking it for three centuries. Doubters had

1

said that no one and nothing could prove that Arthur had ever existed, had ever reigned over all of Britain and Gallic Normandy. Anglo-Saxon fools! In his hands was the evidence that Arthur was real, far grander than even legend had made him. He had conquered Gaul.

As a lad, Brother Gruffyd had listened for hours while his father, a bard of great renown, recounted tales of King Arthur and the old Wales, ancient Cymru. For the young Gruffyd, his jewel-green land had been dressed in a mist of enchantment, where Celtic goddesses led and heroes followed, where strength and valor were proved not only by might but by virtue.

Now Cymru's time was here again. Prince Owain Glyndwr had united his country against the English infidels, just as Arthur had. He even flew Arthur's standard, the Red Dragon.

To be sure, the Welsh prince was in peril at the moment, besieged at the castell close by. Henry, that cursed son of the English king, claimed to be victorious. Cymru was black with his burning and pillaging. If Glyndwr's forces could not hold him, he would take the castell.

Brother Gruffyd put up his rough cowl and thrust the manuscript inside one loose sleeve. There was no doubt about what he must do—take it immediately by the monks' secret entrance to the castell. The power of this omen was inestimable. There was no more magic name in all of Cymru than that of King Arthur. Awaiting the day of his return, Cymru alone had remained the guardian of his legends, his language, his ancient religion. Now! An account of the triumphant Gallic campaign—just at the moment when Prince Owain was fighting this descendant of the Gauls, the Norman pretender, the barbarian who had decreed himself the Prince of Wales.

To know he was on Arthur's quest, repeating Arthur's deeds,

would surely invest Prince Owain with the powers of the Divine. Brother Gruffyd knew his timely find was no accident.

The night air was cold and raw, but spring was approaching. He could almost smell the scent of the summer's wild roses that would cover the slate wall that bounded Dafydd ab Huw's fields. Barefoot on the rocky slope, Brother Gruffyd made his way down the hidden path below the monastery leading to the castell. Even at this season, it was nearly impassable with wiry heather and boulders.

Squinting in the darkness, he made out what looked like a small, moving torch. Alarmed, he scurried back up the trail, secreting himself behind a boulder, clutching at the parchment in his sleeve. His toes were freezing, but he tried not to heed them.

Sounds carried in the still spring night, low, deep laughter and voices—English voices. An advance party of Henry's men, come to spy out the land.

His heart thundered so that he could hardly hear. Gritting his teeth, he willed it to slow. He must think. Should he still try to reach Prince Owain?

Brother Gruffyd agonized as sweat broke out all over his body, running rivers inside his habit despite the cold. Could he, an old man, possibly outwit these young, fit soldiers and make it to the castell? The pasture was an open field. Without doubt, he would be caught before he could get there. If it were only his life, of course, he wouldn't hesitate. But what of the manuscript? What would happen to it, if he were captured? It could be lost again, perhaps forever. Destroyed by infidels.

He watched helplessly as a party of three spies scrambled past him. They smelled foreign, barbaric. He sensed their bloodlust and hate.

If the prince had fled, they would believe he had come here, to this obscure place in the mountains, for safety. But they would not ask questions. Henry was the destroyer. These men would return with an army that would burn and smash Brother Gruffyd's monastery until not two stones were left standing one atop another. And everyone would be slain. Henry would never forgive the Brothers of Castell *cadarn a'i safle grymus ar ben y graig* for supporting Owain Glyndwr against the English king. The old monk had no doubt that the soldiers would leave behind only smoking ruins and the bodies of holy men for the crows to gorge upon.

Panic galvanized him at last. He must secure the manuscript. He knew a more direct though far more tortuous way to the monastery. Luckily, the moon was half full, and it was a clear night. The heather impeded him but cushioned his feet from the sharp rocks as he labored up the hill. Once the spies located the monk's retreat, they would be back with an army by dawn.

Reaching his cell, Brother Gruffyd debated what to do with his treasure. This, he knew, was his first responsibility. If the monastery were to burn . . . the floor! The floor was made of fitted stones, one of which he had carved in the long night hours when he couldn't sleep. It bore the sign of Arthur's dragon holding aloft the Celtic cross. It would not burn. Going to the stables, he secured a large pitchfork.

He worked steadily to dislodge the stone, sweat streaking down his face, his heart beating erratically. Doubtless it was a bad sign, but he could not stop. What he was doing was too important. It was his sacred duty to preserve this relic of Arthur for some future day. Some day more favorable than this one. Such a day would come. The so-called Prince Henry might ravage the country until no one was left, but he could never destroy the spirit of Cymru. It was eternal. It would live on in the hills, the rivers, the land, until Arthur returned to reclaim them.

Finally, the stone loosened, and Brother Gruffyd dug out a cavity beneath. He savored the strong smell of earth. This was his Cymru—

thick, black, magical. This piece of ground had not been disturbed in almost two hundred years. It would make a fitting vault. Carefully wrapping the manuscript in the skins his father had given him years before, he put them into a pewter box that formerly had stored candles. He secreted his treasure in the ground, fitted the stone back into place, and beat it with the handle of the pitchfork. Then he prayed.

The monastery bell chimed out the futile alarm. Henry's army was upon them. Now that the manuscript was safe, Brother Gruffyd felt nothing but relief. Replacing the cowl over his head, he fled toward the giant mountain that had sheltered his community for centuries.

Some time later, as he sought a foothold on the cliff face, the monk turned to look back down at the monastery that had been his home for fifty years. As he watched the flames, a bitter wind carried the smoke to his nostrils. The acrid smell of defeat. Grief overwhelmed his former relief. Tears filmed his eyes. Below him, Henry's men rode into sight, their torches ablaze. He could hear their shouts, and though the words were unfamiliar, their meaning was clear.

Black remorse seized him. He turned his eyes from the flames destroying the monastery and his former life. There was no place for him in Cymru now. He lacked the faith of his forefathers. He should have trusted to the magic of the omen and reached Prince Owain in time for him to stage a miraculous victory.

Turning his face to the cliff wall, he felt his heart convulse, as though it would wrench itself free from him in shame. Pain shot through his back and down his arm. Even as he fought to hang onto the rocks of the cliff face, he could sense his strength ebbing. Now in his darkening mind's eye, he saw the precious document trampled under the feet of Henry's men. Arthur and all his glory under the feet of these infidels! It was too much. His old heart broke, his hands released their hold, and his body arced through the morning mist, two hundred feet down toward the valley floor.

chapter one

The telephone call came at the end of a frustrating day. Maren had just pulled off her long black wig and given her daughter some frozen yogurt when she heard the ring.

"Maren? It's Rachael."

She sat down on a nearby chair with a thump. Her sister, who was in Oxford for the summer, hadn't called her in five years. "Hi" was all she could manage in her surprise.

"Listen. I think I know where it is—the Breton manuscript."

"The what?" Maren tried to switch gears from a day of tracking drug dealers to Rachael's world of Celtic scholarship. Why in the world was she calling?

"Remember when Geoffrey Ashe came out with that book, *Discovering King Arthur?*" Maren detected her sister's impatience.

"The one you and Daddy were so excited about?"

"Yes. Oh, Maren, I wish Daddy were still alive. He'd be so excited about this! It's the ultimate treasure hunt. Ashe built his whole theory

7

of who Arthur really was on the secondhand evidence of this manuscript. But no one even knew for sure it existed."

Some of her sister's enthusiasm penetrated her tired brain. Arthur was still common ground between them. From the time they were little girls their Welsh father had nurtured them on legends of the great King of the Britons, taking them to Arthur's supposed birthplace on the angry coast of Cornwall and then to pastoral Cadbury Castle, the hypothetical site of Camelot.

"Yes," Maren said slowly. "I think I remember now. Ashe thought Arthur was some Roman general who conquered Gaul, didn't he?"

"Right!" Rachael crowed. "He based it all on the theory that this fifth-century manuscript told about Arthur's deeds in Gaul—the same deeds the Roman general is *known* to have done."

"I don't remember the details, Rachael. But I'll take your word for it. And you think you've found this manuscript?"

"I think I know where to find it. I want you to come over and help me hunt for it. It would be just like old times, Mareny. It would make me so happy."

Maren was stunned. Rachael wanted *her*? It would make her *happy*? Then her practical mind took over. "You realize what it would mean to the world if you found this?" she asked. "If you could prove for sure who King Arthur was and that he really existed?"

"It's probably priceless, I know. But I don't care about that. I'm going to give it to the Arthurian Society. It could be the beginning of a whole new era . . ."

"Rachael, you must take care. There are people who would kill for such a thing! It could be the greatest find since Tutankhamen!"

"You've spent too much time chasing drug dealers. Don't worry, I haven't told a soul. You will come, won't you?"

Maren thought frantically, casting her eyes around her small and tidy kitchen and then resting them on her flame-haired daughter who was looking at her out of Patrick's big blue eyes. There was almost nothing she wanted more than to be happily reconciled with her sister. This was clearly the opportunity of a lifetime, but . . . "I'm sorry, Rach. I can't go into it, but things are really unsettled right now. I don't think I should leave Claire." Her four-year-old daughter was the only person in the world who could take priority over her sister's plea.

"If you don't want to leave her with Ian, you can always take her to stay with Mother or Robert and Kathryn. They're crazy about her."

Maren wondered at Rachael's instinct that what was wrong was connected to Ian. But, of course, she was right. And Claire's uncle and aunt had provided a lot of stability in her life since Maren's remarriage. Her daughter had a complete wardrobe, a playhouse, and even a pony at their lakeshore mansion. She needn't tell Ian where she was going. She could just leave. If Claire were safely taken care of, there was nothing to keep her.

"Any clues about what I need to pack?" she asked, allowing a wave of excitement to overcome the weariness that never left her.

"Jeans and boots. And bring me some while you're at it."

"I'll try to catch a plane tomorrow night, Rach. Where are you?"

"Somerville College. I'll expect you. And remember, not a word to anyone."

"You, too. I know what you're like when you get carried away."

When Rachael at last hung up, Maren kept the phone to her ear in wonderment. That's how she happened to hear the click. Ian, her husband of three months, had been listening on the extension.

chapter two

The man who sometimes knew himself as Prince Owain Glyndwr sat, unaware of his more dangerous personality, looking at the woman across the table from him in the candlelight. "So what is it you think you've found?" He smiled the smile that won hearts without effort. Waiters clattered about them with plates of oysters and steaming bowls of onion soup.

Rachael looked like the cat who'd swallowed the canary, her classic features framed by burning red hair. "What makes you think I've found something?"

"I'm a trained observer. I know you're on some kind of quest. You've spent all day in the Bodleian Library. Your eyes are sparkling. You look impish." He toyed idly with his crème brûlée. This was all a game. Would she tell him?

"It's really the magic, though, isn't it?" she asked, seeming to test him.

"The magic?" He raised an eyebrow.

"You're a Celt. You know exactly what I'm talking about."

Puzzled, he wondered if she was a bit daft. "I'm afraid you're wrong. I actually have no idea."

Laughter gurgled from her. "You look so uncomfortable. So British. Relax. I'm not nuts."

For some reason, her words offended him. He could feel anger stirring somewhere inside his breast. Closing his eyes for a moment, he took a deep breath. What was wrong with him? These powerful emotions were coming so often now that he seemed a stranger to himself. And he suspected there were blanks in his memory, as well.

"How much do you know about King Arthur?" she asked.

The query kaleidoscoped his world. Lightning struck in the back of his head, and the restaurant became a baronial hall, the waiters, minions. He knew suddenly he was a ruler of legendary power. "Arthur is my liege lord," he said solemnly.

"I thought you might feel like that," she said, her grin merry. "You're Celtic to the bone, aren't you?"

He swelled in rage. "My country is dissolving, Rachael. The English are committing cultural genocide. Only a quarter of the Welsh know their own language." Ancient passions roiled within him. "We've been gutted by the miners and the slate barons. Arthur wouldn't recognize his own homeland. The Celts are losing their identity."

"What if I told you I knew the location of a manuscript that could prove King Arthur was a real person, not just a legend?"

Now there was only Rachael, curiously sexless—a sprite out of myth. Had she been summoned by the magic?

"What are you saying?"

She leaned toward him, confiding. "I know all about the divine void you feel. I feel it, too. I think Arthur has the answers. And I can prove he was real."

It *was* the magic. The timing could not be accidental. "You have found the Breton manuscript?"

"So you know what it is, then?"

"Of course I do. Where is it?" This must be the divine seal to his plans. It was the eleventh hour—a matter of days. Arthur's omen would rally his countrymen behind him as nothing else could.

She gave a tiny, knowing smile. "My sister is coming. I know right where to look. We're going to find it together."

All at once, he was maddened beyond reason. Did this woman have any idea what she had discovered? How could she? How could some naive American schoolteacher possibly understand the importance of such a document to the future of the world? Tossing a handful of five-pound notes on the table, he rose. "Let's leave."

The night had the crystal perfection of early September. The moon was full, shining down on Rachael's hair. Infuriating fairy sprite. He would choke the secret out of her if he couldn't get it any other way.

CHAPTER THREE

APPROACHING HEATHROW AIRPORT
ENGLAND

As her plane circled to land, Maren closed her briefcase. She knew she was missing a vital link somewhere. Every time she and Agent Sam Reynolds found a witness who was ready to plea bargain what he knew about the Don Benito drug cartel in exchange for a lighter sentence, that witness disappeared. Someone close to them knew exactly what they were trying to do—find the American kingpin of the cartel, nail him for Patrick's death, and put him out of business. And that someone was always a step ahead of them. His or her identity remained a mystery.

Oh, Patrick, why were you so secretive? Why didn't you trust Sam or me with the name? And why, oh, why did you drive off without your bodyguards?

The familiar pain churned through her body, crushing her heart. Though the police had considered her first husband's death an accident, she knew that someone had forced his motorcycle over the median into oncoming traffic. A United States attorney, he was going to name the cartel's leader to the grand jury the very next day. But his case died with him. Cocaine still flowed into the United States from Colombia in even greater quantities now than it had a year and a half ago when Patrick had smashed himself against the great buttress of this American addiction.

Finishing the last of her cola, Maren handed her cup to the flight attendant. She hadn't slept at all, instead spending the flight looking over Sam's latest reports. She had been on hiatus from her job as a public defender since Claire's birth, but she might as well be working full time now that she had joined Sam on this crusade. Robert, her brother-in-law, spoke scathingly of her posing as a "Charlie's Angel." He didn't understand that this was the only alternative to pitching headlong into the bottomless void left in her life by Patrick's death. She had thought for a time that her remarriage would answer that need . . .

She wouldn't think of Ian now. She was going to see Rachael. They would make up for the past five years, and they were going to have an adventure together. Just like old times.

Oxford in the early morning had an almost reverential hush. Mists rose and swirled in the streets and up the golden walls, giving the spires that rose above the city an otherworldly feel. Old Tom, the bell at Christ Church, tolled the six o'clock hour. Somerville College should have just been awakening when Maren arrived.

But black and white police cars were parked next to the honey-stoned buildings. Paying her driver, Maren hoisted her duffel and briefcase and walked in her hiking boots and jeans to the porter's lodge. She stopped before she got there. Across the green lawn of the inner quadrangle, a team of paramedics was carrying a stretcher with a body bag on top of it. Ignoring the porter's shout, she ran, a terrible presentiment clawing its way to her brain.

"What's happened?" she asked a tall man in a plain gray suit who walked beside the stretcher. He looked like Cary Grant, her favorite actor in the old movies she loved. "Who is it?"

"Just let us by, please," he said impatiently.

"I'm Maren Southcott. From the States. I've just arrived to see my sister. Dr. Rachael Williams."

The handsome man stopped and searched her face, his peat brown eyes suddenly alert. "I'm sorry?"

"Who *is* that?" she asked again.

"Do you have any reason to believe it's your sister?"

"Just *tell* me!"

"Mrs.—er . . . Southcott, is it? I'm afraid it is Dr. Williams . . ."

Her heart dropped to her stomach, and she could feel the blood in her head following it. Rachael hadn't listened to her, after all. "How did she die? Are you a policeman or a doctor?"

"Scotland Yard. Chief Inspector Llewellyn. Why don't you come with me to the porter's lodge? I think you need to sit down. You look very faint . . ."

Gripping her arm, he supported her as they walked the short distance to the porter's lodge, a homely little room warmed by a small electric space heater. "She was murdered, wasn't she?" Maren asked, fighting off the blackness that narrowed her vision to a pinpoint.

She didn't know how many minutes she had been unconscious when she came to, lying stretched out on the floor. A paramedic was holding something vile under her nose. The Cary Grant policeman loomed over her.

"How are you feeling?" he asked.

"Have they taken her away yet?" She murmured the question, trying to quell her nausea. "I want to see her."

"I'm afraid she's not a pretty sight, Mrs. Southcott."

"I won't faint again. It's just that I haven't had much to eat and no sleep . . ."

"Fetch Mrs. Southcott a cup of hot sweet tea, porter, will you?"

When they unzipped the body bag, the first thing Maren saw was the brilliant color of her sister's hair, still alive as it framed her purple face with the bulging, vacant eyes.

"I warned her," she whispered, kneeling to clutch a handful of hair and hold it to her cheek. How had two girls who had played so happily in the back garden at dawn come to this gray, horrifying day? Into her mind sailed memories of innumerable treasure hunts— finding jade earrings in the rock garden, jeweled chopsticks in the Japanese garden, and a pair of tickets to France amid the hollyhocks. Tears fell on her cheeks. Rachael's last treasure hunt had undoubtedly been her undoing.

Chief Inspector Llewellyn helped Maren to her feet, while another policeman, whippet thin with colorless hair, zipped the bag closed once more.

"Did I hear you say you had warned her?" asked the chief inspector. "You expected this might happen?"

"Yes. She was on the track of a priceless manuscript, you see . . ."

He replied impatiently, "She was brutally strangled by someone's bare hands. I don't think this is a case of academic jealousy."

"I'd like to see her room," Maren said.

"When the forensics team is finished," he promised.

"Just what was this manuscript supposed to be?" the other policeman asked in a cultured accent.

"It would have proved the identity of King Arthur."

Llewellyn shook his head.

His subordinate whistled. "That would have been a find, indeed."

"How was she found?"

"A woman a couple of doors down came to borrow a tea coil. We suspect the killer was still in the room and escaped when the woman ran screaming into the hall."

When at last Maren was allowed into Rachael's temporary home, she tried to put herself in her sister's shoes. It was a standard

Somerville College room—blue walls, two narrow twin beds, one rumpled, with white chenille spreads. Between them was a window with a window seat overlooking the quadrangle and its plantings of autumn chrysanthemums. Llewellyn's theory was that the murderer had hidden behind the heavy drapes.

Rachael's laptop sat unmolested on her computer table. Shelves of books, a few written by her sister, dealt with some aspect or another of Celtic mythology or the Arthurian legend.

Her murder proves she was on to something, Maren thought, the first glimmer of feeling penetrating the black numbness. She would take her sister's body back to Chicago and hold a funeral for her mother's sake. Rachael herself would have preferred a windy pyre somewhere in Wales, but her mother needed her oldest daughter close by, next to her husband, so she could mourn them together. She would be heartbroken that her daughters hadn't fully mended the breach between them before Rachael's death. She had been so happy when she took Maren to the airport.

"Your father would be so pleased!" she had said.

Once the funeral was over, Maren would return. The killer hadn't been able to search for the clue, so unless Rachael had confided in him before she died, Maren and the murderer were crouching together at the starting line. She would find Rachael's manuscript— one last treasure hunt in honor of her slain sister—and she would present the treasure to the Arthurian society in her name.

In the process, Rachael's killer would undoubtedly have to be dealt with as well. Fortunately, Maren had had some self-defense training in the martial arts. Unfortunately, she was riddled with new grief that was almost more than she could bear.

chapter four

Chicago

The day of Rachael's funeral was made for a travel poster. The lake sparkled, the Gold Coast gleamed, and Michigan Avenue's opulence invited even the most world-weary shopper. After a long, humid summer, it was the first day to feel like fall. A new wind blew off Lake Michigan, fresh and clean-smelling, like a crisp schoolteacher coming to banish the lazy sultriness of summer.

Rachael had always loved school. How many autumns had they spent together, choosing their new school clothes at Marshall Fields, buying their school supplies at Walgreens? The smell of new crayons and rubber erasers inspired excitement—life was starting over. Anything could happen.

Almost choking on the nauseating sweetness of lilies and roses in the funeral chapel, Maren tried to banish the sight of her dead sister's face from her mind.

Rachael had been so lighthearted on the telephone. But the hand that had proffered the olive branch was now cold and lifeless and about to be interred. And her secret would go with her.

Remembering her last conversation with Rachael, Maren was tormented by the tiny click of the extension in Ian's office. She faced unthinkable possibilities. Did Ian, whom she had unaccountably married after knowing him scarcely a month, have anything to do with Rachael's death? He dealt in antiques. He would know what such a find would mean. And he was crooked. He undoubtedly had unscrupulous partners in the U.K. But why would they have killed Rachael before they found the manuscript? Had the clue been so obvious? Had they killed her to keep her from talking? The thought wouldn't leave Maren alone, haunting her night and day, causing her muscles to bunch and tangle, preventing her from eating, sleeping. It didn't really make any sense. It was just lately that she had come to realize she actually knew very little about her husband except that he was a very good actor. Despite her trained legal mind, she had always tended to think the best of people. That was why she was a public defender, for heaven's sake.

She had met Ian just last June at the garden party her brother-in-law Robert had bribed her into attending by buying a pony for Claire.

"Funny," said the stranger, who wore a silk cravat and spoke with a perfect BBC accent. "You don't look at all like a hog butcher."

She burst out laughing in spite of herself. "Carl Sandburg? Does all of Europe think that Chicago is still 'hog butcher to the world'?"

"'Stormy, husky, brawling,' and you all of five foot two."

"I do kickbox."

"I suppose it comes in handy, working on the South Side. Robert told me what you do for a living."

"Well, I've never actually had to use it," she admitted.

"Nevertheless, I'm forewarned. Would you like to go for a sail tomorrow? I've a new sloop."

Life had been so earnest lately. Would it hurt to take a day off? To go out on the lake? She hadn't been sailing since Patrick died. Maren felt a *sudden need to relax the springs of her obsession, even if it were just for a Sunday. "Is it all right if my daughter comes? She's my chaperone."*

"By all means. I adore her already. She has an excellent seat on a horse."

Life had been so complicated since Patrick's death. Ian seemed to offer nothing more complex than smooth, British wit, which was all she felt she could cope with. He made her smile and feel almost light-hearted again—and he was so seemingly civilized and fond of Claire. It had been a struggle to bring up her child without a father when Maren's own father had been the center of her world. In the weeks before their marriage, Ian took Claire on outings to the zoo and sailing on his boat. He had watched her gymnastics meet. And he had said he wanted other children, brothers and sisters for Claire. Maren hadn't wanted Claire to be an only child when her own life had been so rich because of her sister. And she knew it was foolish to think she could ever love anyone the way she had loved Patrick, so what more could she ask?

The question now was, Could Ian be so monstrous as to engineer the murder of her sister? Why did she even suspect it?

It was the other evidence. The robberies. She was still in shock over her husband's outright thievery.

Her vision of him had shattered. With her all-or-nothing thinking, it was but a short step to believing he might be behind Rachael's murder. And now she had two, seemingly unconnected murders in her life. What were the odds of such a thing? Guilt and grief combined like a tsunami to drag her out into the depths. Then she was gathered up by the wave and smashed against the shore of the make-do life she had constructed. It lay like sticks around her—her disastrous second marriage, Patrick's unsolved murder, the rift with her sister. And now, Rachael's strange death. That click. Ian had known about the manuscript. But what would anyone have to gain from killing Rachael? She hadn't even found the manuscript yet. It didn't add up. The same thoughts chased round and round in Maren's weary brain. She was back where she started.

"Where has Aunt Rachael gone? Why can't I see her?" The little flame-haired being by her side pulled her to the surface. Only Claire had kept her afloat this last week.

As a mediocre soprano dealt with "You Are the Wind beneath My Wings," Maren thought of how she could explain the inexplicable to her daughter. She felt piercingly inadequate. She knew in that moment that the last year and a half would have been more profitably spent on a quest for spiritual answers rather than on a personal vendetta. But how could Claire ever really be safe with Patrick's killer still at large?

"I don't know, Claire. There are some things even mommies don't know."

chapter five

OXFORD

Prince Owain Glyndwr slashed Rachael's mattress in fury. He could not accept that she had left no clue, no record of her find. Close to fifty books were strewn on the floor of the Somerville College room. Even the muesli jar was empty, its contents scattered across the linoleum floor.

Confound the woman! He hadn't suspected her of so much guile. Her secrecy had maddened him into murdering her when that was the last thing he should have done. Rachael's fear had made him feel invincible, half-beast, like the heroes of his Cymric bedtime stories. Poor Rachael had certainly not gone gentle into that good night.

Grabbing the muesli jar, he threw it against the wall and watched it shatter. The date was set. The plans were laid. The English prince's days were numbered, and soon he would know it. Failure was not a possibility.

If only he hadn't been interrupted that night. Some female named Cynthia knocking and barging in to borrow Rachael's hot water coil. He'd barely had time to withdraw into the shadow of the window embrasure before her screams began. At least she'd run out, giving him time to make his exit.

His hero's visage reflected back at him from Rachael's mirror. That manuscript could make the crucial difference, proving Arthur to be a man greater than legend and not some foppish myth. It was just what Cymru needed to give the fiery Celts a reason to burn again. The magic.

He smiled. As though making allowances for his temper, destiny was still with him. Rachael's sister. Maren Southcott, his own personal Celtic enchantress. Every great hero must be empowered by the magic of his beloved, and he had, at last, found her. He wasn't certain how or when it had happened, but suddenly she was *there* in his life. She would ensure his safety when the bullets of his enemies sought him.

Fingering one of Rachael's dresses—a moss green velvet—he recognized the color of his homeland, the color of Maren's round, expressive eyes. When she came back to Oxford to take up the search, he would be ready for her. Though not a classic beauty like her sister, she had a lithe athlete's body with straight mahogany brown hair that just brushed her shoulders. And that smile! She had been subdued at her sister's death, of course, but he had seen her smile once from a distance when someone had done her a kindness. She had pocketed his soul in that moment. One day soon, she would be his. No woman could resist him for long.

Her magic was potent. It was the elixir he needed. The people wanted a hero, and they would have one. It was time, past time, for a true prince to step to the fore with Arthur's omen, Arthur's power, Arthur's vision. Britain would rise again, no longer a sycophantic island off an emasculated continent but a brilliant power under the banner of Arthur, the Once and Future King!

Moving over to the small window, he stared out into the night, his mind full of words.

The dead of Cymru will not sleep.
The moon their signal, the Omen their light
The stars their shield, they shall fight.
They rise from long-forgotten tombs
Redeeming strangled holy lands.

Upon their bones, the flesh returns.
Within their skulls, the rage still burns,
Ne'er forgotten dreams live once again.
Through ancient fears and ancient tears,
Ever their King, Arthur
Returns to ancient thrones.

Green Britain breathes.
Free. Free. Free. Free.

chapter six

B y the time they left Maren's childhood home and her heartbroken mother, it was well past one o'clock. Claire was dozing in her car seat looking like a Pre-Raphaelite angel when Maren pulled up to their stone cottage in Glen Ellyn.

Ian's Jag? What was he doing home at this hour? He'd skipped the funeral, claiming he had business. Maren hadn't pressed it. Everything concerning Ian was on hold in her life.

Easing Claire out of her car seat, she tried hard not to jostle her daughter unnecessarily. So it was that entering quietly by the back door, she heard her husband's crisp accent through the front hallway back into the kitchen.

"I tell you, Griffith, it's the genuine article. I'm absolutely certain of it. You must try to have another look. Go in disguise and bribe the char or something. Maren's sister knew her Celts, but she couldn't possibly have had a clue to the real monetary value of her discovery."

Pause. Maren's heart raced, and she tightened her grip on her daughter.

"Listen, if this manuscript actually proves that King Arthur existed, it is one hot antiquity. He is the center of true religion to modern-day Celts. It will certainly rival the Book of Kells."

So! He *was* involved. Only her maternal instinct kept her daughter clasped in her arms as Maren absorbed the shock. He was speaking in an enthusiastic rush, far different from his lazy, upper-class drawl.

"She had found something concrete. Some sort of clue. She referred to a treasure hunt. And Maren told me this morning that she's going back to Oxford to finish up Rachael's 'business.' She's like a terrier with a bone. You can't imagine what she's like when she sets out to investigate something. I may have to finagle a little something with Claire to keep her here, or we won't stand a chance. I'll be there as soon as I can satisfactorily arrange things."

Like a mother bear with her cub, Maren backed out the door. She fumbled a still-dozing Claire back into her car seat and put the car in neutral with shaking hands, coasting backwards down her driveway. She didn't start the car until she was in the street.

Finagle a little something with Claire? Her mind spun, trying to attach itself to the reality of what she had heard. The man she had married *was* a monster.

Robert. She had to get Claire to Patrick's brother. To safety. She wasn't ever going back to that house. But first she had to get to the bank.

Maren gripped the wheel of her car with enough force to choke the life out of a human being. A specific human being. Her husband of three months. How had she come to marry such a man?

A cry escaped her, and Maren forced herself to pull over to the side of the road. Preoccupied with calming her mother, she hadn't cried at the funeral. But now, tears were smearing the streets, and sobs threatened to explode her chest and larynx. To punish herself as much as to divert her pain, she banged her head hard against the steering wheel.

She had to admit, deep inside, that it was more than Ian's seeming fondness for Claire. Like some modern-day Jane Eyre, she must have had a desire to conquer the elusive, the enigma. Since Patrick's murder, she had been casting about, striving to come to terms with the emptiness. How could she ever have thought Ian was the answer? Marriage was not a thing to be undertaken on a whim. Now she had to deal with the results. Not just for herself, but for Claire. And possibly, even probably, she had been responsible for the death of her sister. Who else could have killed her but this Griffith that Ian had been speaking to? According to Rachael, no one else knew about her lead. But why kill her *before* he had her secret? According to the conversation, she had not divulged it.

"Robert," she said breathlessly, as his secretary ushered her into the forest green enclave of her brother-in-law's office suite. Its tremendous effusion of tropical plants always reminded her of the Amazon. "I've got to make this quick. I may know who murdered Rachael."

Robert O'Neill's eyebrows rose toward the line of his thick red hair. He automatically strode toward her and took Claire. Her daughter cuddled into his white silk shirt, still sleepy.

"You've rushed in here to tell me this as if you're inviting us to dinner or something?"

"Listen, I don't have time to explain. I'm pretty sure Ian's involved. You were right about him. So right, in fact, that once he finds out I'm on to him, I don't think my life will be worth much. He's ruthless."

"You're serious." He collapsed into his chair, still holding his niece to him but clearly startled. His heavy Irish features, so ferocious in the courtroom, were accusing. "You're doing it again, aren't you, Maren? Just like after Patrick died. You think you can play detective."

"I know I'm not like Kathryn," she said, sinking into a dark green leather armchair that promptly swallowed her. "But I have taken a hiatus since Claire was born. It's just that I've got to straighten out this awful mess."

"You know, it absolutely amazes me that it was Rachael and not you who was murdered," her brother-in-law said. "She lived a quiet life in libraries. You say you've taken a hiatus, but you live in a state of risk—haunting crack houses, tracking informants, posing as a buyer."

"Robert . . ." Here she paused. She knew he couldn't understand that she was driven, not by revenge as much as a need to keep the world safe for Claire. While Patrick's nemesis was at large, while the drug cartel continued to flourish, countless lives were at risk, including that of her precious daughter. But now she must keep her temper at all costs. "Ian threatened Claire. I heard him. You're the only one who can keep her safe."

"What are you talking about?"

"He's crooked, Robert. I meant to tell you before the whole thing with Rachael. I'd just found out that he's a thief. And I think Rachael's death had something to do with this really valuable manuscript she knew about that he wants. I don't have time to go into it . . . I've got to get back to Oxford before Ian discovers what I'm up to." Looking at her daughter snuggled to Robert's chest, she felt tears sting again. "I heard him on the phone. I heard him threaten to do something to Claire to keep me away from Oxford."

"He did? The filthy Englishman! Maren, I know you think you're in the ring with him, but can't you resist a fight for once in your life? Why don't you just stay here?"

Not even Patrick had known the depth of the breach with Rachael. And now, if Ian was involved, there was the guilt for her death, as well. The tears fell, and she sniffed. "It's a sister thing," she said. "I've got to take responsibility for this, Robert. I'm the only one who heard that conversation. I'm the only one who knows Ian's involved." She sat up straighter in the womblike chair, keeping her head above the floodwaters. "And I'm going to find this thing for Rachael before Ian's bloodhounds do."

Robert's face was now speculative, his bright blue eyes narrowed. Like Claire's, they were the same color as Patrick's, but unlike his brother's, they were hard and calculating. Maren's daughter had fallen back asleep, unaware of the drama surrounding her. Robert put one hand to his face and rubbed the red stubble that always appeared in the afternoon, appraising her with a maddening coolness.

"I don't understand, Maren. What makes you so sure he had Rachael murdered?"

She told him about Ian overhearing the phone call from Rachael. It seemed years ago instead of just last week. "She wasn't confiding in anyone, so who else could it be but this Griffith character he was talking to today? He's probably a hit man or something."

He appeared to consider this. "All this must have been quite a shock to you."

She took a deep breath. "My world is upside down at the moment. I need your help. Two things. No, three. Are you with me?"

Robert put his head on one side. "Are you sure this is wise?"

"Claire is my family. I'm doing this to keep her safe. But I can't do it alone. That's why I want you and Kathryn to take her. Patrick knew how much you loved her, no matter how many squabbles the two of you had." Though Robert's criminal law practice consisted mostly of white collar criminals, Patrick had had little tolerance for his brother's occasional representation of petty drug traffickers.

"Well, of course we'll take Claire. She is obviously in danger. But I think it's crazy and unnecessary for you to go to England. A telephone call to Scotland Yard would take care of things, you know."

"Not to find Rachael's clue, whatever that is. Who knows what Ian's connections are? I tell you, someone's going to get their hands on that manuscript, and it's going to disappear. Ian will sell it to some wealthy Arab or someone like that.

"Now, that brings me to the second thing. I told you he was crooked. I've been thinking about this for a couple of weeks. I think he must be part of some stolen antiques ring."

Robert's eyes were suddenly keen. "What evidence do you have?"

"I'll put it all down in a statement in case something happens to me," she hedged. "It's not anything too concrete, but with your connections, I'm sure you could make something of it. I'll type something up and have a notary witness it."

His phone buzzed.

"It's all right, Madge," the lawyer said into the telephone. "Put him through." Covering the receiver, he mouthed, "Ian."

Robert scarcely had a chance to say hello before her husband began pelting him with staccato speech. Even on the other side of the desk, Maren could hear his sophisticated squawk. She gathered he had received a call from the bank about the withdrawal of all her funds. She had converted them to traveler's checks before coming to Robert's office, getting her passport and Rachael's laptop from her safety deposit box.

Ian was apparently alarmed because she hadn't come home from the funeral. Or so he said.

Her heart sped as it did when she began a marathon. Adrenaline infused her.

"I don't think you need to worry, Ian. She came to see me. Rachael's death made her realize she had never provided for Claire. She wanted to set up a will and trust without delay. You know how impulsive she is."

More squawks.

"She's not actually in the office at the moment. She just stepped down the hall. I can have her call you back, if you like."

Emphatic squawk. Then he lowered his tone, and Maren could no longer follow the conversation.

When he hung up, Robert was a changed man. His slightly patronizing air had gone, and he was someone she'd never seen before. Instead of the overweight ex-Notre Dame halfback who had viewed her with disfavor, he morphed into a steely executive, used to command. "I think the sooner you write that statement down and get out of here, the better," he told her.

His abrupt change of attitude surprised her. What had Ian said?

"Thank you, Robert, you're the only one I can turn to, right now."

"Mind you," his voice was gruff. "Claire's already lost one parent. Be careful." He stood. "You can use my computer for your statement. I'm going to take Claire with me into the coffee room. We have things to eat in there. My paralegal, Valerie, is a notary."

Maren sat down in Robert's desk chair. She knew she was as different from Kathryn as any woman could be. If anyone had been born to be a mother, it was Robert's wife. But fate had apparently decreed differently. And children were very important in the O'Neill clan. Patrick's sisters had half a dozen each.

Jerking her mind back to the here and now, she typed out her suspicions about her present husband.

Near the middle of August, I found a snuffbox in the pocket of Ian Southcott's sport coat. I recognized it immediately as one recently stolen from the home of my friend Alice Shipmann in Winnetka. Before I could photograph it, it was gone. I gradually became aware that many of my friends were missing small, portable antiques. Their losses coincided with our visits. They didn't put it together, but I did. I know that Ian must have criminal connections in order to fence the goods so quickly. I can identify people who have come to the house to see him. He has a very tight-knit group of friends. And then, in the UK is this man Griffith . . . Maren concluded her statement with an account of the phone call. *I think it very probable that Ian Southcott is behind the murder of my sister, Rachael Williams. His telephone conversation confirms that his contacts are international.*

There. She'd said it, in black and white. "Could you send in Mr. O'Neill's paralegal?" she asked Madge on the intercom.

Valerie Kensington proved to be a bleached blonde with acrylic fingernails, long-legged, stylish, and thin. Everything Maren was not. For an instant she seemed familiar, but Maren couldn't place her.

"Good to meet you," the paralegal said. "Call me Valerie, please." Despite her appearance, the woman had an air of studied competence.

"I have a statement here for you to notarize." Maren passed her the typed page.

Scanning it quickly, the blonde said, "This shouldn't be any problem. Just come with me a moment and show me some identification."

When she returned to Robert's office, Maren found her daughter sitting in the big leather wing chair eating Oreos. Robert was on the telephone.

Kneeling by Claire's chair, she said, "You're going to stay with Uncle Robert and Aunt Kathryn for a week or so. Will that be all right with you?"

"What about Ian?" the child asked, her big blue eyes showing concern.

"Ian's going on a trip, and so am I," Maren explained patiently. "It would be much too boring for you. I'm just going to be doing a lot of research and stuff."

"With Aunt Rachael?"

"No, honey. Aunt Rachael's gone. But she had a secret. I'm going to try to find it."

Claire appeared to ponder this. "Okay. Uncle Robert says Strawberry's been missing me." Her daughter was referring to the pony she had lost her heart to. Looking impeccable in the navy blue pleated skirt and gray flannel blazer that Maren had purchased for the funeral, Claire tilted her head to one side. Maren felt a qualm. Was all the time her daughter spent with her benevolent uncle spoiling her? Would the day come when she no longer wanted to come home to her distracted mother?

"You know I love you very much."

Looking into the confiding eyes, it was as though she were confronting Patrick. *How could she possibly contemplate jeopardizing the most important relationship in her life?* Claire's fingers stole into her hand, and her daughter clung with a child's trust.

"I'll miss you, Mommy. Who will tuck me in?"

Her daughter was the best part of her, the only real joy left. Through her childlike eyes, Maren saw a world that still had the promise of becoming a better place. Her whole life had been dedicated to making that a reality. But Claire couldn't possibly know that.

Then she heard Ian's silky threat—*I may have to finagle a little something with Claire.* Who knew what the man was capable of? Neither of them was safe at the moment. Even if she were to stay in the States, the child needed to be under the protection of her large, intimidating uncle. "Aunt Kathryn will tuck you in. Here, Peanut. I was saving these for you." Maren handed her daughter a roll of peppermints.

Claire took the candy solemnly as though it were a talisman. Maren suddenly wrenched Patrick's signet ring off her middle finger and disconnected the light gold chain around her neck. Sliding the ring onto the chain, she clasped it around her daughter's neck.

"This belonged to your daddy. It will always remind you that no matter what, you are part of a family who loves you. I would do anything for you, Peanut. I would kill the scariest dragon for you."

"Did you get everything taken care of?" Robert was off the telephone. "Valerie can get you a reservation if you like."

Maren assumed a tone of good cheer. "That'd be great. Here," she said, handing him her MasterCard.

Buzzing his paralegal, he took a moment to look over the statement. He whistled. "This is pretty damning."

Valerie strode into the room purposefully, wearing four-inch spiked, pointed-toed shoes. Maren felt as short and beautiful as a fireplug. Robert handed his employee the card and instructed her to reserve a space on the first flight to London.

Only later, just as she was surrendering Claire with one last hug, did Maren remember the final question she was going to ask Robert.

"I met Ian at your garden party in June. How did he happen to be there? Do you know?"

"No." Robert stretched back in his chair and rubbed his beard, trying to remember. "Oh the devil's in it!" he exclaimed suddenly.

"What have you remembered?"

"I could be wrong, but I think he was Valerie's date."

"The same Valerie who notarized my statement and made my plane reservations?" She stared at him.

"Unfortunately. What an idiot I am!" His heavy red eyebrows came together in patent ferocity. "I hate to slander a member of my staff, but Ian's charm is notorious, isn't it? Ten to one, she'll let him know what his wife is up to, on the off chance she can get him back."

Claire, sensing disaster in the air, was clinging to the skirt of her mother's black suit.

Robert punched the intercom. "Madge, order a taxi." Turning to Maren, he said, "All the cabbies in this town are crazy. If you tell them to step on it, you'll be on board that plane before Ian even makes it to the airport. I want you safe, out of his clutches. I'll deal with Valerie."

34

chapter seven

CHICAGO

O'Hare. Hurry!" Maren told the cabbie in a voice that sounded as if it belonged to someone else. Thus commenced the ride of her life. Grinning so widely she could detect it from the back of his head, her East Indian driver threw out the motor vehicle code and drove like a demon. His furious pace gave her little time for reflection. Once, when they were backed up behind a light, he pulled into the lane meant for oncoming traffic, now mercifully empty, and darted up to the intersection, beating out the number one car just as the signal changed. He swerved back to their side of the road in time to avoid collision by the narrowest of margins. Even in her present mood, she admired his audacity.

Once she reached O'Hare, she sought a ticket kiosk, pushed in her credit card, and obtained her boarding pass. Twenty minutes to take off, and heaven only knew how far it was to the gate. Craning her neck, she looked around for Ian. He would be here, she was certain. As narcissistic as he was, he would never see that his charisma had limits.

Instead of her suave husband, however, she saw a Mediterranean type with a day's growth of beard. He was studying her with dead black eyes. Though the temperature was in the sixties, he wore a heavy black trench coat. His hands, unhampered by luggage, were stuffed into deep pockets. In her heightened state of awareness, was she imagining it or was this man a killer?

"No luggage?" a TSA attendant inquired as she bypassed the line where she should have stood with the bags she didn't have.

"What? No."

"Security is up the escalator and along the terminal hallway," the attendant informed her automatically.

The intuition of danger prickling on the back of her neck, Maren began to sprint, clutching her boarding pass. Her straight skirt and the high heels she had worn to Rachael's funeral hampered her. But if she could just get to the vicinity of security, she would be safe.

The escalator was in sight through the throng of people. Surely he wouldn't shoot her in this crowd. Her pulse pounded as fight-or-flight hormones kicked in.

She took the moving stairs two at a time and soon found herself at the end of the long security line with armed men and women in clear sight. Hands shaking with adrenaline overload, she opened her handbag and took out her driver's license, handing it to the TSA attendant with her boarding pass and passport. Taking Rachael's laptop out of her bag, she placed it on the conveyer belt.

Once she was through security, she remained in her stockinged feet and, carrying her shoes, sprinted again through the crowd to her gate. It seemed a mile away, and she had exactly five minutes until takeoff.

She was the last one to board the plane. It wasn't until she was looking for her seat that she realized Valerie had booked her into first class.

Sitting through the seat belt demonstration, her mind spun off into a universe populated by pulses of light and men in black trench coats. As she attempted to slow her breathing, she remembered Ian as she had last seen him in his sky-blue silk dressing gown, calmly sipping tea over the morning crossword. And the man with the dead, psychopathic eyes—had he been after her, or was it all her over-charged imagination? She had never seen that particular man before. Had Valerie the Valkyrie communicated her knowledge? Ian could have panicked at what Maren had revealed in her statement. If he knew what she had done, he would have a double reason for wanting her out of the way.

By now he must know that she had made her flight. Would there be someone waiting for her at Heathrow? She couldn't risk it. It wasn't just her life. It was Claire's mother's life.

Maren pulled out her cell phone while there was still time.

"Madge? This is Maren. Put me through to Robert, please. It's an emergency."

"Mr. O'Neill has gone home with your little girl," the secretary said, a sour note sounding in her voice.

"I'll try his cell."

Just as the flight attendant was telling them they must turn off all electronic devices, she got through to Robert's voice mail.

"Maybe I'm just paranoid, but a guy may have been waiting for me at the airport," she said. "Could you notify Scotland Yard and see that someone meets me at Heathrow? If you tell them it's connected to Rachael's murder, there shouldn't be any problem. Gotta go. The flight attendant's giving me the evil eye. Thanks."

Maren tried to relax against the back of her seat and drew a deep breath. She was aware that her seatmate, a prosperous looking middle-aged man with heavy gold jewelry, was looking at her surreptitiously, but she felt as though she were in her own private bubble.

As her plane took off down the runway and soared into the air, she felt her trembling ease. She was on her way. But maybe, if it hadn't been for her disastrous choice of husbands, her sister would still be alive and they would be happily pursuing Rachael's treasure hunt for the Arthurian manuscript together.

CHAPTER EIGHT

CHICAGO

Ian Southcott stood on his back deck, a whiskey in his hand, and looked out over his garden. The lawn wanted mowing, but his fall plantings were doing well. Particularly the chrysanthemums. They studded the fence line like a heavy border of tiny snowballs. There were still a few climbing roses, and the begonias were brilliant coral, healthier than ever.

Where could the woman be? What would cause her to act so irrationally? Maren was odd, it was true. One never knew what she was thinking. She had a kind of kink in her brain that shunned the obvious. She was also fearless.

But why would she choose now to draw up a will and disappear? Ten minutes ago he had rung Robert again. The lawyer wasn't in.

Ian had remained relatively calm. It wasn't the time to panic. The only explanation was that she was off to Oxford in search of her sister's "find." She couldn't possibly know about the other. Perhaps she was miffed at him for shunning the funeral and had chosen this way of punishing him. It wouldn't be the first time she had run off without telling him. There was the time, right before Rachael's death, when she had taken Claire to Wisconsin for a week with absolutely no explanation. She had unconventional ideas about marriage—or maybe it was just him.

Since he had overheard the telephone call from Rachael, she had been less open than ever, as though hiding a guilty secret. Not that she had ever confided much. His wife of three months remained a mystery to him. The marriage had been a command performance for his part; nevertheless, she intrigued him. On the whole he liked mysteries. She kept herself tantalizingly separate, and her small face was interesting. He, who had loved so many gorgeous women, preferred that to movie star perfection. And she was a challenge. It was unsettling not to have a woman, particularly his wife, totally absorbed in him.

Sighing, he took a long drink of his whiskey and went inside to place a telephone call to Oxford. There was only one thing to do.

"Griffith, here."

"Southcott. Listen, I think my wife may be on her way over. If she arrives, she'll go straight to her sister's room. She chose not to confide in me, unfortunately."

"What do you want me to do about it?"

"I don't expect you to kill her. At least, not yet. Tail her. She has a better chance of finding this thing than we do. She must have Rachael's 'clue.'"

"Right. What do I do when she finds it?"

"Detain her. Then call me. I'll be over right away. I think if I showed up any sooner, I'd give the game away."

His listener sighed audibly. "I'll attempt to amp up the old charm, then. Is she susceptible?"

"I used to think so, but I'm beginning to wonder. She may prefer your type more than mine, however."

"Well, I must say, I am intrigued. Always did have a soft spot for King Arthur."

"This should be right up your street, then. Come to think of it, you do have Welsh blood in your veins, haven't you?"

"Sometimes your brilliance is stunning, Southcott."

Stifling his annoyance at this sarcasm, Ian hung up and went back out to the garden and his whiskey. He must not get overexcited about this or it would start the headaches again.

What he wanted was something fuchsia colored that did well in the shade. He needed a spot of brightness at the foot of the old elm.

chapter nine

*W*hen Maren leaned her seat back and closed her eyes, she tried once again to come to terms with what had just happened. Surely she was being melodramatic. In this day of terrorists, no one would have dared shoot her in an airport.

She felt only a flat detachment. Perhaps she was in denial over Ian's perfidy. She needed a more self-preserving state of mind before she landed at Heathrow. Just in case Robert didn't get her voice mail, she used the airphone, calling London information for the number of Scotland Yard. She was connected.

"This is Maren Southcott calling. I'm on my way to Heathrow." The man next to her didn't take his eyes off his newspaper, but he was as still as a hunter listening for prey. "I believe I may be in some danger connected with my sister's murder at Oxford last week. Dr. Rachael Williams."

"I'll connect you with CID," the receptionist said coolly. "Do you happen to remember the name of the inspector who handled the case?"

"Umm, it was Chief Inspector . . . something Welsh. Very stoic, though."

"Davies, Llewellyn?"

"Llewellyn, yes. That was it."

"He's off duty, but I'll contact him on his mobile and have him call back on this number. Then I can connect you."

"Okay, I'll hold."

Maren drummed her fingernails on the armrest and tried to rein in her impatience. Her neighbor actually put down his newspaper and looked at her with his slightly bulbous brown eyes. He fit the profile of a wealthy Greek shipping magnate. "It sounds like you are in trouble . . ." His accent was thick. It could have been Greek.

"Family matter," she said, giving him an absent smile. The possible Greek went back to his newspaper but didn't turn any pages.

Inspector Llewellyn's voice finally greeted her with aplomb. "Mrs. Southcott, where are you?"

"Over the Atlantic, by the skin of my teeth. Could you please meet my flight at Heathrow? I think someone may try to detain me."

A moment's pause. Then, "What's your flight number?"

She turned to her seatmate. "Can you please tell me our flight number?"

He produced his boarding pass from the breast pocket of his designer sports coat. "British Airways Flight 587. Arriving at six A.M."

"Right. I'll pull some strings and meet you at the gate myself."

After a dinner of cold lobster salad, a hard roll, and marinated corn, Maren decided she would look at Rachael's laptop. Her neighbor was toying with his Blackberry.

Turning on the computer, she waited as the screen scrolled through its loading scenario. Then it asked for a password. Maren rolled her eyes. When she had helped the police download the contents of the hard drive onto a CD, she had had a few bad moments.

A password! What in the world would Rachael choose for her password? She had wondered.

She had tried her sister's birthday first. No dice. Then, opening her sister's bag, Maren had taken out Rachael's wallet and keyed in her Social Security number. Nothing. She had tried Travis, their mother's maiden name. Zip.

Rachael, help me! What in the world were you thinking of when you configured this computer?

Celts. Of course. Rachael never thought of anything else. Maren had typed in C-E-L-T. Bingo! She had downloaded everything for Scotland Yard, and then they had let her take the computer home with her.

Now, checking the directory for the first time, she saw that her sister had only a few programs listed—Quicken, Word, and what looked like an encryption program. Great. All the computers in the Pentagon would have to work a thousand years to crack this encryption program. And of course Rachael would have encrypted everything Maren wanted.

She called up a promising file named "hunt." The screen responded by displaying garbage. Wonderful. Now she had to think of another password. And knowing Rachael, this would be something esoteric. When riding her hobby horse, no one could be more erudite than she. Maren exited in exasperation and switched off the computer.

As she shoved it back into its bag, her feelings of inadequacy swirled down into the familiar refrain: *Oh, Patrick! Why did you go off that day?* That familiar feeling of never being wise enough sent automatic flares of guilt rocketing through her. Why had she been so stubborn about not leaving his side?

What's so unreasonable about asking you to stay at your mother's? Have you any idea what's at stake here? Do you think I could hold out for a moment if I thought anything were going to happen to you or Claire? I've got a bodyguard waiting at your mom's in Kenilworth. Get over this idea that you're deserting me. I don't need your protection. Think of Claire. Deal with it, Maren!

If they hadn't had that quarrel, he wouldn't have rushed off on his motorcycle without his FBI bodyguards. Mr. Tough Guy. She could see him still, as piratical and devastatingly handsome as any Johnny Depp, silhouetted against the dusk in the back doorway, his black eyebrows raised in paralyzing hauteur.

That was the last time she had seen him alive. Now she heard his curt voice in her head. It was Patrick at his sharpest, looking at her out of Claire's eyes. *What kind of woman would leave her only child and go running off into certain danger because of some quixotic sense that she owed something to her sister? Who was more important? Dead sisters or live daughters?*

Whichever way she turned, webs of guilt ensnared her. She *must* try to think of something to break these sticky strands that made her a prisoner of her own mind. Lowering the shade over the aircraft window, she forced herself into the mental exercise of unraveling all the convoluted Celtic legends she could recall, attempting to figure out Rachael's password. As she was trying to recall the details of the "Four Branches of the Mabinogi," she mercifully fell asleep in the numbing aftermath of her adrenaline rush.

chapter ten

HEATHROW AIRPORT
LONDON

hief Inspector Llewellyn waited for Maren Southcott by the gate. One thing he didn't have to worry about. She hadn't been noticeably smitten by his looks. He was glad, because they had never caused him anything but trouble. No one on the force took him seriously. Running his hand ruthlessly through his hair, he wished he could rid himself of the forelock that insisted on falling over his eyes and had caused the detective superintendent to nickname him Lover Boy.

He didn't like this case. He'd been at Oxford on holiday, singing in a choir competition, when the call came through. They needed a Yard man because a foreigner had been strangled at one of the colleges. They'd assigned him Cole, with his old school tie and Cambridge degree, and already they were at odds. Cole thought the American's death was a smash and grab, but that didn't ring true to Llewellyn.

"Strangulation isn't a burglar's style," he'd told his sergeant.

"Whoever this perpetrator was, he was mad with anger. Besides, the computer's still here. And all her jewelry."

The computer was a sore spot. He'd allowed Mrs. Southcott to take it to the States and was relieved she was returning so promptly. Not until he looked at the printouts taken from it had he realized one of the files was encrypted. Cole had leapt on that one.

"She told me it was full of research about King Arthur, of all things," replied Llewellyn coolly. "Didn't think it could possibly be relevant."

"Thought she was a nutcase, didn't you?" Cole had challenged.

"Let's just say I didn't buy her story about some ancient manuscript being the motive for as brutal a strangling as I've ever seen. Still don't."

Cole, tall, bony, and languid, had simply raised an eyebrow.

There she was now. Looking a bit weary around the edges but grinning for some reason.

"Darling, I knew you'd come!" she greeted him.

"Laying it on a bit thick, aren't you?" Llewellyn concealed his surprise.

"Smile. You don't want anyone to know you're not delighted to see me." With a wicked glint she stood on her tiptoes and planted a kiss on his cheek.

"What is going on?" the chief inspector asked.

"Maybe it was just my imagination, but there was someone unsavory at O'Hare. My husband had threatened to keep me from coming to Oxford, so I didn't want to take any chances at this end. Anything new?"

"Nothing to speak of. Did you bring the computer?"

"In my handbag. But the file's encrypted."

"I know. I'm counting on you to decrypt it."

"Well, let's hope your confidence isn't misplaced. As I recall, you thought I was missing a few essentials when we met before."

He grimaced. "Sorry. I don't like this case. I was positively over-joyed when I found out you were on your way. You're going to save my skin."

"Don't get your hopes up. You've got to save mine first. And I promise I won't faint this time."

Llewellyn speeded their departure by taking her to the front of the passport control line, where he showed his credentials. As they moved into the swarm of humanity awaiting arriving passengers, he said, "This makes me frightfully uncomfortable. Fortunately, I know another way out. Do you have any luggage?"

"No."

"Good. We'll just walk this way, and then we'll make for the WC."

Between the men's and women's rest rooms was a plain gray door. Llewellyn produced a passkey, opened the door, and pushed her through.

"I alerted security," he said tightly as he slammed the metal door shut. "Cole is waiting for us with the Range Rover."

She stood rooted to the concrete floor while he rang Cole on his mobile. *Something has spooked her,* he thought. For some reason, she seemed to have touched a protective chord in him. Like when she had fainted.

"Don't worry. They can't get past here without a key." Leading her through a maze of grimy, dark corridors, he took her to a side door of the terminal, where Cole and the Range Rover were waiting.

"Just who is threatening to detain you?" Llewellyn asked once they were underway. He had joined her in the rear seat.

"My husband." She was unconsciously turning her wedding ring.

"He wants to kill you?"

"Well, he certainly wants to keep me from getting to Oxford ahead of him. I heard him threaten my daughter."

"Is this something different from your sister's murder?"

"No," she answered with a little sigh. "I think he may have been responsible indirectly for her murder."

She seemed calm enough now, but what she said sounded preposterous. "You're serious?"

"Totally. Do you think I'd make a joke about something like this? But then you think I'm crazy, don't you?"

Exasperated, he raked back his forelock. "Let's start at the beginning, shall we? Why would your husband want Professor Williams dead?"

"I don't think he wanted her dead, exactly. I think things got out of hand. A man named Griffith, his henchman who was supposed to get her clue to the manuscript—I think he must be a maniac or something. She didn't confide in anyone but me as far as I know, so I can't see who else could have attacked her but Ian's man."

"Ah—the research she was doing?"

"Are you ready to hear about it now?"

"By all means." He settled back to hear what he was certain would be a lot of imaginative nonsense.

She took a deep breath and looked straight into his eyes. "She had found a clue to the whereabouts of a manuscript scholars have been hunting for hundreds of years. It's a fifth-century Breton document, possibly owned by someone called Walter. He was an archdeacon at Oxford." She paused, looking at him just as his nanny had when dispensing particularly disgusting medicine. "He showed it to his friend Geoffrey of Monmouth in the thirteenth century. Geoffrey wrote a book, long considered fantasy, about the history of the kings of England, particularly about King Arthur. Got it so far?"

"Faint but pursuing."

"He hinted at the existence of this manuscript. A twentieth-century scholar, Geoffrey Ashe, has determined that it has some missing details about Arthur's life that would prove his identity, if they were known."

"But Arthur is nothing but a fairy tale for children!"

"And you're named Llewellyn?"

"My people haven't lived in Wales for a century or more. I'm a Londoner."

"Then why do you talk with a lilt?"

He looked at her in amazement. "A what?"

"You have the Welsh lilt in your speech. It's unmistakable."

"Professor Henry Higgins, I presume?" He didn't appreciate her observation in the least.

But she smiled disarmingly. "I'm nearly as crazy about Wales as my sister was. My maiden name was Williams. Our family's originally from Dolgellau. My first husband and I honeymooned there. But you never answered my question."

"I assume it."

"Assume it?" she echoed in astonishment.

"Drives the women wild," he said, keeping his face dead sober.

"Seriously."

"Seriously, I didn't even know I had a lilt. Must have picked it up from my nanny. She was a tiny Welsh lady from Llangollen."

"Did she speak Welsh to you in your cradle?"

He squirmed. "Probably."

"And she never told you stories about the Once and Future King?"

"That's just what they were. Stories. I never believed there was anything to them. I enjoyed Camelot, though. Splendid play."

"Well, Arthur was like some kind of god to Rachael. Some people see him still as the great 'restorer.' You know, the urge for sanity in an insane world. She belonged to the American Arthurian Society.

Dedicated to the propagation of Arthurian ideals and that sort of thing. They were funding her research."

They had pulled onto the motorway now. "Where to?" the sergeant asked over his shoulder.

"Someplace I'll be safe."

"I'd recommend the Randolph, then," the sergeant said. Without giving Maren or his chief a chance to agree, he used his mobile phone to call the Oxford hotel, identified himself as Kendall Cole, and reserved a room for her. "Thankfully, it's not tourist season," he said. "I've got you a suite."

"Another chunk out of my trust fund, I see."

Llewellyn could tell she was irritated and that made him obscurely happy.

"You want to be safe, don't you?" Cole demanded. "The more people around and the higher visibility you keep, the better. Also, the doors at the Randolph are solid hardwood."

"You sound as though you're pretty familiar with the place."

"I wasn't always a policeman."

She ignored this invitation to inquire into Cole's other life, Llewellyn noted. Better and better. Maybe she'd put the blighter in his place. Now if only she could figure out how to get into her sister's encrypted file.

Almost as if she had read his mind, Maren turned back to face Llewellyn. "It has to be something Celtic," she said.

"What does?"

"The password to the encrypted file. My sister was a monomaniac about the Celts. It's probably some Welsh word or place or something like that."

"Have you any idea what she encrypted?"

"The clue to the whereabouts of the manuscript, I imagine. By the time I arrived here, she was dead, remember. I never got to talk to her."

"And what exactly makes you think your husband is behind this?"

"I heard him on the telephone to that person called Griffith, who's over here somewhere. He said it could be as valuable as the Book of Kells. Ian told him to find it." Then, seeming to notice her wedding ring for the first time, she removed it and sat scrutinizing it for a moment. "He's crooked," she said finally. "He deals in stolen antiques. He probably has a record in this country, as a matter of fact. His name is Ian Southcott."

The inspector ruminated. "I don't suppose you have a picture of him?"

Maren opened her bag and pulled out her wallet. "As a matter of fact, I do. It's our wedding photo. We were married only three months ago."

"Rotten for you," he observed, feeling he should say something.

"I'd only known him a month, so I guess I got what I deserved."

Looking at the picture with some curiosity, Llewellyn observed that the man appeared as thin and whispery as Cole. There was a spiritual kinship between the two, he felt certain. "Don't know the bloke. Do you mind if we scan it and e-mail a copy to the Yard when we get to Oxford?"

"Do as you like," she said, removing the picture from its plastic holder. "I really don't care if I ever see it again." Dropping her wedding ring into her bag, she turned away from him, looking out the window as the dreaming spires of Oxford appeared.

chapter eleven

The phone buzzed on Chief Commissioner Braden's desk. "Braden here."

"Chief Commissioner, I have the director general for you."

Straightening in his chair, Braden unconsciously ran a hand through his bristle-short hair.

"Braden?" his boss queried a moment later.

"Yes, sir."

"We've got a situation. The Prince of Wales has received a letter from some fool calling himself Owain Glyndwr. He's threatening assassination and revolution and all the usual. The Queen is most upset. I want you to look into it right away. I'm sending it over."

"Right, sir. I'll be on the lookout."

"There's some rubbish in it about King Arthur. Can't make head or tail of it."

Braden sighed as he rang off. With all the home-grown terrorists threatening his country in the name of Allah, he had enough on his plate without some Welsh nutcase.

chapter twelve

OXFORD

aren had a problem with full English breakfasts. She loved them, but she couldn't help calculating every gram of fat she was consuming—fried eggs, fried sausages, fried toast, fried potatoes, fried mushrooms, even fried tomatoes. After all, she was only five foot two.

Of course, once she ate such a breakfast, she didn't require food until late evening. The way her life had gone for the past twenty-four hours, that point obviated the fat gram factor. Chief Inspector Llewellyn was arriving to escort her to Somerville College in half an hour to go through Rachael's books and try to figure out what her sister had been thinking of when she had encrypted her computer. It was only ten A.M. British time and who knew what the rest of the day would bring with it?

With this rationalization, Maren entered the dining room of the Randolph, still dressed in her black funeral suit and emerald green shirt, but having showered, combed her hair into a ponytail, and reapplied her makeup. The room was stately, as was everything about the old hotel. Oriental rugs covered the floor, white linen and fresh flowers—carnations this morning—adorned the tables. A massive stone fireplace took up most of one wall, and Victorian chandeliers hung from the twelve-foot ceiling.

Unfortunately, she had chosen a popular hour for breakfast, compelling her to share a table with a man eating alone.

"I'm sorry," she apologized as she was seated by the maitre d'. "Please continue with your newspaper."

Her companion smiled brightly and nodded for her to be seated. A medium-built, ginger-haired man, he was a fair-toned specimen of the British species, complete with close-cropped beard. Rachael would say he had Celtic blood in his veins.

She needed to court Rachael's ghost in this manner, painful though it was. She needed to see everything from her sister's perspective if she were to have any chance of tracking her "treasure." It was obvious that Rachael's murderer was on the quest and that that would be the best way of snaring him.

In spite of exhaustion and jet lag, she must keep going. She was certain one of the mythic Celtic heroes or heroines was the password. The right one would strike her. There had been a link between Rachael and Maren that her father used to call "pure witchery" when they were children. Though they had pursued different professional paths, their interests had remained intertwined. At least until five years ago . . .

"I say, are you a baseball fan?" Her tablemate offered her a section of what looked like the *International Herald Tribune.*

Maren smiled. "Rabid Cubs fan. I absolutely abhor the Cardinals, so I'm not interested in the playoffs."

The man relaxed back in his chair and looked directly into her eyes. His were a sparkling, inquisitive gray. "I really fail to understand

American sports. It seems your players are more like superstars than athletes."

"They never used to be such narcissists. My sister would say it's all part of the demise of the hero. A combination of their egotism and our cynicism. The same thing's happening in this country with your royal family."

He smiled grimly. "They're not *my* royal family. All the same, I'd like to see them try going on strike." He held out a hand across the table. "David Morgan, by the way."

Shaking hands, she replied, "I'm Maren." She couldn't bring herself to use "Southcott."

A waiter appeared, poured coffee, took their orders, and left.

Morgan folded his newspaper. "Are you a root-digger?" he hazarded.

Surprised, Maren was taken off guard. "A what?"

"A genealogist."

"What makes you think that?"

"I've met a fair number. You have all the signs—sense of purpose, the vital notebook, an air of democratized aristocracy . . ."

"What is that?"

"It's undefinable, really. Just something one knows. Am I right?"

"No. And my roots aren't English. They're Welsh."

"Ah, the wise foreigner who knows the distinction."

"Your name is Welsh, too, isn't it?"

"Yes. But I'm hopelessly polluted with Anglo-Saxon blood. My mother was a Tennyson."

"The same Tennyson who was obsessed with King Arthur?"

"Distant relation."

The conversation seemed in danger of lapsing. Maren had no intention of elaborating on her purpose in coming to Oxford, nor did she particularly care about his. He struck her as a bit too forthcoming for an authentic Englishman. Or perhaps it was just that her experience with Ian had made her overly suspicious.

At that moment, their breakfasts arrived, and Maren attacked her meal with enthusiasm.

"I'm an anthropologist, by the way, which must serve as an excuse for my curiosity. I can't resist interviewing an American. You see, I'm studying the effects of language on culture, and I find the fact that we share a common language is a vastly overrated link between us."

Now he was starting to intrigue her. "You do?"

"Yes. I really think there's much more of a Romantic influence on the American culture than people realize. You've far more in common with the Welsh, for instance, with their Romano-Celtic background. Americans are capable of tremendous enthusiasm and loyalty. Your mention of the hero is telling. Americans feel they ought to have heroes. It's the Romantic tradition."

Maren finished eating quickly. Folding her napkin, she placed it on the table. "There *are* strong Celtic underpinnings in our culture. Besides the Welsh, we have a huge number of people descended from the Scots and the Irish. As a matter of fact, there's a sort of Celtic revival going on in the States right now. Music and so on. It's interesting how broad the appeal is. You may just have accounted for it."

"Are you interested in Celts, then?"

"My sister was a Celtic scholar. *The* American expert, as a matter of fact."

"Was? Has she switched fields, then?"

"She's dead." Try as she might, she couldn't keep her voice on an even note. Here in Oxford, it seemed that Rachael should be more alive than ever.

"Oh . . . I am sorry. I didn't mean . . ."

She felt a qualm at inflicting her emotions on this hapless

stranger. "You weren't to know. Now. I really must go, Mr.—or is it Professor— Morgan?"

"Professor, as a matter of fact. I'm here for a conference. From Birmingham, actually."

"Then perhaps I'll see you again, Professor. I need to get going now. Thank you for the interesting chat."

The chief inspector awaited her in the lobby. He explained that Sergeant Cole was running the check on her husband.

"I've got to buy some clothes and things," she told him. "But that can wait until after I've seen Rachael's room."

He nodded and held the door open for her. She stepped out into the street and breathed the particular sweetish smell laced with gasoline fumes that she associated with Oxford. Bright autumn sunshine shone on the honey Cotswold stone walls of the colleges, and students raced by on their bicycles, weaving in and out of the more stolid motorized traffic. Ringing the hour in their myriad tones— from a deep tolling to a light chiming—the bells of Oxford were a comfort to Maren. The fact that they had been presiding over the university for hundreds of years was reassuring. Some things did endure.

In this repository of genius and inquiry, you could become entirely immersed in the realm of your choice. The essence of many of the world's greatest thinkers emanated from the architecture, the gardens, and even the qualities of the light and shadow. The atmosphere was palpable. But all that was spoiled for Maren as she remembered her previous visit to Oxford and Somerville College. Murder shouldn't happen in a place like this.

The same porter who had fetched her tea after her faint (an old man with an ancient pince-nez) was quick to surrender the key to Rachael's domain.

Maren stood stunned at the entrance to her sister's room. It was in indescribable chaos. Catching her breath, she said, "Are you responsible for this?"

"No." The chief inspector was frowning deeply. "Someone has broken our seal. We did leave a modest amount of upset—fingerprint powder and so on. But this . . ."

"Ian . . ."

"I beg your pardon?"

"This is Ian's henchman's work. Remember Griffith? That's who my husband was talking to on the telephone, anyway."

"You can't have it both ways, Mrs. Southcott. If your husband ordered Dr. Williams's death, wouldn't it have been for the purpose of getting this manuscript? Wouldn't his henchman have taken the clue, whatever it was, while he was at it? Why come back later?"

"Because he didn't find it the first time. Besides, I think it's here." Maren placed the laptop computer on Rachael's cluttered table, sweeping off the muesli with her sleeve. Opening up the computer, she turned it on and entered the password CELT. "Somewhere in this mass of books, there have to be some about mythology."

Llewellyn was crouched on the floor, inspecting the volumes with his gloved hands. Maren heard the crunch of glass under his feet. "Rather a nice Dylan Thomas here. He's one Welshman I do admire." He read the flyleaf. "Do you know someone called Anthony?"

Maren looked over his shoulder and read the inscription, *May you lose sleep over this one. My love always, Anthony.*

A frisson of shock buzzed through her. Rachael had had a love interest! Someone who knew her weird taste in poetry and shared it.

"No. She never mentioned him. But there were reasons she might not have. And of course, by the time I got here, she was dead."

"Nothing in her e-mail or anything that would help us trace him?"

Maren said sadly, "No. We didn't e-mail."

"Pity."

She eyed the slim volume of poetry still in the policeman's hand. It would be doubly tragic if Rachael had been killed by someone she loved and trusted. She didn't do either easily. Tossing her head impatiently, Maren was emphatic. "I'm sure this mess is Ian's work. Unless this Anthony doubles as Griffith, I don't think he enters into it."

"It doesn't pay to take anything for granted in an investigation," Llewellyn advised. "Here. I think this is what you're looking for." He handed her a book written by her sister, *The Celtic Myth in Modern Wales*.

"Yes, that's what I need. Is it okay if I take it? I'd like to get out of here."

"I understand how you feel, but with the threat from your husband, I'd rather you stayed with me." The chief inspector pulled out his mobile phone. "I just need to get someone down here to photograph this and dust for prints, though I haven't much hope of finding anything."

"There ought to be some on that poetry."

"It might actually be more interesting if there weren't."

Maren thought this over while the chief inspector made his call. "You mean if someone wiped it clean?" she asked once he had hung up.

"Precisely. That would tend to indicate that Anthony Whomever was the one who made this jolly little mess."

"I think you're wrong."

"Suppose you concentrate on cracking that code right now." He pulled a chair over to the table for her.

Sighing, she sat down. She saw this as simply more evidence of her husband's dual personality. "But this has got to be Ian's doing. I heard him telling Griffith to look for 'it,' whatever 'it' is. He told him to bribe a char."

"There may be a completely separate action going on here."

She looked at him, stunned. How could he even think that? "But that doesn't seem logical. How many people could possibly know about this? Rachael was playing it very close to the chest."

Llewellyn returned her look, one handsome eyebrow raised in irritation. "How about if you let me worry about it? I'm the chief inspector."

"She was my sister."

"I'm well aware of that. But the best way to find out who did this is not to limit our paradigms."

"What do you mean by that?"

"Do you know anything about chaos theory?"

Rolling her eyes, Maren looked around her. "No. And I don't want to. I have enough chaos in my life. Look at this room, for heaven's sake."

Rachael had been such a neat soul. Now her bed was not only unmade but completely dismantled, the baby blue sheets in tatters. Her modest wardrobe had been pulled out of the cupboards and thrown about the room, its civilized colors screaming of the wrongness of the picture. Dresser drawers had been dumped and pawed through. Maren detected the glint of her grandmother's emerald brooch, newly fashionable in its antique setting, and bent to retrieve it. It had particularly become her sister, with her red hair and green eyes. Claire would have it.

As for the clothes, she and Rachael were exactly the same size. Rachael had been more inclined towards the whimsical, the eclectic; Maren, to tailored suits for work and jeans for leisure and undercover work. But she pulled Rachael's duffel out of the mess and began folding skirts and blouses, shawls, and underwear into it. She needed to get into Rachael's skin, didn't she? She would wear Rachael's clothes. Llewellyn nodded his permission for her to remove these personal items. When she was finished with this task, she paged through her sister's mythology with determination. The faster she got to the bottom of this, the sooner she could be home safe with Claire. *If she could elude her husband and his comrades long enough.* Actually, it was quite comforting to have the chief inspector sticking to her like glue.

Beginning with the mythic foundations of Welsh literature, Maren entered into the computer the names of all the gods and goddesses she came across, trying to find the password that would enable her to break the code. *Pwyll, Arawn, Rhiannon, Pryderi* . . . None of them worked. Somewhat dispiritedly, she admitted to herself that this was at best a random exercise. Rachael would have had some logic behind the name she chose.

She heard Llewellyn's reinforcements arrive but paid no attention. *Taliesin, Ceridwen, Gwyddion, Amaethon* . . . nothing. What would Rachael have associated with this treasure hunt? Danger, excitement. Unfortunately, all the Welsh myths dealt with danger and excitement. Beings were forever going and coming from quests in the dangerous Otherworld. The Otherworld was the place where they proved themselves, where they earned their blessings. *Wait a minute.* Wouldn't Rachael see this quest, this mystery, as the equivalent of a venture into the Otherworld? And encrypting her message in this latest code would all be part of it. Going into this file would be, for her, like walking through the looking glass, literally entering the world of her dreams, her obsessions. Her Otherworld.

Hands shaking, Maren looked in the English-Welsh dictionary Rachael had provided at the back of her book. *Otherworld: Annwn.* She entered the word into the computer. Yes! Punching the air with her fist, she exclaimed, "I'm in!"

chapter thirteen

S he was here! Prince Owain Glyndwr tried to quell his impatience. It wouldn't do to make himself known just yet. For a time he must make do with poetry.

> *Twin suns rising*
> *One red, one white*
> *Twin orbs racing*
> *To a single place*
> *Destiny's terminus*
> *Unity or death*

chapter fourteen

T he chief inspector peered over her shoulder. "What was it?"

"*Annwn.*"

"Of course. The Otherworld."

The document was decrypting before their eyes. In an instant, they had it. Maren read it aloud:

In the Bodleian Library is a twelfth-century manuscript on Celtic myths, "The Romano-Celtic Tradition of Life After Death." It hadn't been touched in years because it is in Old English, and J. R. R. Tolkien had done a modern translation that has been in common usage for some time. Near the end of the manuscript is a note that doesn't appear in Tolkien's translation. It is a seemingly unrelated page referring to Walter, Archdeacon of Oxford, who had gone to retire in Wales at the monastery called the Brothers of (here Maren hesitated and spelled out the words) *Castell cadarn a'i safle grymus ar ben y graig, taking his library with him. I have no idea why this particular note is with the manuscript. Perhaps Walter was an unacknowledged source. Tolkien, at any rate, thought him irrelevant and reasoned that the note was not part of the original document. I have looked for the monastery, and no such place exists at present. Dr. Rachael Williams. August 31.*

"Hmm." Maren felt deflated. "That's not much to go on. But it is written on the day she phoned me. The day before she was murdered."

"But if this manuscript is so sought after, why would no one have picked up on this note before?" the chief inspector wanted to know.

"Because no one had any reason to associate Walter with Celts, only with Arthur, I suppose. The people who studied this wouldn't have been Arthurians. It was only comparatively recently that Geoffrey of Monmouth's *History of the Kings of England* was given any credibility at all." She bit her lip. "Walter's evidence is key in identifying King Arthur as a real person. His library would be invaluable." Looking absently at the mess around her, she picked up Geoffrey Ashe's *The Discovery of King Arthur.* A page was dog-eared. Glancing it over briefly, she handed it to the chief inspector. "The reference to Walter is slight. It's not something you would remember unless you saw it as the vital piece of the puzzle, as Geoffrey Ashe did. Tolkien wasn't an Arthurian. He was more interested in the Nordic legends."

Llewellyn whistled. "So who did this chap Geoffrey Ashe think King Arthur was?"

"I looked up Ashe on the Internet before I came over here to meet Rachael. He says Arthur was a famous king-general known by the Roman name of Riothamus. He was a real historical figure, not a myth, who did many of the things Arthur is reputed to have done. Most of them were in Gaul, which is what this Breton manuscript is all about. Ashe deduced that Arthur must be Riothamus on the basis of what this Archdeacon Walter told Geoffrey of Monmouth about the manuscript. But the manuscript has never been found."

"Do you think it would be valuable enough to kill for, then?"

Maren took a deep breath. "Look. There is a whole Arthurian

culture that has been active since the fifth century. They live and breathe Arthur. Ian told Griffith that this would be a greater find than the Book of Kells. I think he may be right."

"Well, well. Now I suppose all you have to do is find out where this monastery disappeared to."

"Yes, it sort of looks like Rachael jumped the gun on this one. I can see her getting excited and projecting all of this into something concrete. It's tragic, really, because if Griffith or whoever it was had known how slim her lead really was, he never would have killed her for it."

Exiting from the encrypted file, Maren turned off the computer and closed it. Rachael's computer—it had turned out to be her death warrant. For a moment she forgot the thrill of the chase and remembered her sister's purple, swollen face in the body bag.

Llewellyn's mobile rang. Opening it, he strode to the window that overlooked the green quadrangle below.

"Chief Inspector Llewellyn here. . . .Yes. . . . Yes. I see. . . . Hmm. Interesting. That rather puts the cat among the pigeons, doesn't it? Well done, Detective Sergeant."

He turned to Maren. "How do you react to a shock?"

"It depends. Why?" she replied, puzzled.

"I can only hope you won't throw something at me, then."

"What is it?"

"Cole's had some success. Your husband *is* known to the authorities in this country. He went by the name of James Hubbard, but they've lost track of him in recent years." He pocketed his phone. "Interpol wants him for smuggling, among other things. The FBI should be picking him up this morning in the States. They're going to let me know."

Maren exhaled slowly and felt heat flush through her body. Her mistake was assuming epic proportions. "What sort of smuggling?"

"Drugs. Hubbard worked with a fairly well-known ring, but we haven't been able to trace any of its known operatives to this country."

Drugs. Patrick. She froze. What had she done? "There was no one called Griffith?"

"No. Most of the people we know about are Colombian."

She nodded, unable to speak. She had actually gone and married the big, bad wolf.

"His antiques business might have been used as a money-laundering cover," the chief inspector continued. "And his interest in this lot," he indicated the trashed room, "might have been a little something he had on the side."

Maren wrapped her arms around herself and held tight. Drugs! Patrick would absolutely crucify her if he knew she had entrusted his daughter to a member of some drug gang. That would be as bad as if he were a murderer.

"You'll let me know as soon as you find out he's been arrested?" she asked.

"Of course."

A chubby detective constable handed the book of poetry back to Llewellyn. "Now it looks like we've got another problem."

"What?"

"There are no prints on this Dylan Thomas. It's been wiped clean. And whoever did this," the detective indicated the pandemonium surrounding them, "wore gloves."

Llewellyn addressed his assistant. "Have you found anything different this go round?"

The man shook his head. "Don't think so, sir. Only careful analysis will tell, but right now it appears there were no prints other than those of the deceased. A lot of surfaces have been wiped clean."

"What about the first time you investigated, right after the murder?" Maren wanted to know.

"It was the same then. But until this discovery," Llewellyn held up the book of poetry, "we didn't attach much significance to it. We just thought it was a murderer being extraordinarily careful. But if this Anthony is our man, he may have been in the habit of spending time here. And he may have missed a print somewhere or another. Of course, unless we can identify those prints from a police record, they won't do us much good at this stage."

"Was there anything in her appointment diary?"

"She seems to have given up keeping it the last month. There aren't any entries since July."

"That surprises me. Rachael was meticulous. She must have been very excited if she gave up her record keeping. That makes this encrypted message all the more important. I wonder if she felt she was in danger."

"Was she inclined to be melodramatic?"

Maren nodded, feeling the familiar melancholy settle on her as an image of her sister surfaced. She saw a twelve-year-old redhead triumphantly holding up the gilt coronet of leaves their father had hidden in the laundry chute, the object of their treasure hunt. Poor Rachael. She had been like a kid at play. To her, it had all been one step removed from fantasy. All part of the Arthurian mystique. She hadn't the least idea what she'd let herself in for.

The chief inspector cleared his throat. "Now, the thing to do is put yourself in this fellow's shoes. What would you do if you were Anthony?"

Putting her hand to her forehead, Maren tried to think. The forensics team made a noisy exit. "If this mess doesn't have anything to do with Ian and Company, my guess is that Rachael must have told this Anthony something about what she was doing."

"Then why this?" Again the chief inspector indicated the mess around them.

"She could be absolutely maddening when she had a secret. Look how she made me fly over here. She wouldn't tell me anything on the telephone."

"Right. So she tells him enough to tempt him, and he kills her. Why, we don't know. Perhaps she told him it was encrypted somewhere, and he thought he could find it and decode it. What would he do when he couldn't find it?"

Maren said, "Wait for me to get here, I suppose. He must have known I was coming. Probably thinks I'll lead him to it."

"Right. Anyone this cold-blooded isn't going to give up very easily. I suggest you beware of strangers."

For the first time, Maren noted the chain lock that hung on her sister's door. "Whoever killed her wasn't a stranger to Rachael. She didn't have casual affairs. She would be very careful about who she let in."

Did that eliminate Ian's cohort, then? But perhaps Griffith had ingratiated himself. She grew more intrigued about the man who had done Ian's dirty work. Had he romanced her unsuspecting sister?

CHAPTER FIFTEEN

Chief Commissioner Braden folded hands roughened from gardening and looked around the table at his team. Projected on the screen before them was Prince Charles's letter from "Prince Owain Glyndwr."

To the Pretender:

Your conduct in the sacred position you hold does nothing but bring condemnation down upon the heads of all Britons. You shamefully hounded your lawful wife to her death. She was a true Princess of Wales, worthy and gracious in all ways. You compounded your perfidy by marrying the woman who did more harm to Princess Diana than anyone except yourself. Perhaps more importantly, your government has done nothing to rid this land of the invasion of infidels who are blowing themselves and others to bits in their insanity. Are we to sink into the Dark Ages again?

The House of Windsor is doomed. King Arthur would not own you. He is the true King of our Country, of all Britons, and whoever stands in his place does so only as a steward. You have proved to be an unworthy steward and will be removed, along with your sons. You have never been anything but unworthy Saxons—a scourge to all.

Cymru has been too long in subjection. We are prepared to step forth in the name of Arthur and once again rule Briton according to his just and righteous principles, which have no place for adultery. For the good of this country, the Celts will rise again and make it the great nation it once was. We will rule with the power that righteousness lends and rid this country of heathen zealots. You have been warned.

Prince Owain Glyndwr

"Comments?" Braden asked.

Handwriting expert Inspector Wolff spoke up. "Accustomed to command. Frustrated. Dangerous. Definitely delusional." He pushed rimless spectacles toward the bridge of his long, thin nose. "Once saw a specimen of Hitler's handwriting. Similar."

"What's the date today?" a small, hairy man with pink ears asked vaguely from the end of the table, his eyes surveying the ceiling.

"The eighth of September, Keates," Chief Commissioner Braden said patiently.

"We have eight days, then," pronounced the little man with an air of unconcern.

"Eight days until what?" Keates's tall, stooped partner, Chief Inspector Evans, asked sharply.

"September sixteenth. Date Owain Glydwr raised his standard in rebellion. Welsh have been trying to make it a national holiday for years."

Chief Commissioner Braden passed around the folders that had been resting on a stack before him. They were labeled *Meibion Glyndwr.*

"What the devil does this mean?" complained the querulous Evans.

"It's the group that was burning homes in Wales twenty-some years ago. We have to start somewhere. Let's get to work," the chief commissioner said. "His Royal Highness is going to be attending services in Bangor Cathedral in Wales on the sixteenth. It's on his Website."

CHAPTER SIXTEEN

OXFORD

Even being a chief inspector of Scotland Yard was not enough recommendation for Llewellyn and Maren to obtain readers' cards at the Bodleian Library. At the inquiries desk, the dapper little man with a silver toothbrush mustache informed them that they must go through regular channels, managing to imply that Scotland Yard was a relatively new institution, whereas the Bodleian was eternal.

Llewellyn was able to turn up a professor of vocal performance at Magdelene College he had become acquainted with during the choir competition. Professor Tompkins vouched for the chief inspector and Maren to the librarian. In his presence, they then took an oath in Latin that they would not deface, burn, or remove any of the books, manuscripts, or other materials from the library. They also promised faithfully not to kindle any fires in the stacks. After paying five pounds apiece, they were each presented with the coveted reader's card.

"I'm glad you agree this is necessary," Maren told Llewellyn as they made their way up the ancient staircase.

"Detective work is based on the same principles as good scholarship. You've read your Holmes, of course?"

"Sure. But policemen in the States aren't quite as broad-minded as you. They go in more for Mickey Spillane."

The library was just as she had imagined it. Old. Maren breathed in the smell of leather, aging paper, and book paste. Dust motes played in the gray beams of light filtering through the leaded glass windows. The place had an almost spooky aura—the repository of men's minds. Every thought, great or small, published on this island since before the invention of the printing press had its own special niche here. Fielding and Defoe, Austen and Brontë shared housing with the ancient illuminated manuscripts that monks had toiled over for a lifetime. If you let your imagination run wild, it was an exhilarating place to be.

They introduced themselves to a small woman whose hair was pinned in a tight gray bun. She showed them, with obvious unwillingness, into a dim room where the manuscripts were kept in folios. Her underslung jaw gave her a Churchillian appearance and, like the former prime minister, reminded Maren of a bulldog. "This is the stack your sister was working on," she told Maren. "You might as well know, I don't approve of all this sensationalism. If she had been British, I'm certain *this* never would have happened."

With difficulty Maren managed not to further alienate the tartar by telling her that someone British had undoubtedly done "this." Removing the large folio to a scarred and ancient table, Maren thought of Rachael and wondered if she knew of the bulldog's disapproval. No, she had probably been oblivious. It was easy to feel her sister's presence here in the ancient library. Her room had been ransacked, but this place was eternally the same, and it was one of the last places her sister had been. How vivid the flame of her hair must have been against the old wood and diamond-paned glass! And she would have used the large, Holmesian magnifying glass that had been Maren's gift to her when she received her Ph.D. For Rachael, this would have been a sacred citadel. The Celts had left no written records, so the closest she could get to her beloved people were the accounts of them written in monasteries, the only institutions that had survived the barbarian Anglo-Saxons' defeat of the Romans. She would have handled these old papers with all the reverence due them.

"Do you know what you're looking for?" Llewellyn asked.

"Yes. But you needn't hang around. Why don't you take a nice walk?" Maren wanted to be alone with her sister's presence.

Thrusting his hands into the pockets of his trench coat, he said, "If you need me, I'll be in the current periodicals."

Twenty minutes later, she found the manuscript Rachael had discovered: "The Romano-Celtic Tradition of Life After Death." Paging through it slowly, being very careful of the ancient parchment, she finally came to the end. Though her knowledge of Old English was slight, it was good enough that Maren knew the note Rachael had referred to on her computer was not there. Leafing through the document once more, Maren shook her head. Someone had been awfully quick. Rachael's murderer?

Maren went looking for the small librarian. "Someone has removed something from that folio," Maren told her. "Can you tell me who was working with it last?"

"No one's been interested in that folder since your sister, last week," the bulldog snarled.

Was it just last week Rachael had been murdered? It seemed like a million years ago. Her murder was one of those landmark events that seem to start time all over again.

Maren thought furiously. "How do you know what each patron looks at in there? I mean, I had to sign in. But is there any way of knowing for certain which folio a person reads?"

The woman pulled herself up and looked at her with patent hostility. "You must understand, young woman, that this is a very busy job. I have this entire wing to look after."

Maren ignored her tone. "Do you have a list of who has been in that room in the last week?"

"I can tell you that without looking. There's only been Professor Jones. He was a colleague of your sister's, as a matter of fact. They were working together."

"Would you mind terribly showing me his signature?"

"You must realize Professor Jones is a renowned Celtic scholar."

"Granted. So was my sister. His signature?"

Mutely passing her the clipboard Maren herself had signed, the bulldog turned back a couple of pages. "See, here it is. Room 17. Professor Anthony Jones."

Dated the day after Rachael's murder. Maren clutched the edge of the table in her excitement. The writing was the same as the inscription in Rachael's Dylan Thomas. "Would you happen to know where I could find the professor?"

"If you mean what college he is affiliated with, I can tell you that he is a most respectable fellow of Christ Church College."

Descending the stairway, Maren asked the way to current periodicals, where she found the chief inspector. "It looks like a Professor Anthony Jones of Christ Church College broke his Bodleian oath. The note is missing."

The desiccated porter at Christ Church College was obviously spiritual kin to the bulldog. He looked at Chief Inspector Llewellyn as though he had a bad smell about him. "Professor Jones is not on the premises."

"Perhaps you can tell me when he's likely to be in?"

"He left this morning for a week's leave."

"Did he mention where he was going?"

The porter inspected his fingernails.

Llewellyn said bluntly, "This is a murder investigation. Would you like me to take you into headquarters for questioning?"

"Wales," the porter sighed. "He has a sister there who is ill. No forwarding address. Said to hold his mail."

Maren looked at Llewellyn. One edge of his mouth quirked upwards. "And Bob's your uncle," he said with understated triumph.

"He's obviously on the track of this monastery," the chief inspector said on their way to Boots, where Maren intended to buy toiletries. He carried the duffel with Rachael's clothing.

"Yes. Undoubtedly he speaks Welsh. I don't suppose you do?"

"I can say *bore da*."

"What's that, for heaven's sake?"

"'Good morning.' Not much help."

Maren stopped still in the middle of the path. A student swerved his bike around her. She looked into the inspector's puzzled face. "I have an idea! Does the Randolph have an Internet connection?"

"Undoubtedly. This *is* Oxford."

"We need to do a little surfing on the Internet. But first I have to buy a toothbrush."

chapter seventeen

The man Maren knew as Ian Southcott got off the Lufthansa 747. From the airport, he placed a telephone call to London. "Susan? James here. Has anyone been asking for me?"

"The police were around this morning, if that's what you mean. They probably have the phone tapped. Stay out of my life, James."

"What did you tell them?"

"The photo they showed me was of your wedding. Committing bigamy now, are you?"

"Did you tell them that?"

"I didn't need to. They know I'm married to you. But not for long."

"Do me a favor. If any of our old friends come calling, you don't know anything."

Susan cut the connection. Probably just as well. If the phone were tapped, the boys at the Yard wouldn't be able to trace the call.

Wedding photo. That meant Maren was definitely on to him.

Somehow, he hadn't wanted to believe it. But a sixth sense that he had learned to trust unequivocally had warned him to get out of the States.

Placing a second call to Griffith's mobile, he got only voice mail. Why didn't the man answer? Was he screening his calls? Well, there was no help for it. He must get to Oxford himself.

Using an Irish passport in the name of O'Leary, he went about chartering a private plane. His American wife seemed to know about his curiosity concerning Rachael—he must have betrayed himself somehow. And now, thanks to the wedding photo, she probably knew about the other.

He swore. Her being able to identify him as Ian Southcott alias James Hubbard was a serious problem. James Hubbard had been compromised. If he showed himself, she could lead Interpol straight to Ian Southcott. And from him, it was only a short hop to his Chicago connections. Once his bosses found out his alias was known, no place would be safe enough for him.

It was past time he dealt with the errant Mrs. Southcott. He didn't dare leave it to Griffith. From now on, this was his operation. After making a further detailed call to Chicago, he climbed aboard his rented jet.

Chapter Eighteen

Oxford

Chief Inspector Llewellyn stood over Maren's shoulder as she typed the name of the monastery into the Welsh-English dictionary on the Internet. Her suite was large enough that she didn't feel crowded by his presence. The king-sized bed was ready for her weary body, and the gentle fragrance of lavender potpourri and the roaring fire were welcoming after the stiff September wind.

"'A mighty castle superbly situated on a rocky crag,'" she read. "Oh, brother."

"Does that bring anything immediately to mind?" Llewellyn asked.

"You're the Llewellyn," she told him. "Llewellyn the Great fought in castles all over Wales. As far as I can tell, it could be any of them."

"I think we ought to order tea," the chief inspector said, his tone suddenly weary. "I can't really believe this is going to lead anywhere."

"Go ahead." Maren waved towards the telephone vaguely. "Be my guest."

She typed the words *Castle Wales* into Google, and an impossible number of sites appeared on the screen. She was still scrolling through, eliminating only a few, when the tea came.

Llewellyn wheeled the tea cart over to her elbow at the little table. "Lemon? Sugar? Milk?" he asked.

"Milk and sugar," she answered. Then, looking at the cart, she spied the scones and clotted cream. Sighing, she abandoned the computer. It had, after all, been a long time since breakfast.

As she was endeavoring to eat the scone without getting cream all over herself, a new idea sprouted in her head. "I wonder if that would work?" she said aloud.

"What?" the chief inspector asked.

Without answering, Maren finished her scone as delicately as possible, took a swig of tea, wiped her hands, and turned once more to the computer. This time she typed in "Brothers of *Castell cadarn a'i safle grymus ar ben y graig.*"

An instant later, the Arthurian standard of the red dragon and a picture of a medieval knight astride a horse appeared on the screen. The caption read "Owain Glyndwr, Prince of Wales."

"What?" Maren expostulated. Scanning through the site, she saw no reference to a monastery, only pages and pages of dates and places and battles. She vaguely remembered from her honeymoon visit that Owain Glyndwr was some kind of Welsh hero.

"What did your nanny tell you about Owain Glyndwr?" Maren asked. "A printer sure would come in handy right now."

"He led a rebellion against the English," Llewellyn said. "I know that much. There was a tremendous anniversary celebration in Wales in 2000. What does he have to do with anything?"

"I haven't a clue. All I know is that the computer pulled up this site when I typed in the name of the monastery. There are tons of castles here."

"I'll get my notebook," the chief inspector said phlegmatically. "Though what the Super would say about chasing Owain Glyndwr around Wales doesn't bear thinking of."

"The monastery's got to be near one of these. This writing is so small, I can hardly make it out." Looking over her shoulder, she saw that Llewellyn had taken out his notebook. "Ready?"

"Ready."

"Good grief. It says here the blood was 'fetlock deep' in one of these battles."

She felt the chief inspector stir behind her. He went to the door to let in the waiter to retrieve the tea cart.

"Okay, okay, I'm getting to it now. The first castle looks like Conwy. Then Ruthin. Let's see . . . more battles . . . but not at castles . . . Okay, here we are. Cardiff. Hotspur! That name's familiar! Wasn't he a character in Shakespeare?"

"I have no idea. Is that all?"

"No. We've got Mach-y-n-l-l-e-t-h. Man, these Welsh names are murder. Glyndwr was crowned Prince of Wales there, so I'd say that was a good possibility. But there doesn't seem to be a castle. Hold on. There's more. Criccieth. Harlech. Oh, I remember Harlech. I went there on my honeymoon. Grosmont. But he was apparently defeated there. Okay. From here on out it's the same castles, just defeats. I think that's it."

"That's six castles!" the chief inspector groaned.

"Cheer up!" Maren said lightly. "You don't have to come. I'm looking for a manuscript, remember? If I run into a murderer in the course of my investigations, I'll be sure to tie his feet and hands and hand him over to you."

The inspector looked irritated. "It's our best lead, I suppose. We'll have to take Cole, you know."

She rolled her eyes. "I'm not planning a romantic getaway for two, Chief Inspector. Detective Sergeant Cole will be very welcome. We'll get a map and plot the castles out. We just about have time to get to Blackwell's before they close."

"Remember one thing," he said.

"What?"

"This isn't an amateur show. Cole and I are looking for a murderer."

She turned serious. "This was my sister's quest, Chief Inspector. Most likely, she died because of it. Believe me, I'm just as anxious as you to find the murderer. Whether it's Griffith or Professor Jones, the murderer's looking for the manuscript, so it stands to reason we'll run into each other."

chapter nineteen

ENGLAND

O wain Glyndwr stepped up to the window and looked out into the September night. The wind was blowing, as restless as he was. His muscles were coiled for action. It was getting harder and harder to restrain himself when it was so close.

Well, that arrogant "Prince of Wales" had his ultimatum. Word had just come that the weapons had arrived. They were stashed and waiting for the uprising to start.

How wonderful it would be to be in Cymru again! Among his people, on the track of Arthur's magic. What was it that Rachael had said about the "void"? She spoke more truly than she knew.

The void inside him yawned, hungry for power, justice, and a world where there would be Divine Order. Everyone would see he was Arthur's instrument. And his goddess would reign at his side, passionate, full of awe at his incomprehensible power. She would know him for who he really was. Her magic would be his protection against the heathens.

Yes, Arthur. I, Glyndwr, will finish what I started six hundred years ago. You have slept long enough. Death shall have no dominion.

chapter twenty

aren lay awake long after her midnight chat with
her daughter.

"Mommy? When are you coming home?"

"Aren't you having a good time with Uncle Robert and Aunt Kathryn?"

"They aren't my mommy."

"I'm sorry, Peanut." She felt bereft, wishing for a hug from those skinny
little arms and not knowing what to say to ease their mutual loneliness.
"What did you do today?"

"Uncle Robert taught me to pitch."

"So he stayed home with you?" Poor Robert. He really must be smitten
with Claire to have forgone a Saturday at the golf course.

*"Uh-huh. He bought me a candy apple. We're watching baseball right
now."*

"Is it fun?"

"It's boring." Like herself, Claire liked action and plenty of it. At her
age, she was far too young to appreciate the nuances of baseball. On the
other hand, she had a wide-ranging imagination.

"I'm playing a game of hide and seek, Claire. Remember the story I told you about King Arthur?"

"The one who had the magic sword?"

"Yes. Excalibur. Well, I'm trying to find out if he was real or not."

"What do you mean real?*" Sometimes Maren forgot that her daughter was only four. To her, every story must be real. And she had only one mommy. What she knew very well was that Mommy wasn't with her.*

She would take Claire to Wisconsin. They would buy that derelict little farm she had seen on their visit. She'd fix it up and teach her daughter at home. Claire would have a dog, a cat, a chicken, and maybe a goat. There would be a tire swing, a garden of sweet peas, and of course a big apple tree.

"Would you like to live on a farm, Claire?" she asked.

"Like Old McDonald's ee-eye-ee-eye-oh?"

Maren had a flash vision—Patrick kneeling in front of the infant Claire. "And a honk, honk here, and a honk honk there . . ."

Telephones were worse than unsatisfactory. They called up longings that only touch and sight and smell could satisfy. And some that nothing in this world could satisfy.

Maren felt her throat thicken. "Yes, Peanut. Ee-eye-ee-eye-oh."

The sooner she got home, the better. Of course, the farm was only a fantasy—a longing for peace and order. A normal childhood for Claire. Somehow she had to find a balance in her life. She didn't really think she *could* escape the world and all its problems. She had to be bringing peace and order to a chaotic world. Maybe she had a bit of an Arthur complex herself. Nevertheless, she knew very well that that was what had made Patrick fall in love with her.

The following morning, determined to begin Rachael's quest, Maren brushed her teeth with her new toothbrush and applied a spare amount of blush and a generous amount of charcoal eye shadow. Feeling a little spooky in Rachael's multicolored peasant skirt, lace blouse, and camel's hair shawl, she heard the housekeeper's knock.

"Come in," she replied.

A moment later, a man in a ski mask appeared in the mirror. Before she could think, he had grabbed her from behind, an arm around her throat, his forearm choking her as his other hand clamped over her mouth. His muscles were like steel. Something hard and cold was digging into her neck. In seconds, she was seeing stars as her vision began to blacken.

Her mind scrambled, desperate for some means of escape. Was this how Rachael had felt? Had she seen stars as her oxygen went?

Maren struggled with new desperation. She was *not* Rachael. What could she use as a weapon? Kicking her bare feet wouldn't help. Mousse. She had her spray-on mousse. Groping on the counter blindly, she found it, grabbed it, and aimed for her attacker's eyes.

He howled and loosened his hold. Turning in his slackened grasp, she moved back as far as she could against the sink and gave him a roundhouse kick to the solar plexus. He staggered back, clawing at his eyes. Escaping from the bathroom over his writhing figure, Maren raced for the hall.

"Help!" she yelled. "Someone call the police!" She held a shoulder against the door as though keeping it shut by main force. But no one attempted to come out.

Professor Morgan flew out of the doorway next to hers, his eyes wide with alarm.

"What's wrong?"

Her hands went to her throat. It hurt from the crushing pressure of her assailant's arm. "Someone just attacked me. He's in there."

"Go into my room and call security," the ginger-bearded man told her. "I'll stay here."

He was clad in a paisley dressing gown, but she could see that the scholar was as well built as a wrestler. Leaving him at her door, she ran into his room and picked up the telephone from the bedside table that showed the remains of his morning tea. Still clutching her throat, Maren sucked in a long, grateful breath and summoned her wits before ringing the desk. *That had been too close.* The man had been no amateur. If she hadn't been trained in self-defense, she would be dead right now.

"This is Maren Southcott. A man just attacked me in my room. 208. Please send security right away."

"Are you all right, Mrs. Southcott?" the receptionist asked, clearly alarmed.

"Just send someone please. Someone big."

She sat down on the bed and commenced to shake. *Focus. You weren't killed. You're all right.* Rachael had been strangled until her breath was gone permanently. They said the killer had used his bare hands. Was this the same attacker?

Then she heard the professor's voice in the hall. "No one's come out of here." Getting up on trembling legs, she went out. A muscular, middle-aged man in the outmoded tails and starched shirt of a butler was fitting a passkey card into the slot on her door. Seeing her, he asked, "Did he have a gun, Missus?"

"No. At least, he didn't use a weapon on me." Her hands went to her throat again, remembering the hard coldness of whatever had pressed into her neck. The security man threw open the door. Walking in boldly, his fists clenched, he reported immediately, "The window's open." Maren followed him back into her room. There had been no disturbance to her things, she noticed. Rachael's laptop still sat on her table. If he hadn't been after that, what had he been after?

Professor Morgan went to the telephone. "I'm ordering you a pot of tea. You've had a shock."

A shock. That was putting it mildly. Suddenly she was ferociously angry. Her assailant had nearly succeeded. Ian had to be behind it. He must have had someone scouring the hotels in Oxford.

She clenched her hands. "I thought it was housekeeping," she explained to the security guard. "How did he get a key to my room?"

"I'll be looking into this," the man said, his voice low and with a cockney twang that contrasted oddly with his "uniform."

"The coppers have been called, Missus."

Professor Morgan excused himself to get dressed, and by the time her tea had arrived, the security guard had discovered the Pakistani chambermaid kicking the door of her housekeeping closet. She was bound, gagged, and frightened. The security guard ("Call me Toby, Missus") reported that she had seen nothing. She had been hit from behind.

The phone rang as Maren was taking her first sip of hot, sweet tea. Chief Inspector Llewellyn was calling from the lobby where he had arranged to meet her. "I've been attacked," she told him. "I'm with security. Just let me get my things together. Believe me, I want to get out of here."

"Wait a moment. Are you quite certain you're all right?"

"Not entirely. I'm afraid I'm still in shock. I'll be with you soon."

Hands still shaking, she threw her toiletries into their plastic shopping bag and tossed them on top of the clothes in her duffel. She zipped it shut under Toby's dubious little eyes. "You'll have to talk to the coppers, Missus."

"Actually, I have my own private copper," she told him. "That's who just called me."

When she arrived in the lobby, Chief Inspector Llewellyn's peat brown eyes assessed her face with concern, his customary *sangfroid* having deserted him. "What happened?"

She told him. "He wore a ski mask. Medium height, gloves, street clothes. Nothing out of the ordinary. I think he had something metal on his wrist. Bulkier than a wristwatch." Maren fingered her bruised windpipe.

"I say." Professor Morgan appeared by her side, fully dressed in a tweed jacket and slacks, clutching a suitcase. "Are you in any kind of trouble, or was this just a random attack?"

Maren told Llewellyn how the professor had assisted her. The chief inspector answered the question for her. "We're following up on a case. Mrs. Southcott was in the wrong place at the wrong time. Thank you for your assistance, Mr. . . . . ?"

"Doctor. David Morgan. Professor from Birmingham. Pleased to be of help. I'll be on my way, then."

Maren gave him a smile and put out her hand. "Thanks. You were my knight in shining armor." She hoisted her duffel and her bag containing Rachael's laptop, her new ordnance survey maps and guide to Wales in her other hand.

"You'll need to make a statement before we can go," Llewellyn told her, indicating the stout Oxford policeman in the corner.

Resigned to the delay, Maren followed the chief inspector into an alcove. The departing professor gave her a wave.

"Friend of yours?" Llewellyn asked.

"He finds me anthropologically interesting."

"Hmm. That's a new line."

While she was being questioned by the police, Maren felt a geyser-like impatience pressuring her to get on and away before Griffith could follow. She told the short, stubby Oxford inspector that her assailant was unrecognizable but was likely her sister's murderer and that the CID chief inspector had the case well in hand. Llewellyn reassured him of this, and finally he left.

As they reentered the lobby, the effete Detective Sergeant Cole stepped forward. "Car ready?" the chief inspector asked, his voice flat and colorless. Whereas Llewellyn was dressed in a shirt and tie, even for this excursion into the country, his sergeant wore a weathered leather jacket and a cashmere sweater. He breathed that indefinable English *class* that was impossible for the uninitiated to imitate. His almost colorless hair was tousled, his light blue eyes insouciant. He merely nodded to his chief.

Maren acknowledged him with a handshake and then asked, "Any word on Ian?"

"Sorry," the sergeant said, his tone clipped. He pinched the bridge of his nose and closed his eyes tightly, as though this news had given him a headache. "He seems to have disappeared. Hasn't entered this country, though. Not as James Hubbard or Ian Southcott, at any rate. Interpol's been alerted. There's a watch out for him."

Maren's chest felt suddenly leaden. Ian was still at large. Perhaps it had been too much to expect her smooth husband to be caught so easily. He was like quicksilver.

The chief inspector cleared his throat. "One other thing I ought to just mention." He seemed hesitant to go on. Almost embarrassed.

D.S. Cole had no inhibitions, apparently. His pale blue eyes looking straight into hers, he said, "Fellow's married. Got a wife in London."

The relief she felt at this news was surprising and instantaneous. Though he might still be after her and determined to kill her, she felt as though she had been given an unexpected gift. She wasn't married to a member of a drug cartel or a murderer! She could wipe out the last three months and consign her nonhusband to the devil. And Ian or James or whatever his name was had absolutely no relationship to Claire. Smiling broadly, she said, "Good."

D.S. Cole smiled back with a laziness that was almost insolent.

They drove away from the Randolph, the subtly elegant Cole at the wheel.

"Where are we off to?" he asked, negotiating the early morning traffic that was brisk and noisy. With its dreaming spires, Oxford was a town clearly not meant for automobiles.

"It depends. I found all the castles on the map, and it looks like we can take our pick of North Wales or South Wales."

"Geographically, we're closer to South Wales, of course," the chief inspector said.

"Actually," Maren looked up from her map, "if we take the A40 to Cheltenham and then on to Ross-on-Wye, we'll be within striking distance of Grosmont Castle. It's fairly isolated, so I wouldn't be at all surprised to find a monastery hidden somewhere around there."

"The trouble is, you're American," Cole said, his tone almost bored. "You can't possibly understand that every square inch of this country has been inhabited continuously for eons. Every speck of ruin is accounted for. I seriously doubt there could be a monastery anywhere in Wales that hasn't been the subject of the bards for centuries."

"Then why doesn't anyone know about this one?" Maren wanted to know. "It existed at one time, and somehow the Internet associates it with Owain Glyndwr."

"Yes," the elegant sergeant drawled. "The chief inspector has told me about your Internet search. Curious."

Llewellyn had remained stolid throughout this exchange. His former personality seemed to have effaced itself, the tenuous bond between him and Maren disappearing. His sergeant, though less prepossessing and clearly disapproving of her, reminded her of British aristocracy between the wars. Indeed, Cole was the personification of Lord Peter Wimsey, her favorite detective. Cole was like a lazy leopard, languid but with the potential for quick, lethal action. In short, he was dangerous.

Maren caught herself. She was fantasizing, a habit she shared with Rachael, though she would rather die than admit it. There were absolutely no grounds for her conclusions about the sergeant other than his seeming likeness to a fictional character who had come quite vividly alive in the mind of his creator, Dorothy L. Sayers.

"How did you come to know so much about the Once and Future King, Mrs. Southcott?" D.S. Cole asked.

"Please, Detective Sergeant. That name is completely bogus. Call me Maren. You, too, of course, Chief Inspector."

As they traveled through the Cotswolds, some of the most enchanting countryside in England, with its thatched golden stone cottages covered with the last of the summer's climbing roses, the attack upon her took on an unreal quality. Especially when she began entertaining her listeners with tales of her father and the "magic" quests he had set for his daughters to while away long summer days. "He was an Arthur fanatic. His grandparents were born in Wales, and he was raised to be very superior about his heritage. He took us to Tintagel once, to show us where Arthur was born. Then we went on to Cadbury Castle. You know, where scholars think Camelot was. Rachael was hooked for good."

"But not you?" the sergeant inquired.

"As I say, I was young. But I've more or less grown up with Arthur, and I really don't see the good of sitting around and waiting for some Once and Future King to come and make everything right." She paused, examining her mind on the subject. "It would be far more likely to be a lunatic. I just don't look for any kind of political solution. I think we get right in and give it our all." She knew she was echoing her husband. Patrick had literally given it his all. Sighing, she continued, "I know it's not enough, but we have to try."

"You haven't begun to grasp Arthur's mystique," Cole told her, his bored tone reappearing. "It's not political. It's metaphorical."

"Oh, I understand the psychology behind the mystique," she said, feeling a bit defensive. "That's clear enough. Everyone needs hope. But I think it comes from the inside out, if you see what I mean."

"I'm not sure that I do. Are you a Christian?"

"Yes, but I believe in a personal God. I don't think anyone's going to wave a magic wand and make everything all right for all of us, whether we like it or not."

"Arthur is symbolic. Absolute good. Absolute truth," the sergeant argued.

"I see that. But it's no good trying to force that on people. They have to decide for themselves."

The chief inspector warned, "Don't argue with his Cambridge education. It won't get you anywhere."

There was an uncomfortable silence. Maren looked at the landscape once more and fingered her throat. Ian couldn't know she was going to Wales. That thought was reassuring.

chapter twenty-one

"S he's gone to Wales," Griffith told him over the phone.

Ian Southcott, aka Shamus O'Leary, cursed.

"Do you know where?"

"Look, I'm after the manuscript. Those were my instructions. I've got an idea, but it's rather hazy."

"Where is she?" Maren's bigamous husband demanded, feeling a headache start. Why had she left the Randolph so suddenly?

Griffith responded, "Someone tried to kill her this morning. How do I know it wasn't you?"

His head throbbed tremendously behind his left eye. Who could be after Maren? "Someone tried to kill her?"

"Right. He got into her room with a passkey. Tried to strangle her."

"Where are you?"

"On the track of the manuscript."

Pain made his annoyance sharper than ever. "Griffith, need I remind you that I have the whip hand?"

There was a pause. "I'm not sure where I'm going. I'll call you when I get there." Griffith cut the connection.

When Southcott/O'Leary tried to call back, he got only voice mail.

CHAPTER TWENTY-TWO

THE A40 WEST
GREAT BRITAIN

The traveling party had lapsed into silence, and Maren nodded off into a jet-lagged snooze. She dreamed she was being pursued by a large band of knights astride armored horses, bearing wicked lances. Patrick rescued her, singing loudly in his lusty tenor voice, "Ee-eye-ee-eye-oh!"

She opened her eyes to find that they had stopped at the charming medieval village called Ross-on-Wye. They enjoyed a quick pub lunch of sausages, bread, and pickles.

"We'll soon be officially in Wales," the sergeant told her. "The Wye travels through the Black Mountains."

Maren looked around her as they walked out of the pub, admiring the tidy town with its market spire.

"We've got to get along if we're going to make Grosmont before they shut it down. The rest of the drive is on secondary roads," Llewellyn spurred her, his voice impatient.

"There's no one following us, is there?" she demanded as they turned off onto a scantily traveled road.

"No," said the sergeant, "we're alone. We ought to reach Grosmont by about three P.M. What's the program?"

"If there's an old church, that's our best bet. But from what I read on the Owain Glyndwr site, most of the old Welsh churches were burned by Prince Henry during the rebellion," Maren said. "He's probably the one who destroyed the monastery, too."

Llewellyn nodded. "My nanny told me about Henry. She called him a scurrilous rat."

"The Internet site said Glyndwr was the first one since Llewellyn the Great to unite Wales. He aimed to emulate Arthur and take the rest of Britain, too," she told him. "Henry didn't react well."

With that, Maren sat back and watched the scenery. Wales always affected her like magic. She and Rachael had often said it must be the voices in their blood. Once they crossed the border, the signposts pointed to tiny towns with unpronounceable names: Llangarron, Llanrothal, Lingoed . . . the names always struck her as Tolkienesque, reminding her of the consonant-laden Elven tongue in *Lord of the Rings.*

In fact, the whole landscape might have been a slice of Middle Earth. It seemed older here, as though the hills and dales had been worn smooth eons ago, covered with a rich green blanket of sod, and then continuously inhabited by those who loved them. Trees and shrubs were twisted and black with age, miniature streams and water-falls created small, magical scenes where she half expected to see an elf or dwarf whisk out from behind an aged boulder. Her scare of the morning seemed far, far away in another world. Ian could never find her here among the fairies.

She shared none of these fancies with Llewellyn, who struck her as far too prosaic to be an authentic Welshman. When they reached it at long last, Grosmont Castle proved to be a classic ruin. A guide in a houndstooth-checked coat and woolen cap greeted them with obvious enthusiasm.

"More visitors! And in September! This is certainly my lucky day!" He smiled a broad yellow-toothed grin. His voice was distinctly British with none of the singsong lilt Maren associated with the true Welshman. But then, they were in South Wales, which Maren knew to be far more English than Welsh.

Their guide led the three of them across the moat by way of a modern wooden bridge. The castle was built of honey-yellow stone, overgrown with vegetation. Its most distinctive feature was a great chimney, built, the guide told them, by Prince Edmund some time between 1274 and 1294.

As he chatted on conversationally about William Fitz Osbern and his invasion of South Wales, Maren's mind drifted. This place seemed too English to be what they were looking for. All its owners in its great long chronicle had been English. Surely it wouldn't provide a refuge for Welsh monks. But since they were here, she had to ask.

"Pardon me," she broke in upon the tale of the death of someone called Payn Fitz John at the hands of the Welsh. "Do you happen to know if there was ever a Welsh monastery near here?"

Their guide's face changed from polite enthusiasm to incredulity. "How extraordinary! You're the second person today to ask me that very question!"

Llewellyn stepped forward and showed his credentials. "I'll have to ask you for a description, I'm afraid."

"CID? You're investigating a murder? At Grosmont Castle? That's absurd!" The man gave a forced laugh.

"It's a long story," Maren told him, guessing that his vanity needed to be appeased. "The victim was my sister, actually. She was searching for a monastery by a castle in Wales. One that was conquered by Owain Glyndwr . . ."

"Glendower! That bag of wind! You won't find many here who appreciate him, no matter what they think of him in the rest of Wales. We were on the side of Prince Hal! Glendower never conquered Grosmont!" He had drawn himself up and was looking distinctly bellicose.

"Yes, I realize that, of course," Maren calmed him, holding up a palm. "But this person, the one who was inquiring about the monastery . . ."

"He didn't mention Glendower, I can tell you that!"

"What did he look like?" D.S. Cole asked quietly.

His BBC accent seemed to have the desired effect.

"Perfectly respectable. Very high class, actually. Oxford. Dark hair. He had a beard, too. Smoked a pipe. Very interested in the history of the castle. Polite."

From this description, Maren gathered that their guide intended to slur the present company. "Did he give you a name?" she asked.

"Well . . . ," he hesitated. Then, coming to a decision, he pulled a card from the pocket of his cream-colored vest and handed it to her.

"Dr. Anthony Jones," she read aloud. "Christ Church. Oxford."

chapter twenty-three

GROSMONT CASTLE
WALES

The chief inspector's face hardened. "Jones. You were right, Mrs.—er, Maren. We're right behind him."

"How long ago was he here?" D.S. Cole inquired.

"Earlier this afternoon. Sent him on to Abergavenny down the road. They've an Augustinian monastery there—Llanthony Priory— he wanted to have a look at."

Maren exchanged glances with the chief inspector. He was frowning intently.

"Jones?" the D.S. asked.

"My sister's love interest." The words were bitter in her mouth. Rachael loved rarely and wholeheartedly. Maren felt this betrayal keenly.

"Possibly her murderer," Llewellyn added.

Abergavenny proved to be a bustling Welsh farm village in a hollow of the Black Mountains. Sheep grazed on emerald hillsides, and Maren's group found themselves sharing the road with pony trekkers as they made their way slowly into the village. Their guide had failed to tell them today was market day. Pulling up in front of a slate roofed, white-washed pub, Llewellyn got out to ask the way to the monastery.

The streets were bursting with local merchants and farmers with their sheep, cattle, and ponies. Colorful canopies along the main streets sheltered displays of harvested vegetables sold by doughty, red-faced farmers in worn dungarees. Their wives were selling homemade butter, free-range eggs, and fresh-cut flowers.

Despite her preoccupation with Rachael's murderer, Maren could not resist the sight. How her sister would have loved this place! She would have charmed everyone and ended by being their darling. Getting out of the Range Rover, Maren browsed among the stalls. She picked up a heavy fisherman's sweater and asked the tiny gray woman attending the stall if it were her work.

"Yes, ma'am. The wool's from my own sheep. "

"My husband would look wonderful in it." Then, biting her lip, she realized she had been thinking of Patrick with his black beard and pipe. *Will I never realize Patrick is really and truly gone?*

Feeling someone's eyes on her, she turned, expecting to see Llewellyn's movie star visage. Instead, she met the glance of a tall, bearded, black-haired man not unlike Patrick. He was even smoking a pipe. Seemingly unabashed at having been caught staring, he took the pipe out of his mouth, saluted her briefly with it, and walked away.

Maren's heart pounded. Who *was* that? How extraordinary that he had appeared just as she was thinking of Patrick!

Absently replacing the fisherman's sweater, she wandered back to the Range Rover, where she found Chief Inspector Llewellyn fuming and D.S. Cole trimming his nails.

"Must you go off like that? Can't you remember as far back as this morning?" Llewellyn berated her.

"I'm sorry. I was seduced by the market. Rachael would have loved it."

"Well, it's being market day makes it a nuisance. Turns out this Llanthony Priory has a lodge that's been turned into a hotel and restaurant. We might as well go there and put up for the night—if we can get rooms."

"Sounds uncomfortable," Cole opined. "Just how far away is it?"

"About eleven miles. We'd best get going now that the market is shutting down. The traffic will be horrific."

At her first glimpse of Llanthony Priory, Maren gasped. It was like something out of Claire's fairy tales. Only a ruin now, its rows of graceful arches stood out against the purpling dusk. It was a perfect antique diadem set down gracefully in green velvet. Could Walter's Arthurian manuscript be here? Surely someone would have found it long ago, if that were the case. Detective Sergeant Cole was right.

The guide at the Prior's Lodge in the southwest tower told them that the site was closed for the day but offered them pamphlets and showed them the way to the hotel and restaurant. There, the concierge, a severe-looking man, who might in another age have been a monk, allowed that they had two rooms available, both doubles.

The sergeant winced, and Maren knew that he did not fancy sharing with his superior officer. Maren thought Llewellyn probably felt the same way. Booking her own room, she told the others she would join them in the restaurant in half an hour. She left Llewellyn showing his ID and trying to cajole better accommodations from the concierge.

She wondered what she would find up the stone stairway. Though stark, her room, surprisingly, was not uncomfortable. A crisp white duvet over a comfortable feather quilt furnished the ancient four-poster bed. On the washstand stood a delft blue pitcher full of white chrysanthemums. The walls were hung with inexpert watercolors of the Priory. A walnut wardrobe was more than adequate for her few items of clothing.

Discovering a bathroom down the hall, Maren was pleased to find that plenty of hot water flowed into the clawed Victorian bathtub. After bathing, she dressed in Rachael's bottle green, floor-length velvety gown with the three-quarter-length sleeves and the draped cowl neck. It was most suited to her surroundings and warmer than her other clothes. Returning to her room and turning on the brass lamp at her bedside, she sat down to study the brochure on the ruins for the few remaining minutes before she was due downstairs.

The priory was Augustinian, dating back to the early twelfth century. It had been devastated in the rebellion under Owain Glyndwr in the fifteenth century and never recovered. She could find no mention anywhere of the Brothers of Castell *cadarn a'i safle grymus ar ben y graig.* She would have to ask.

When she entered the little restaurant, which was snug and pub-like in atmosphere with its low-beamed ceiling and womblike booths, she found neither of her escorts; however, the man with the beard and pipe whom she had seen in the marketplace was sitting alone, looking into the fireplace. At her entrance, he glanced up, and his countenance rapidly changed from abstraction to astonishment. Maren stood completely still while he appeared to master himself. Getting to his feet, he said, "Excuse me. That dress . . . your eyes. . . . Are you by any chance Rachael Williams's sister?"

Now it was Maren's turn to be astonished. Someone who knew Rachael *here,* in this remote valley in Wales? "I am," she said slowly. "And you are . . . ?"

He offered a hand. "Anthony Jones. I'm . . . I'm truly sorry about Rachael's death. It was such a ghastly thing. Do they know yet who did it?"

Stunned by his identity, Maren swallowed, ignoring the

outstretched hand. All the clues certainly pointed to him. The chain on the door, the lack of prints on the Dylan Thomas, the missing note from the Bodleian. And it did appear that he was hunting down the manuscript. She just needed to ignore her instincts. They had been wildly off where Ian was concerned. This man just happened to look like Patrick.

"They think you did, actually," she said, keeping her voice cool. "You were working with Rachael, weren't you? On the lost Breton manuscript?"

He stood looking at her for a moment, one of his eyebrows raised. It was absolutely bizarre how much he resembled Patrick. "I was," he said. The warmth in his voice had gone.

"And now you're after it for yourself," she stated bluntly.

She was wrong. He wasn't a clone of Patrick. His eyes weren't blue. Nevertheless, they were the most beautiful eyes she had ever seen. With a charcoal rim around the iris, they were gold, merging into clear green, and fringed densely with long black lashes. Now they narrowed, and she saw a glint of challenge there. It was like the light in Patrick's eyes before he went into the courtroom. "You're wrong. I'm after it for Britain. I belong to the Oxford Arthurian Society. So did Rachael. I'm doing this in her memory."

"Well, I think you should know that I'm here with Chief Inspector Llewellyn, who's investigating my sister's murder."

"And he thinks for some misguided reason that I'm the killer?" he asked, his tone completely glacial.

"The Dylan Thomas. There were no fingerprints on it. And you took the note from the Bodleian."

Professor Anthony Jones lowered his eyes. "How do you know about that?"

"I decrypted the file on Rachael's computer. When I went to the library to look for the note, it was gone. Yours was the only signature in the book, Professor."

He refrained from answering. At that moment, the chief inspector and his sergeant came up behind her.

"Chief Inspector Llewellyn, Detective Sergeant Cole, I'd like you to meet Professor Anthony Jones of Christ Church College, Oxford."

Llewellyn stood still as a statue, looking at the professor. He was clearly having some difficulty taking the information on board. His handsome features showed no response whatsoever. D.S. Cole was studying Maren, an odd expression of detachment in his eyes, as though she were some form of exotic beetle.

"Uh, Mrs.—uh, Maren," the chief inspector stammered, "we have something of a private nature to discuss with you. Perhaps it would be best if we took a stroll outside?"

She looked at him in surprise. Why was he looking at her in that tortured way, like Cary Grant when he rescued the poisoned Ingrid Bergman in *Notorious?* "Didn't you hear what I said? This is Professor Jones. The man we came here to find."

"I'll leave Detective Sergeant Cole with him. Don't worry." Rather stiffly, he gestured towards the doorway. "Shall we?"

The night air was chilly, with a brisk wind blowing through the valley. The stars and a thin crescent of moon shown down eerily on the skeletal ruins of the old priory. Maren was suddenly afraid.

"I'm sorry to be the bearer of bad tidings," Llewellyn began, "but I'm afraid I have some rather serious news. I just rang the Yard. My mobile phone needed a recharge. They've been trying to reach me all day."

He looked down at her, and his eyes were disturbingly sad.

"What is it?" She scanned his face anxiously.

"Your daughter. Your brother-in-law says she's been kidnapped. Your husband seems to have taken her."

Chapter Twenty-Four

Maren stared at the chief inspector. "Claire?" she said without understanding. "What are you talking about?"

"Your brother-in-law telephoned Scotland Yard today. Claire has been kidnapped. He's received instructions from your husband for her ransom."

"Ransom?" The edges of her vision were beginning to shrink oddly, as though her world were closing in on itself. A flash of heat started between her shoulder blades and spread while her stomach revolted.

"He wants the manuscript. You're to meet him with it at a place as yet to be specified."

Maren stared blindly at the black shapes that were the ruined arches of the monastery. She reflected in part of her mind that it didn't seem like a fairy tale anymore but rather like some twisted gothic horror story. Llewellyn was telling her that Claire, her daughter, whom she had left safely in the care of the child's Uncle Robert, had been kidnapped by Ian. Straightforward. Devastating.

Who will tuck me in, Mommy? Kidnapped! Red waves of horror shook her body, and black spots appeared before her eyes. The fresh cut of pain struck clear through her breast and remorse filled the hollow, almost stopping her heart. Why had she left Claire in danger? Why? *Why?* Her arms, aching to hold her daughter against harm, tensed with futility, and she clenched her fists. For a moment she stood, trembling until great heaving sobs made it to the surface. The chief inspector stood by helplessly.

Ian. He had pretended to care for Claire. Had bought her frilly dresses (which her daughter despised but wore to please him), had taken her to the Lincoln Park Zoo, had picked little bouquets for her out of the garden . . . but he was a fraud, a bigamist, affiliated with a drug ring. Possibly a murderer. He had tried to have her killed. What would he do to her daughter? Horrifying images chased through her mind.

In desperation, she seized at the chief inspector's jacket. "The FBI? Has the FBI been called?"

"He's left the country with her," Llewellyn told her quietly. "I've put Interpol on it, but we don't know what name he's traveling under."

Everything in the world distilled into the memory of a pair of trusting blue eyes looking up into hers. "I've got to talk to Robert," she said fiercely. "Can you arrange it?"

Her brother-in-law said before she could even ask him, "They're going after Valerie. I expect they're questioning her now. We should know something one way or the other soon."

"But . . . Claire's gone! Robert, how could you let it happen? You knew she was in danger. How could he get her out of your house?"

"The very devil's in it, Maren. We were out last night. Left Claire

108

with Louise, our maid. She put her to bed after your call, and that's the last anyone saw her." He paused, and the illusion of his closeness disappeared. Robert was a long way off. "I still can't take it in. I keep expecting to see her . . . I think you know how much we care for her. We did know she was in danger . . . I blame myself . . . I am so, so sorry . . ."

"This Louise . . ."

"Used to be Kathryn's nanny. Been with the family for years. She's having a regular breakdown."

"So am I! I've never felt so helpless. She's just a little girl! Who knows what could be happening to her?" She began sobbing again. The images in her head wouldn't leave. When she could speak, she said, "I'm on the next plane out of here!"

"Don't you understand? She's with Ian! He's left the country. It wouldn't do a bit of good for you to come home!"

"How do you know?" she demanded, anger welling up inside her, stifling her sobs. She had to take action. Some sort of action. Now.

"It's all in a note on her bed. Typed. I have no doubt he's behind it, but he could have ordered it done. That's what's giving me fits. She knows Ian, but . . ."

"Oh, Robert!" Maren felt as though her cut-up heart were being wrung from her by savages. It was bad enough to think of Claire with Ian. But with strangers!

"I know you," he said calmly. "I know what you've been like since Patrick died. You think you've got to find Claire yourself. You think . . ."

"Robert! You don't understand at all! Any mother would feel the same! I've got to *do* something!"

"The FBI has been all over the house, and they've found nothing. There was just the note. Now, I'll follow up here on Valerie. We'll find out what she knows, don't worry. After all, she works for me. Your best chance of getting Claire back lies in finding whatever it is he wants—that manuscript or whatever it is. Focus on that. We don't have a clue where he is, but he'll find you, don't worry." He cleared his throat. "And I honestly don't think he would hurt her."

Maren closed her eyes against the appalling pictures in her head. Claire in the hands of the psychopath in the airport. Claire being transported by plane to some unknown destination in the middle of the night. *Who will tuck me in, Mommy?* She suddenly couldn't think at all. All she could do was feel that wretched, black fear that was every mother's worst nightmare. It was as though she were falling down a bottomless well.

"He wants me dead, Robert," she murmured at last.

"What?" her brother-in-law demanded.

She recounted the attack of that morning.

"You've got to get police protection."

"I have it. But they're not going to help me get Claire back."

"You don't know that. They can do more than anyone. Ian is going to turn up there, looking for that thing. Maybe they can nab him. Just level with them. Tell them you've got to get that manuscript. Use it as bait. It's the only thing you can do. Seriously."

Maren hit the bottom of the well suddenly. She was a long way down, and it seemed there was only one possible way up. She didn't honestly care if she ever found the cursed thing. It had caused Rachael's death and now Claire's kidnapping. But it was the only way out she had. The only possible thing she could do. Robert was right.

"It must be that statement that's caused him to go after me. The one Valerie read. She had to have told him about it. And the police over here have connected him with a drug cartel. Colombians. This is nasty, Robert. He is *not* a nice guy." Down in her dark black hole, another terrible idea jolted her. "You know, I wouldn't be surprised if these are the people Patrick was prosecuting."

There was silence on the other end of the line. Finally, "How could you have married him, Maren? After one month? After what you had with my brother?"

Despair wiped out her incipient anger. "You won't understand this, Robert, but I was looking for some way to prove that I was still alive. Ironic, isn't it?"

That night in the old priory she did not sleep. She lay staring at the fragment of willow branch that scratched against her window in the moonlight, thinking about how miserably she had failed as a parent. Patrick was dead. Claire had needed a mother more than ever. Would he have been pleased at her rushing around, trying to round up a drug cartel? No. Claire had been his pride and joy. In spite of his own demanding schedule, he had been there every single night since she was born to tuck her in and sing silly songs to her. He had been so proud of her red hair—a throwback to his immigrant mother's. He used to brush it for her on Sunday mornings before carrying her off to mass. And her diet! He had read every pediatric book there was on food, insisting that she be fed plenty of vegetables from the moment she could gum solids.

No. Patrick would not have been pleased at the choices she had made. The thought of what he would have had to say about Ian made her writhe. She had betrayed him at the most basic of levels, entrusting his daughter to his enemy.

And never having known the reasons behind her split with Rachael, he surely wouldn't have understood her involvement in this chase after an ancient manuscript. She had failed Patrick. And she had definitely failed Claire. She had thought she was doing the right thing to go after Ian, especially after his threat against Claire, but she would have been better off staying where she was, forgetting Rachael and the manuscript, letting Ian go his own way. What was some relic compared to the life of her child? It was impossible to slay every dragon, face down every threat. You just had to take the hours you were given and make them count.

In agony, Maren buried her face in the goose down pillow. She promised the God she pictured as the shepherd she remembered from Sunday School that if only she could get Claire back, she would take care of her. Not just entertain her but relate to her as the true, unique person she was. Raise her to be the daughter of Patrick O'Neill.

But *would* she get her back? She only had so much control. And that lay in the things she knew that Ian didn't. He and his pal, Griffith, couldn't possibly find the manuscript without her.

Here she stopped short. *Then why had he tried to kill her?* It didn't make any sense at all. There had been an attack on her life the very morning after Claire was taken and the ransom note left.

Something was very, very wrong. Then she remembered that the police were questioning Valerie. Maybe that would shed some light on the situation. She could only hope. And pray to that Shepherd she didn't know very well.

Oh, God, watch over her! I would rather she die and be with you than suffer something terrible at the hands of some psychopath!

Twisted images continued to visit her in the bleak night, and she couldn't see anything through the psychic, spiritual darkness. Her remorse was as real and searing as a rod of steel, hot and red from the refiner's furnace.

chapter twenty-five

O wain Glyndwr was strolling amongst the old ruins in the moonlight. It had been six hundred years since he'd been here. And that had been a defeat that would never be repeated.

Innocence rested upon the Garden.
Fruit abundant, red and gold.

Secret slitherings through blessed stillness.
The bite. The blood. The fall from grace.

Winds gathered about them.
Storm blew them and drew them

Apart from innocence and silence,
Tumbling into velvet black.

No gold, no sun, no light.
Sweat, thorns, tears, truth,

Followed forever, never relenting,
Always behind them, ever at hand.

Death dropped in and never departed.

He had found his Eve. With her by his side, even this mortal misery could be changed into gladness. She would see. He must not reveal himself too soon, but he couldn't keep his distance for much longer. He had to draw from her all the light and strength he needed in this time of waiting.

Death to the Anglo-Saxons.

chapter twenty-six

LLANTHONY PRIORY
WALES

One thing Maren learned from her sleepless night was that time didn't stop, wouldn't stop, just because you couldn't bear for it to go on. She had to face this day, Monday, knowing that Claire was somewhere out of reach and in danger. She didn't know if it would be possible.

Then she remembered something she had totally forgotten in the night. Dr. Anthony Jones. Possibly Rachael's murderer. Had he taken her sister in with his resemblance to Patrick? Played her along as she fell fathoms deep in love again? Then had he, in a fit of passionate anger, strangled her when she wouldn't tell him her secret? It wouldn't do to forget, in her concern for Claire, that Rachael had been brutally murdered. But just how much horror could her brain and heart take in?

The problem was, Dr. Anthony Jones was the one most knowledgeable to help in the quest. What would Rachael want?

Dressing carelessly in her sister's suede boots, tiered knit skirt, and long-sleeved cotton sweater, Maren tried to put herself inside her sister's mind. Rachael had been very good at getting what she wanted. Even if Anthony Jones had murdered Rachael, she would want Maren to use him to find the manuscript, save Claire, and *then* prove him guilty of the murder.

She would watch her back around Dr. Jones, remember that it was possible that he had a hair-trigger temper and was capable of murder, but for Claire's sake she would use his Celtic-obsessed brain to locate the relic. She only hoped the police would cooperate. Just how much evidence did they have against Dr. Jones?

She reflected that her sister's summer wardrobe was becoming inadequate. It was icy cold in this room. But perhaps that was nerves and lack of sleep. Never in her life had she felt this vulnerable. What good were her self-defense techniques now? She gave a hasty glance in the mirror. Never able to compare favorably with Rachael, she appeared positively witchlike now, her eyes puffy and red-rimmed, her hair wild with static electricity from her tossing and turning.

She found Professor Jones breakfasting on a hard roll and reading the *Times* in the small, dark dining room. It was seven A.M., and her escorts were not yet down.

"Dr. Jones," she said, seating herself at his table without ceremony.

"Mrs. Southcott." He nodded briskly, returning to his newspaper.

"Don't call me that!" she said, her nerves snapping at the hated name. "Don't *ever* call me that!"

"I beg your pardon," he said, his voice cool, his beautiful eyes hot with some emotion. "I thought it was your name."

"It's not!" She clenched her fists on top of the table. She was making a mess of this. "Ian Southcott was a fictitious name. On top of that, he is a bigamist. So I am definitely not, nor have I ever been, Mrs. Southcott. My name is Maren O'Neill, and my daughter, Claire, has just been kidnapped by . . . by . . ."

"Kidnapped?" the professor echoed, putting down his newspaper, clearly incredulous. "By whom? Have you any idea?"

Her eyes spilled more tears. "By James Hubbard, I guess we should call him. If that's Ian Southcott's real name, which I am beginning to doubt."

"He's not her father, then?" A frown lowered his brow.

"No! Her father was a wonderful man . . ." Here Maren, to her mortification, broke down in pure shame.

Professor Jones handed her his clean linen napkin. "What can I do to help?" he asked, his voice unexpectedly gentle.

"I'm sorry. I never do this . . . It's been an awful night." Maren mopped her face with the napkin. Then she raised her head. The charcoal ring around his remarkable green-gold irises had darkened, and he was studying her with profound concern. It almost started her off again. What was it about a compassionate man that made you want to weep? In the midst of all her self-condemnation, she suddenly wondered if he had loved Rachael very much. Instead of suspecting that he had killed her sister, she found herself wanting to know how much he had suffered. But then, she had a lousy record for judging character.

"So I would imagine," he responded softly. "Certainly beyond anything I can fathom."

"Dr. Jones, the only way I can get her back is to find that manuscript. That's the ransom."

He was quiet. For a moment, they studied each other. Then she said, "Claire is Rachael's niece. Rachael was . . . well, Rachael was in love with Claire's father."

He looked away, out the small window to where autumn rain lashed steadily against the ruins.

"I know how much that manuscript meant to my sister, " Maren continued. "But as it stands, her death is meaningless. If we can save

Claire by following Rachael's clue, I know she would want us to give it up for Claire. It would make her death count for something."

At that unpropitious moment Chief Inspector Llewellyn joined them, accompanied by D.S. Cole, his relaxed, bony frame dressed in a sky blue cashmere polo neck sweater and blue jeans.

"Am I under arrest?" Anthony Jones asked them, his tone resigned.

"Detective Sergeant Cole briefed me on his interrogation of you," Llewellyn said. "I gather the last time you saw Dr. Williams was the evening of her death?"

"Yes. We had an early night because her sister . . . Mrs.—uh, Mrs. O'Neill was coming in at dawn the next morning."

"And you knew about this manuscript?"

He frowned, taking the pipe from his pocket. "I don't know how well you know academics, Chief Inspector, but it was rather a game between us. I knew she had found something in the Bodleian that she was frightfully excited about. Old Miss Tibbs helped me retrace her steps there." He filled his pipe. "The librarian, you know."

"Down to brass tacks, Jones," Cole said brusquely.

"After reading the note, I decided the manuscript must be associated with a castle on a hill near a monastery. I began here because it was the closest. But they've never heard of the Brethren here. There's no sign of them, and the feel is all wrong. Should have known. This has always been an English stronghold. I intend to go north."

"Were you romantically involved with Dr. Williams?" Llewellyn asked.

Tamping down his tobacco, the professor said, his voice carefully controlled, "She wasn't frightfully keen, actually. Said I reminded her too much of someone she had loved once before. Bad experience, I gathered." He looked up then, straight into Maren's eyes.

The guilt that would never go away stabbed her. "He's telling the truth," she said. "My sister was in love with Patrick O'Neill. He looked remarkably like Dr. Jones. Except for the eyes."

"O'Neill?" the chief inspector queried. "But surely that's your daughter's name?"

"Yes. Patrick was my husband. He was killed. Another little problem for you, Chief Inspector. I suspect the drug ring he was prosecuting was responsible."

Llewellyn looked thoughtful. "Funny how this drug business keeps popping up." Then he cleared his throat. "Now then. What precisely are your plans, Professor Jones?"

"I planned to go north to Valle Crucis Abbey. It's near both Ruthin and Dinas Bran castles in Clwyd."

"Ruthin is on our list, Chief Inspector," Maren informed him.

"Then let me make a suggestion," Llewellyn said. "I must tell you that the case against you, Dr. Jones, is strong, as far as motive and opportunity are concerned. But we've no actual evidence. I'll have the sergeant take your fingerprints and send them to the Yard. Then, I suggest that we all make the journey together. I'm not letting you out of sight to be swallowed up in rural Wales."

Professor Anthony Jones responded by extending his arm to the table beside him. "Breakfast first, then, gentlemen?"

CHAPTER TWENTY-SEVEN

OXFORD

Why didn't you telephone me last night, you idiot? I could have been at the priory in no time!" the man calling himself Shamus O'Leary expostulated as he paced his room at the Randolph like a restless cat.

"And done what? She doesn't have it yet, I tell you. She got a bad start, but I think she's headed in the right direction now. Most of Glyndwr's battles were in the north."

"Who is Glyndwr, and what does he have to do with this manuscript, pray tell?"

"Shakespeare. You're a little rusty, I think. *Henry IV, Part One.* Remember the bloke who claimed the heavens shook when he was born?"

"Hotspur's blowhard crony? Glendower? Why on earth should he matter?"

"Well, for some reason unknown to me as yet, they are following the trail of Glyndwr's campaign through Wales in the fifteenth century."

"And just how did you come upon this piece of information?"

"I'm rather good at impersonating waiters, believe it or not. I intruded upon them while they were planning their route. Tea tray, you know."

O'Leary grumbled, "Why didn't you tell me this yesterday?"

"It wouldn't have done you a speck of good. I'd no idea which way they were headed. The priory took me completely by surprise. They were discussing castles."

"So they're headed for North Wales, now?"

"I've got a tracking device on their car that communicates with my computer. Too early to tell which castle they're headed for yet."

"I'll take the motorway to Chester," O'Leary said. "That will get me into the vicinity. Keep me informed. I want to catch up with Maren tonight."

"Why? You're bound to antagonize her. Why not let her look around?"

"It's between husband and wife, Griffith. Who knows? Maybe I can help her out. And remember I have the name of your superior on autodial. All it takes is a punch of my finger, and you're through."

Griffith hung up.

Shamus O'Leary aka Ian Southcott aka James Hubbard swore. Then he went downstairs to get directions to the nearest Internet café, where he looked up Owain Glyndwr.

Some time later, armed with printouts of four castles and an ordnance survey map of Wales, he set off for Chester on the motorway. So absorbed was he in negotiating traffic that he failed to notice the Volvo on his tail.

chapter twenty-eight

Traveling through Wales

The route to Clwyd was complex and slow as they traveled on two-way roads ever northward through the valleys carved in the mountains of Mid Wales. The chief inspector sat in the rear seat with Maren. Dr. Jones sat in the front next to D.S. Cole.

At first, no one said anything. Horrible visions of what could be happening to her daughter revisited her and kept Maren from noticing or remarking on the pastoral loveliness of the Wye River Valley. The landscape did not suit her mood. The earlier rain had been a far better match than this heartlessly sunny day.

The chief inspector sat, his face averted from hers, staring out his window. She appreciated his attempt to give her an illusion of privacy. In the front seat, Cole had the Range Rover's radio turned to BBC 3, which was currently airing a string of Chopin etudes—alternately stormy and melancholy. Professor Anthony Jones seemed perfectly at ease, paging through a folder of notes and briefly glancing at the scenery now and then. Could a murderer in the custody of two policemen be so self-possessed? But he was rather a cool customer, Rachael's Dr. Jones. Off on the chase the day after her murder . . .

At length, he asked, "If you don't mind my asking, Mrs.—er, O'Neill . . ."

"Maren," she corrected absently.

"Maren, then. What put you on to Llanthony Priory and Ruthin Castle?"

"We didn't know about the priory," she told him, rousing herself. "That was luck. We were visiting Grosmont Castle when the guide told us you had gone there."

"I think it rather extraordinary that we both chose to visit the place yesterday."

"Not really, when you think about it." She shrugged. "Didn't you use the Internet?"

"The Internet?" he queried, as though she were asking about a valley on Mars.

"You must have Googled the monastery!"

"Google? What on earth is that?"

Astonished momentarily out of her preoccupation, she said, "You're a professor at the most prestigious university in the world, and you don't use the Internet?"

He chuckled. "Celtic Studies, remember. Hardly the Internet age."

"The Celts would love the Internet. It's the closest thing there is to magic. I typed in the name of the monastery, and up popped a Website all about Owain Glyndwr. I never in a million years would have made the connection."

"What connection? Glyndwr was fifteenth century. Arthur was a thousand years earlier."

The chief inspector turned his head and joined the conversation. "Are you certain you want to take him into our confidence, Mrs.—uh, Maren?"

"I have a feeling we could use his help," she told him firmly. "We've got to find this thing for Claire." She turned back to the professor. "We don't know what the connection is. I read the site, but all I got out of it was a list of castles. We figured one of them must be this 'mighty castle superbly situated on a rocky crag.' We are just going around looking for ruined monasteries connected with these castles. Do you have a better plan?"

"I started with the monasteries and then connected them with likely castles."

Through the window of the Range Rover, Maren glimpsed a man in a checked hat pulling a wagonload of enormous pumpkins. It was probably the first thing she had noticed all day. "The problem is, these brethren were unrecorded. I think their monastery was destroyed. Maybe by Prince Henry. I think what we need to look for are some unclassified ruins."

D.S. Cole interrupted. "I doubt you'll be able to find anything like that. This isn't the Wild West. It's Britain. We love picturesque ruins. We photograph them. We put them in books and on Websites."

"Then why hasn't anyone ever heard of these monks?" Maren demanded.

"Actually . . ." the professor began.

"Yes?" Maren prompted.

"I was just going to say, there are some fairly wild places in the mountains around Snowdonia."

A mobile telephone rang. "Chief Inspector Llewellyn here. . . . Yes, Sergeant, what have you got for me? I see. Yes. Yes. That's good. Registration number? Excellent." The policeman closed his phone. "I put a man on to the Randolph this morning. On the off chance that someone might come round asking for you, Maren."

She felt a spurt of expectation. "And?"

"I e-mailed the hotel a photo of your . . . er . . . the man you knew as Ian Southcott. He was there. Last night. Under the name of Shamus O'Leary. Alone. No little girl. This morning, he inquired about the whereabouts of an Internet café when he checked out."

Claire wasn't with Ian, then. Though that would have been terrifying, the alternative was worse. Who had her? "And the registration number? What was that about?"

"He was using their car park. It's very small, consequently they ask for vehicle registration numbers in order to monitor it. He was driving a BMW. The sergeant has already radioed the registration number. We should hear something soon."

"That's excellent news!" Maybe the police *were* going to be able to help her after all. Some of her gloom lifted. "He will tell us where Claire is. He has to, once he sees the game is up. Is there any way we can find out what the FBI's report on Valerie was?"

"Valerie?"

"Kensington. Ian's girlfriend. Robert, my brother-in-law, you remember, told me they'd picked up Valerie for questioning. She's the one who must have told Ian about the statement I made. About his being a thief and possibly murdering my sister."

"This is the first I've heard of it," the chief inspector said, his voice curt. "I'll call the Yard."

Maren looked out the window as they pulled into a town called Knighton. She was surprised to see a sign welcoming her to Wales. She had no knowledge of ever having left it. The road had narrowed into one street that climbed sharply towards a clock tower. A group of youths, outfitted for hiking and carrying backpacks, was heading up the hill.

"Offa's Dyke," D.S. Cole said cryptically.

The professor looked up from his papers. "Oh? Have we reached the border, then?"

Shutting his phone, the chief inspector said grimly, "Valerie

Kensington has disappeared. She didn't go into work yesterday, and her flat's empty."

"I'll bet she has Claire," Maren said, feeling as though someone had put cool water on the hot brand of her soul. Valerie hadn't struck her as a monster. Not like the man in the trench coat. "She might never have left the States at all." Tapping her fingernail on her knee, she thought frantically. Sam, Patrick's buddy at the FBI in Chicago, could help on this. This was drug related, because Ian was involved. "I have a friend I can call. He should know about Ian, or whatever his name is, anyway. As soon as we stop, I'll phone the States."

They lunched at the Six Bells Inn, a yellow brick pub next to the church in Bishop's Castle. While the men were ordering the local ale, Maren went to the pub's small office, escorted by a white-aproned hostess who wore Wranglers and Nikes. The hostelry clearly dated back hundreds of years. Wiring in the office was visible and the lighting somewhat dim. Seating herself at a scarred kneehole walnut desk that would have sold for a high price in the States, she wondered how to go about reaching Sam. Looking at her watch, she counted back the hours. Sam wouldn't have left for work yet. Hopefully, she could catch him at home.

The phone rang so long, she didn't think it would be answered. Finally, Sam picked up. "Reynolds."

"Good. I got the right number. I thought I had it memorized," she said.

"Maren? What have you got?"

"Nothing on Patrick's case, but something related possibly." She told him about Ian and his record in the UK. "I'm in Britain right now. The police here think his antiques business was used for money laundering. It's called 'Southcott, Ltd.'"

"Good lead. I'll look into it. But you're married to this dude, right?"

"Wrong. Turns out he has a wife over here already. But the worst thing . . . the reason I called, actually . . . is that . . ." Here she took a deep breath, trying to maintain the professional calm he would expect. "He's taken Claire and is holding her for ransom."

There was a pause. "Kidnapping? Claire? Maren! How in the world are you holding up?"

"Not well," she admitted, tears filling her eyes at his concern. "She's so little, Sam. And I've . . . oh, Sam! I married a man involved with drugs! He took her! At least, she's not actually with him. But she's with someone. Possibly someone really dangerous. It's bad, Sam."

"What can I do? You know I'll do anything."

"That's why I called." She wiped her eyes. "There is a woman friend of Ian's . . . actually, he's known as James Hubbard or Shamus O'Leary over here . . ." She told him about her experience with Valerie and the attempt on her own life at the Randolph. "And now she's disappeared. I think she may have Claire. Ian left a note saying he took her out of the country."

"Who'd he leave the note with?"

"Patrick's brother, Robert. That's where Claire was staying. Robert thinks Ian may have hired it done. Ian's over here. Last seen at Oxford. The police just got a registration number on his car. He didn't have Claire with him."

"I'm going to give this priority, Maren. I'll find Valerie Kensington for you. And for Patrick. I'll start with your brother-in-law."

"He's pretty upset. He blames himself."

"I can see why. How can I get in touch with you?"

"Through Chief Inspector Llewellyn at Scotland Yard. We're traveling through Wales on another matter . . . I won't go into that now, but he has a cell phone and is in touch with the Yard."

"All right. I'm sure sorry about this, Maren. What a louse that guy turned out to be."

"I should have known better," she shuddered. "You'd think I was born yesterday. Probably I should have had you run a check on him."

"Well, you can bet I'm going to look into all his dealings with a fine-toothed comb. Maybe there's even a connection to Patrick's ring."

"I thought of that, too. Irony of ironies. Can you imagine what Patrick would say? On second thought, don't. Say hi to Meg and the kids."

"Will do. What's the ransom, by the way?"

"You would never believe it. An ancient manuscript that might prove that King Arthur really existed. Trying to find it is the only thing that's keeping me going."

chapter twenty-nine

VALLE CRUCIS ABBEY
NORTH WALES

her anxiety to find the manuscript sharpened, Maren was disappointed at the well-preserved state of the ruins of Valle Crucis Abbey. Traveling down the magnificent Horseshoe Pass, trailing narrowly over the steep precipices, they approached the wild and lonely spot, which seemed ideal for their purposes. But the majestic vaulted ruins of the Cistercian monastery were so obviously a tourist attraction that she knew that anything like a manuscript would have been found long ago. More and more, she found herself agreeing with D.S. Cole's assessment of the situation.

Dr. Anthony Jones, however, was not so easily daunted. He approached the guide and paid his two-pound entrance fee. Following his example, she too paid the little red-faced lady in the green plaid dress.

"Corns are bothering me," their guide admitted, handing them each a brochure. "And I have to go home to put my man's pie in the oven. Show yourselves around, will you?"

"Is there someone nearby that knows local history fairly well?" Dr. Jones asked, his tone brisk.

"Oh, you'll be wanting Dr. Davies. He'll be here tomorrow. Talking about doing what he calls 'a dig.' "

"A dig?" Maren asked, perking up. "What for?"

"He thinks those monks may have left something behind. He's after thinking he's found a likely spot."

"Have you ever heard of *Castell cadarn a'i safle grymus ar ben y graig?*" the professor asked, rolling the Welsh off his tongue as if he were a native.

The little woman's tired face lit up at hearing her own language. She replied in rapid accents, clearly excited. Maren couldn't understand a word. The chief inspector and sergeant, who hadn't yet paid their fees, moved forward.

Dr. Jones turned to them all. "She thinks we must mean *Castell Dinas Bran.* She says it is on a mountain right above Llangollen."

"Is that far?" Maren asked.

"We came through Llangollen on the way. It was that last little town. On the other side of Horseshoe Pass. Close enough that the Brethren may have called themselves after the castle. We need to talk to this Dr. Davies."

"Do you know if Owain Glyndwr was ever here, ma'am?" Maren was too impatient to wait for the would-be archaeologist.

Instead of answering Maren, the little woman favored the professor with a pithy reply in Welsh. "She says he was through here many times," Dr. Jones told Maren. "Fought de Grey at Ruthin, north of here, of course."

Feeling stirrings of excitement, she realized she could have easily missed the place on the Website. The writing had been so small, and at times very light, almost illegible. Llangollen probably didn't have Internet cafés so she could check.

D.S. Cole interrupted. "Ask her where we can stay. And where we can get a decent glass of wine and some Welsh lamb."

Another exchange followed. The professor translated, his eyes laughing. "She says that because I speak Welsh so well, she'll tell them to expect us at the Squirrels. It's a guest house in Llangollen. Walking distance from the center of town."

As the Range Rover wound its way back through the green, green valley to Llangollen, she found herself praying once again to a God she didn't understand very well to watch over Claire. Until last night, she hadn't prayed since she was a child and Daddy had taken her to Easter services at his Methodist church, an important part of his Welsh heritage. But what else was there to do? She was going after the manuscript. Sam was following up in Chicago. Recalling the saying that there are no atheists in foxholes, she knew she was as close to desperate as she'd ever been. She clenched her fists in her lap and stared blindly at the Valley of the River Dee.

In her state of mind, she was scarcely able to appreciate the comfortable accommodations their Welsh guide had secured for them. The Squirrels Guest House was an obviously well-loved red-brick bed and breakfast run by a small and homely Welsh couple named Thomas. Mrs. Thomas, stooped with a dowager's hump, had a bright Welsh welcome for them. She stood beaming in her doorway, clearly unaware that no one but Professor Jones could understand a word she was saying.

Dr. Jones replied in Welsh and then introduced the party in English. He inquired after rooms.

"We have a double for you and your wife and a nice twin for the gentlemen," she said.

"I'm sorry to say she's not my wife, Mrs. Thomas. Do you have another room?"

The woman blushed scarlet. "Yes, *cariad.* Another twin."

Maren's room was comfortable and homey with apricot walls, a black four-poster bed furnished with a blue and white quilt, and a window that looked out on the Abbey Road toward the setting sun. Putting down her duffel, she collapsed on the bed, the journey having taken more out of her than she could have imagined. For the moment at least, she was glad to be alone.

Would they find the manuscript here in this place? And if they did, how would she ever convince the scholars involved to let her trade such a monumental relic for a little girl's life?

chapter thirty

G riffith? Where are you?" Shamus O'Leary demanded from his sterile, anonymous hotel room. A migraine had developed during the drive from Oxford, and he was lying on the bed, a wet washcloth over his eyes. The medicine did no more than take the edge off. At least he wasn't seeing lights anymore, and his double vision had cleared. He could drive if he had to. And he certainly had to.

"Just arrived in Llangollen. You know, the place where they hold the Eisteddfod. I'm not exactly certain what we're doing here."

"What do you mean?"

"This isn't one of Owain Glyndwr's haunts, but they've settled into the Squirrels Guest House. On the Abbey Road."

O'Leary sat up slowly. The pain behind his left eye pierced straight through his head. "I'll be there."

"She's got the two policemen and another man with her. I'm not certain where he fits into the scheme of things. They visited Valle Crucis Abbey today but didn't even go inside."

"Good-bye, Griffith. Make a reservation for me at the Tyn Celyn Farmhouse. I'll see you there."

As he checked out of the hotel and climbed behind the wheel of the BMW, he reflected upon the woman who had been his wife. She was so vital, so strong. And so elusive. He found himself longing simply to touch her again and wondered if he could bring himself to kill her.

And so he didn't notice the Volvo that pulled out of the parking lot behind him, as he drove west into the autumn sunset.

ChAPTER ThIRTY-ONE

Apparently, Chief Inspector Llewellyn remembered only too well the attempt on her life and was taking no chances. He insisted that all four of them dine together. Maren wished profoundly that she could be alone with Rachael's professor in order to persuade him to let her have the manuscript, if it were found. Nevertheless, she could see the chief inspector's point. After all, she clearly had no judgment when it came to men, and Professor Anthony Jones was a viable possibility for having murdered Rachael. It was hard to remember that when she was in his presence, though.

They left the snugness of the Squirrels on foot and, crossing an ancient bridge over the River Dee, they were soon in the town center. It was surprisingly well provided with restaurants, wine bars, bistros, and cafés. As she looked around her in surprise, the professor said, "It's the Eisteddfod. An annual international music festival. It brings in so much business that this place thrives."

D.S. Cole said, "Well, we shouldn't have too much trouble finding a decent cut of lamb. How about that place?" He indicated a tiny bistro with a black shingle lettered in gold and green. "The Inn at Dinas Bran."

"Named after the castle," the professor said. "Perhaps we can pick up some local legends."

Surprisingly elegant, the bistro had a scant eight linen-clad tables, with only one of them free. They were seated by a young girl with long brown braids and a ring in her nose. Obviously severely conflicted, Maren reflected. Perhaps that was modern Wales in a nutshell.

Not lingering over their heavy menus, all four of them chose the specialty lamb chops, garden peas, and *pommes frites*. The latter, the professor informed them, was nothing more than that traditional Welsh standby, chips. Or as Maren would say, French fries.

It seemed as though all the men were determined to proceed with business as usual, despite Claire's peril. But then, they weren't mothers. She didn't even know if she could stomach the meal, but Llewellyn had insisted that she could not stay at the Squirrels alone.

"So, Jones, what draws you to Arthur?" D.S. Cole asked, his elegant long fingers clasped before him on the table. Maren remembered inconsequentially that Lord Peter Wimsey's only vanity had been his hands.

"I'm a bit pedantic on the subject, I'm afraid, but I really do feel that we need his vision today," the professor answered, an eager light in his eyes. Their odd gold color gleamed even in the dimness of the restaurant. "I have a theory, you see. Not new. But I feel that each of us has a divine void within us. Philosophers call it different things."

"Existential darkness," Cole remarked.

"It all depends on your point of view," Jones said. "I prefer to see it as an absence that can only be filled by selflessness. Mother Theresa was a good example. But everyone feels the absence, and everyone fills it with something. Drugs, pornography, alcohol . . ."

"And you'd fill it with good works?" There was the vestige of a sneer in the sergeant's voice.

"That's where Arthur comes in. Why do you suppose his legend is so powerful? Because he wasn't dissuaded by the forces of darkness and the disbelief of the barbarians. He started where we all need to start—with the soul of the individual warrior. He believed in the persuasiveness of enlightenment."

"*Jones* is Welsh, isn't it?" Maren inquired, feeling impatience stir within her at his ability to be so abstract about the matter. He seemed to have forgotten Rachael and Claire completely.

"Yes, yes, of course it is. A derivation of *John's men*. King John, more's the pity. But they did come from Wales. That's the saving grace."

"That explains your romanticism," Maren said. "This is the real world, Professor. Ugly things happen. Ugly things like kidnapping and murder."

His eyes deepened with that same well of fellow-feeling she had noted that morning, but he didn't apologize for his enthusiasm. "I share in at least part of your loss, Maren. But I know I can scarcely imagine how black the world must seem to you right now." He looked past her, seeing something in his inner vision. "What keeps me going is that, of all people, your sister viewed Arthur's values as our only hope. You see, barbarism is nothing more than ignorance, in most cases. But more dangerous than barbarism, even, is the prevalent attitude that all is well. All, as you so powerfully demonstrate, is *not* well."

Maren could see him, poised at his college lectern, emphasizing points with the stem of his pipe.

"We have succumbed to the comforts of plenty," he continued. "We're filling the void with things that just don't work. People are pursuing excess now in an attempt to feel. They don't realize that the things that sustain our civilization are personal commitment to the light, to the good. Arthur's creed."

"So you believe a new Dark Age is upon us?" Cole inquired. His superior was looking ill at ease, Maren noted. With a flash of insight, she realized he was uncomfortable with his sergeant's erudition.

"I do," the professor stated flatly. "In 1941, we got up the moral gumption to fight it off. We came out of our prewar excesses and became Arthurian to the core. Right makes might. I don't think we're the same nation anymore."

"So what solution do you propose?" the chief inspector asked as his lamb chops were placed before him. "Another war?"

"A popular philosophical revolution," Dr. Anthony Jones said. "What draws people to Arthur is what used to draw them to church— a sense that there is, somewhere, an absolute good. This manuscript is just what we need to bring Arthur's values back to the public con- sciousness." His eyes sparked with enthusiasm. "We *must* have a nucleus of people who are committed to putting off the natural man, who are willing to embrace ideas that extend beyond their own per- sonal comfort. A new Battle for Britain, if you will."

"Led by whom?" asked Cole, idly spearing a chip. "You?"

"By ideals. Not one person in particular. We have no modern Arthur, so we must depend on his legend. That is why this work we're doing is so important."

"So you worship Arthur, then?" Maren asked.

"No. I merely hold him up as a type. He was a dedicated Chris- tian, you know. But this seems to be the age of the metaphor. Look at the popularity of *Lord of the Rings*, for example, or *The Chronicles of Narnia*. People grasp at the spectacular while being blind to the essence."

She was dismayed to realize that she could see his point of view. The demise of the hero was an insidious thing. With whom had she been speaking of that? Ah, yes. The professor from Birmingham. What chance had one little girl's life against such mighty visions? But the memory of Claire's blue eyes, gazing up so trustingly as she clutched her peppermints, emboldened Maren. Her daughter had no other champion.

"You talk about the soul of the individual," she said, challenging Dr. Jones with her eyes. "In that case, doesn't every choice we make matter?"

Professor Jones raised an eyebrow. "Of course."

"Wouldn't it be barbaric to sacrifice the life of a helpless child to an ideal? Doesn't that smack of idolatry? And isn't that what terrorists do every day?"

Anthony Jones looked as though she had struck him. Chief Inspector Llewellyn said, "It won't come to that, Maren. I'll take care that it doesn't."

D.S. Cole ate his lamb chop in silence.

chapter thirty-two

The A5
Wrexham to Llangollen

As Shamus O'Leary pulled out of the traffic circle outside Wrexham, he was annoyed to find the same narrow set of halogen headlights on his tail. When exactly he had become conscious of them, he couldn't tell. His headache was still tormenting him, and he wondered whether he shouldn't put the whole thing down to imagination. But as he drove into the sudden hills of Wales and the headlights still followed, he began to think.

Wasn't this just what he had feared? Wasn't this why he was trying to find Maren? Somehow, the cartel had gotten a step ahead of him. Experimenting, he pulled off the highway at Ruabon to use the men's convenience. An innocuous silver Volvo, bluish halogen headlights on, was there when he emerged. He was puzzled. If they were who he thought they were, why were they merely following him? Why hadn't they done away with him before he was conscious of their presence? Could it be that they too were on the track of Maren? Were they hoping he'd lead them to her? Was it the cartel that was behind the attempt on her life? Who had she endangered besides himself? He knew she had been making a nuisance of herself in Chicago. He thought he had kept a step ahead of her, but had she stumbled onto something?

His headache vanished. If there were any eliminating to be done, he would be the one to do it.

As his sense of self-preservation kicked in, he thought hard. Volvos were not only unobtrusive but vulnerable in comparison to BMW's. He consulted the GPS. There was a place . . . he remembered it from holidaying here with Susan . . . she had been terrified. Yes, it was that piece of road north of Llangollen. The Horseshoe Pass. One of the wonders of Wales. Steep as a nightmare. The Volvo would labor up that hill, and then there was a convenient precipice . . .

O'Leary calmed as he drew plans in his mind. He had gotten out of tighter scrapes than this. This was child's play. The cartel had over-played its hand.

When he reached Llangollen, instead of going on to the farm-house B&B as he had intended, he drove north on the A542. Ah. There it was. The hill that had made Susan as green as the landscape. What a fear of heights she had! Odd woman. She wasn't afraid of anything else that he knew of.

He accelerated without regard to his safety. He knew the BMW would leave the headlights struggling up behind him. When he reached the summit, he pulled swiftly into the scenic turnout and opened the briefcase that lay next to him on the passenger's seat. Taking out the SIG-Sauer 9 mm pistol he had smuggled in on the private jet, O'Leary opened his car door and moved quickly to the front fender. He crouched behind the car, aiming the pistol in the direction of the oncoming Volvo. It appeared.

chapter thirty-three

*W*hen they arrived back at the Squirrels, Maren went up to her room. She had made the professor think. Good.

Exhausted by the effort of carrying on despite emotional turmoil, she lay across the bed, fully clothed. Her mind went into alpha mode, floating above her, snatching at impressions gained throughout the day, and then flying off in a new direction, remembering the past.

Patrick. Sailing in his sloop on Lake Michigan, his hair unfashionably long, blowing back in the stiff breeze as his Greek-statue profile jutted forward. Jason in search of the Golden Fleece. That is what he'd always been to her. An idealist like Anthony Jones, he'd broken himself against America's hedonism. The professor had it right. It wasn't enough to fight the criminals; you had to fight the natural man. The natural, self-delusional nature of man was at the bottom of everything vile. Was there any hope in appealing to his better nature?

No longer able to keep them at bay, her thoughts returned to

Claire. Where was she? With Valerie? She hoped so with all her heart. At that point in her cogitations, she heard a knock on her door.

"Who is it?" she called out.

"Anthony."

Getting up wearily, she crossed to the door and said, "What do you need?"

"I'd like to talk to you for a moment. Perhaps we might take a short walk?"

She opened the door to him. He stood in his tweed jacket, the collar of his cranberry-colored shirt unbuttoned. He held his pipe in his hand, looking exactly like a professor. A professor with remarkably hypnotic eyes. She looked away. "I'm far too tired for a walk. I'm sorry. There's a chair and a window seat, if you don't mind coming in."

His eyebrows rose in surprise at the invitation.

"If I were to turn up dead, Chief Inspector Llewellyn would know exactly who did it."

His look was somber. "There is that."

Stepping aside, she allowed him to step into the room. He seated himself at the window seat and let her take the chair. Then he began, slowly, to fill his pipe.

"I've been thinking about your rebuke," he said. "And you're absolutely right. Your daughter has to come first. You made an excellent case. I sounded like some sort of fascist. Forcing my ideals on people."

"I'm a lawyer and a mother," she told him. "But I see your side of it, too. I mean, I see why the manuscript is so important. I don't think we ought to count Chief Inspector Llewellyn out. He does seem to be closing in on Ian."

Anthony looked at her with a one-sided smile. "He's gone on you, you realize."

His observation took her by surprise. Llewellyn? Was that true?

Shaking her head, she said, "I don't think so. He's just doing a job."

Anthony had his pipe going. "Tell me about Rachael and your husband."

Struck dumb, she studied her hands but saw only Rachael's countenance, extinguished at the first glimpse she had had of Maren and Patrick when they returned from their honeymoon in Wales. She had never talked to anyone about that. Not even Patrick. "I don't think so," she said finally. "Was there anything else?"

"Do you really think that's why she couldn't . . . well, why she wouldn't give me a chance?"

"Did you love her very much?" Maren asked.

Taking the pipe out of his mouth, he stared vacantly through the tobacco haze. "Yes. Yes, I did. We had so much in common, you see."

Maren felt his heavy sadness. The gleam that had animated him was gone. Then her own grief, displaced by Claire's kidnapping, rose up and smote her. Rachael could have been happy with this man. If she'd given him a chance. They could have spun their Celtic magic together. Maren found suddenly that she couldn't give herself wholly to that image. It had something wrong with it.

"I'm sorry," she said wearily. "I'm very tired. I think you'd better go."

He rose at once. "I'm hopeless. Of course, your grief at a time like this must be enormous. I had no right to impose on you or to force my notions on you at dinner . . ."

His distress was so genuine that she put up a hand for him to stop. "It's all right," she told him.

He stood studying her, obviously at a loss. She looked down, unable otherwise to keep her eyes from seeking his.

"You're not very like Rachael, are you?"

"No," she said. "I'm not. Good night, Anthony."

chapter thirty-four

C hief Inspector Hugh Llewellyn needed to get away from his sergeant. It had been a long and trying day, and Cole's languorous exhibitionism got on his nerves as usual. Not having his sergeant's advantages, he had worked hard to educate himself. But it seemed as though there was any number of things one couldn't assimilate without a public school education.

Turning into a small, anonymous pub with smoky rafters and a fire burning in an open hearth, he went up to the bar and ordered a pint. He took it to a small, circular wooden table in the back of the room. There was the traditional dartboard with its gaggle of working-class players in their dungarees. A fog of cigarette smoke hung over everything, while someone played a melancholy tune on the harmonica. His sergeant would undoubtedly prefer a wine bar.

As he sipped his pint, he allowed his mind to stray to Maren. Diana, the huntress, that's who she reminded him of. Funny, this desire he had to protect her. She could clearly take care of herself. Maybe that was the attraction for him. He had had all that he could take of clinging, possessive women. The love of someone like Maren would be worth something. Recalling his attempts to impress her with his mastery of chaos theory, he smiled into his pint.

She was so full of pluck. The way she had stood up to the professor! It had been a treat to see. But he ached for her, just the same. What could he do about recovering her daughter? He hadn't heard anything from the Yard on the number plate. But there must be something he hadn't thought of. Some angle of the case he hadn't examined properly.

Out of the corner of his eye, he saw someone settle at the table next to his. With a fervent longing for the English reserve, he hoped his neighbor wasn't the average talkative Welshman.

The beard was the first thing he noticed. Ginger-colored. Familiar. His antennae immediately twitched. He had a good memory for faces. Getting up to renew his pint, he looked the man over. The Randolph. He had seen the fellow in the Randolph. Talking to Maren. After the attempt on her life. Odd that he should be here. Dr. David Morgan, he had been. Professor from Birmingham. In the next room to Maren. Yes. Definitely odd. Oddities in a case were quite often turning points. This man would bear watching.

From the corner of his eye, he could tell his quarry was nervous. He was taking something fizzy in a glass. A headache powder? He kept looking at his watch. His mobile phone sat on the table in front of him and he watched it as though it were a snake. Finally, with a sigh, he finished off his drink, pocketed the phone, and stood.

Llewellyn waited until he got to the door and then followed. He trailed the stocky professor through the town center. The evening crowd became thinner, forcing him to lengthen the distance between the two of them. Presently they were alone on the road. The professor appeared to be in a brown study, unaware he was being followed.

Or was he? This was an isolated stretch. Lonely as a coal miner's widow. Now where had that thought come from? Too much time in Wales. Cursed country. It made him uneasy to hear that gibberish they called Welsh. Actually made his flesh crawl.

Just as he had begun to wonder whether he wasn't being set up for an ambush, a farmhouse appeared. Professor David Morgan went inside. The September night had turned downright cold, and a stiff breeze was blowing down the vale. After waiting beside the holly hedge until his fingers grew numb, Llewellyn entered the place that advertised itself as Tyn Celyn Bed and Breakfast.

"Ah! Then you would be Mr. O'Leary?" A stout matron in a print jersey dress asked him. "We've been after wondering if you were held up."

He looked at her blankly. It took a moment to register. *O'Leary? As in Shamus O'Leary? Hubbard's most recent alias?*

He stepped out of the guise of polite stranger into the more familiar figure of authority. Pulling out his identification, he showed it to the matron. "What can you tell me about this Mr. O'Leary?"

The woman's eyes bulged in sudden fear. "What's he done, then? I don't want trouble in this house."

He saw no reason not to tell her. "He's affiliated with a dangerous ring of drug smugglers, as well as being suspected of murder and kidnapping."

Her hands flew to her face, which had whitened in alarm. "And that nice Dr. Griffith made his reservation for him."

"Griffith?" Llewellyn echoed. *Maren's mythical Griffith? The one her husband had phoned from Chicago? The one she suspected of Rachael Williams's murder?*

"Yes. Just came in, he did. Very civil. Very respectable. Not one as like to be mixed up in murder or anything like that."

"No need to alarm him. I'll just wait for my sergeant. And should Mr. O'Leary arrive, act as though you've never seen me."

"A murderer and a kidnapper? I won't have the man in my house!"

"My sergeant will be protection for you, Mrs.—?"

"Carroll, Chief Inspector. Mrs. Carroll. I won't have my name in the papers?"

"We'll keep this as quiet as we can. Just let me telephone to my sergeant." Pulling out his mobile, he dialed his sergeant, summoning both him and the Range Rover, and settled down next to the open fire in the lounge to await their arrival.

chapter thirty-five

"Yes, sir," Braden reported to the director general. "We've had some success. We have a good lead."

"Details, please. The Home Secretary must report to the Queen."

Chief Commissioner Braden looked down at the file on his desk that the dour Evans had assembled, picking up the top sheet. "It's a chap in Llangollen. He was involved in a Glyndwr group in the eighties. They set fire to English holiday homes in Wales."

"Yes, yes. I remember. But that was all a very long time ago."

"But this man actually seems to have some kind of Glyndwr alter ego. He performs at the International Musical Eisteddfod in Llangollen, singing the Welsh national anthem and billing himself as Owain Glyndwr. He's a tenor. He's won awards. Has quite a following, apparently."

"The Home Secretary won't care if he's a soprano!" the director general said, his irritation clear. "Where is he to be found?"

"He's a local, actually. From Llangollen. Sings in a men's choir there."

"So you're off to Llangollen then?"

"Yes, sir."

"Good. You'll keep me informed? The Prince has a trip to Wales in three days' time."

"I'm aware of that. Yes, I'll certainly keep you informed." Braden hung up the telephone and wiped his brow.

After a moment, he telephoned his sergeant and asked her to bring the car around at eight o'clock the following morning. Then, taking his suit coat from the hook behind the door, he went home to his comfortable wife, his steak-and-kidney pie, and his chrysanthemums, glad to have this prickly affair so close to resolution.

chapter thirty-six

Owain Glyndwr felt as though he were in a straight-jacket. This place held too many memories. It was getting more and more difficult to restrain his passions. In his mind, he strode through the late evening among the ruins of Castell Dinas Bran. He could see the world from here. His world. The world that had once been a grand kingdom full of great and worthy men.

Would it be tomorrow? The day the talisman would finally be uncovered? It must happen soon. It *would* happen soon, of course. All the magic was with him. It should not astound him how everything was dropping into his hands. The magic was like that.

> *Therefore rise, look, watch the light.*
> *Comfort shall come after cruel night.*

And his Celtic goddess would oversee his victory with her mystical green eyes. The time had come to court her. She would see that she belonged to him, body and soul.

Chapter Thirty-Seven

Tyn Celyn Farmhouse
Llangollen, Wales

"Chief Inspector, isn't it?" the man Llewellyn knew as Dr. Morgan exclaimed upon seeing him. "What on earth brings you to Llangollen?"

Llewellyn had counted on fear and was unprepared for detached curiosity. "Inquiries," he said shortly. "I'm more interested in what brings you here."

"As far as I can tell, that's my business. But I don't mind telling you. I'm an anthropologist, you see. Very, very interested in the Welsh character. I'm part Welsh myself. And there's this odd dichotomy about Llangollen." Seating himself away from the fire, he stroked his beard. Llewellyn glanced at his sergeant, who, he was amused to see, was looking down his nose at the professor, if that's what he was.

Morgan/Griffith continued, "It's just a sleepy little Welsh town of three thousand people, but every summer it brims with internationals from as far away as Iceland! The Eisteddfod, you know." He looked out from under his brows, as though to make certain the policemen were following him. "It started out as a purely Welsh celebration of national pride. Now that particular festival is separate and distinct, attended by Welsh nationalists, while this other Eisteddfod, the one that was started after the war, brings in people from all over the place. It breeds a type of schizophrenia in people's consciousness."

"One minute they are isolationists, and the next they are globalists," Cole responded curtly. "Yes, dim coppers though we are, we can perceive that much. What we can't perceive is how you come to be staying here under an assumed name."

"Having reserved a room for your associate O'Leary, who is wanted for drug smuggling, kidnapping, and conspiracy to commit murder," Llewellyn added, satisfied to see the detached air slip from the professor's face. He now looked feral, sly. "Just what exactly was your business with Maren O'Neill at the Randolph? Did you try to kill her, perhaps? Like you killed her sister?"

Now the man was gaping. "What on earth are you talking about? I'm completely at sea here."

"How about if we start with the business of the assumed name," Cole suggested.

"Griffith is my pen name," the man said, pulling himself together with obvious effort. "I'm writing rather a steamy work of fiction set in Llangollen during the Eisteddfod. You know, local girl seduced by . . . Well, you get the picture. Need the income. Those things sell like ice cream on the promenade. But they don't do my professional life any good. I endeavor to keep the two halves of my life separate."

Cole nodded. "Fair enough. Now let's move on to your friend O'Leary."

"He's an acquaintance of my publisher. An antiques dealer from London, I believe. Arnold, my publisher, asked if I'd set him up with a room. What I was told is that he's going through a messy divorce and needs to get away."

"Thin, Professor Morgan, very thin," the chief inspector said, at the same time marveling at the man's ingenuity. "I don't suppose you'd mind having your fingerprints taken, then?"

Their suspect drew back. "Fingerprints? Whatever for?"

"Comparison," Llewellyn said, feeling the pleasure he always did at closing in on a someone who thought he could outwit him. "You see, we know all about your conversation with Ian Southcott, also known as Shamus O'Leary, when he was in Chicago. We know about the relic you are pursuing. We know that he instructed you to look for it. Mrs. O'Neill overheard the conversation. She thinks you murdered her sister. There are unidentified fingerprints in Dr. Williams's rooms. I have a feeling they might just match up with yours." He had received that report only this afternoon from the Yard. Now, emboldened by some sixth sense, he baited his trap.

Their suspect said nothing. Bringing his index finger to his mouth, he began, inelegantly, to gnaw on a cuticle.

"Dr. Morgan?" the chief inspector prompted.

"I could say that I need to consult my solicitor, but your charges are absurd. I am guilty of nothing more than taking a look at an empty room. I know nothing of murder or . . . what was that you said? Kidnapping? Who has been kidnapped?"

"Mrs. O'Neill's daughter, Claire."

"And what is that to do with me? I know of no one called Mrs. O'Neill."

"You know her as Maren Southcott. And there is the little matter of the attack at the Randolph."

He was clearly taken aback. "*She* told you I attacked her? But that's impossible. I came to her aid!"

"You were in the room next door," Cole insisted.

"There was no connecting door between our suites. You can check, if you like. I don't know how she can possibly think I was the one who attacked her!"

154

"But you did know she was your partner's bigamous wife when you chatted her up, didn't you?" Cole pressed him.

"*She* sat down at *my* table. It was coincidence. Just as it was coincidence that our rooms were next to one another. Listen, I had absolutely nothing to do with any murder, and I don't think Hubbard did, either. He *is* an antiques dealer. A shady one, perhaps. We *are* trying to get our hands on this relic, but as the Americans say, 'Finders keepers,' in this situation."

"That doesn't justify breaking and entering. Or kidnapping."

"Why do you keep harping on this kidnapping? Who says Hubbard had anything to do with any kidnapping?"

"He does. He's demanding the relic as ransom."

The stocky professor stared at them. "He is, is he? Well, I'll not have anything to do with that, thank you very much."

"Just when is Mr. Hubbard expected?" Llewellyn inquired.

"He should have been here long ago. He was just motoring over from Chester."

"You've been following us, I suppose," Cole asked, his lazy air back in place.

"In a manner of speaking."

The fire crackled, and a log fell, splintering. Their hostess entered the room resolutely. "Dr. Griffith, I won't have that Mr. O'Leary in my house. Murder, kidnapping, drugs! It's that Eisteddfod!"

"It's all right, Mrs. Carroll," the chief inspector said. "If Mr. O'Leary puts in an appearance, he'll be coming with us. Now, then, perhaps you'd be good enough to leave us?"

The woman looked at each of them with equal measures of distrust and then departed.

"You had a tracking device, then?" Llewellyn said. "You are aware that that is illegal?"

"Who said anything about a tracking device? You won't find any-thing."

"Removed it, have you? Well, Dr. Morgan, you've spun us a fair number of tales here tonight, so I don't know how you expect us to believe anything you say. But I will tell you that it will go down bet-ter in a court of law if you agree to help us capture your accomplice."

"You can't possibly charge me with anything," he said, sounding mulish.

"Breaking and entering, at the very least. Fingerprints, remem-ber?" Cole said, his voice caressing and cool. "Though how you came not to be wearing gloves is more than I can understand. Smacks of the amateur, if you see what I mean."

"In spite of what you may think, I've never done anything like that before. And I found the place a perfect ruin. It looked like it had been visited by the furies."

Llewellyn considered this. Was the man, at last, telling the truth? "It wouldn't do your reputation with your university any good if you were found guilty of this charge, you realize."

The man hung his head, at last conceding defeat.

"Hubbard is a wanted drug smuggler," Cole said. "He is part of a well-known ring. He is also a kidnapper, as we have mentioned. Entering into a conspiracy with him won't go down well, either. It would be far better for your cause if you were to cooperate with us. Now. How can we find the man?"

"I have his mobile number," Professor Morgan muttered.

Llewellyn's gratification at this victory was cut short by the ringing of his own mobile.

"Chief Inspector Llewellyn here."

"Sergeant Graves, sir, at the Yard."

"Yes, Sergeant?"

"We just received a report, sir, on that number plate."

"Yes, sergeant?"

"The car was found, sir. On Horseshoe Pass outside Llangollen. Empty."

Llewellyn sighed. Hubbard/Southcott/O'Leary was tough quarry, indeed. Closing his phone, he asked Morgan, "What was that mobile number?"

After the dispirited professor gave it, the chief inspector dialed. A cultured voice said in his ear, "Leave a message after the tone."

chapter thirty-eight

Maren awoke sharply at five A.M. *Claire!* Confused at her own sense of urgency, her exhausted mind fumbled. Was it the croup? Had she heard a cry? Or had she left the window open?

Reality assailed her with sickening dread. Her heart thudded hollowly in her chest. How could she go on living with this uncertainty?

Trying to prevent her dread from paralyzing her, she concentrated on what she knew. Ian was here. He didn't have her. Valerie, his known girlfriend, disappeared the same time Claire did. It made sense that she must have her.

Like a warm breath in the quiet of the dark morning came her father's steadying voice, "Don't take counsel from your fears." How could she go on if she dwelt on the worst? Was it better to lie here, wound up tight with fear? Or to get up and do something, anything?

If only it weren't the middle of the night in the Chicago, she would call Sam. Running. She would go running and release all these destructive fear hormones. Swinging her legs onto the floor, she was thankful she'd grabbed her sister's track shoes. They weren't first rate, as Rachael's idea of exercise was a brisk walk, but they would do.

Running along the towpath of the River Dee in the dark, Maren felt the damp fog on her face and breathed in the scent of wet grass and running water. As thoughts of her daughter crowded her mind, she pushed harder. The exercise began to purge her, and she reached heavenward. "I know awful things happen in this world," she prayed. "I know I have no right to ask for special favors. But, please, God, please, watch after my little girl. Help Sam to find her. Help me to find the manuscript."

She thought of Rachael as she skirted a fishing boat, pulled up onto the path. Pounding across an ancient bridge, she thought of Patrick. "The only one I have left is Claire. I've failed everyone else, God. Please, please help me to save her."

As dawn began to gray the sky, a fine drizzle commenced, and she turned and started running back to the Squirrels. Endorphins were now flooding her system. The sharp desperation of fear was gone, but she knew her own resources weren't enough. If there were such a thing as divine intervention, Maren needed it badly.

Entering her room, exhausted and damp, she saw that a square of white notepaper lay just inside the door. Puzzled, she picked it up. It appeared to be verses of poetry.

> *Emerald goddess of the waters*
> *Swaying with the waves,*
> *I am trapped on this dry shore.*
> *I may not go your way.*
>
> *I can dream of watery worlds,*
> *Of light and joy and love.*
> *But I am weighted by the earth,*
> *And ne'er can float above.*

Calm the sea, O goddess good.
Stretch out your milk-white arms
And keep the savage shark at bay
That he may do no harm.

Float across the endless oceans,
Go to meet your destiny.
But don't forget the beachbound one
And let me see, oh let me see.

I'm coming for you someday soon.

Glyndwr

Love poetry? Glyndwr? As in Owain Glyndwr? What was this? A joke?

She sank onto her bed, staring at the paper. It must be a joke. But there was something creepy about it. She didn't like the idea of being compared to a fish. It sounded uncomfortably suggestive for some reason. But who could have done it?

Anthony? No. She mentally kicked herself. Anthony had loved Rachael and had made it all too plain that she was not his type. But if not Anthony, who? Was she being stalked? Had Ian found her? But no, it wasn't Ian's flowing script. The poetry was written in small, neat capital letters. What about her anonymous attacker?

She began to shiver in her damp clothing. What had she been thinking of to go running alone in the dark, for crying out loud? This creep might have caught her! But what could her unknown assailant know about Owain Glyndwr? And what if she had been in this room, alone, when he came?

Suddenly, she wanted the chief inspector with his Cary Grant Englishness. He would take care of it. He would bring her down to earth. And there might be fingerprints.

160

But when she was showered and dressed for the day in Rachael's flowered peasant skirt, long-sleeved T-shirt, and sage Shetland shawl, Maren met only Anthony in the breakfast room. As on the day before, he was breakfasting on a roll, reading the *Times.* He got up as she entered.

"I heard you go out before dawn this morning," he said, his eyes dark with concern. "Are you all right?"

"I went for a run," she told him, helping herself to muesli. "Sorry if I woke you. Couldn't sleep. Is the chief inspector down yet?"

"He just left for the local station. He didn't tell me why, just that he'd meet us at the abbey. We're to take the Range Rover. He'll arrange for official transport." His brow was furrowed. "I'm sure you want to hear the latest word on your daughter."

She took a deep breath and tried to sound more positive than she felt. "I think she's in the States. My friend Sam is with the FBI. He's looking into it. I think Ian's girlfriend may have her. At least, I hope she does. The alternatives are too scary."

"I can't even imagine. I . . . I thought Rachael's murder was bad, but this . . . somehow this is even worse."

She gave him a grateful smile. "You don't even know Claire."

"She's just a little girl." He had been looking at her intently, but now he pulled out a chair for her. "Tea?"

She shook her head. "At this particular moment, it reminds me too much of Ian. I'll just have cocoa."

"Rachael thought you were happy."

Maren shuddered at the thought of Ian's hands on her skin. "I was a fool. I knew him no better than I know you."

He looked a bit taken aback at the comparison.

"For all I know, you murdered Rachael," she said brutally, battering down the clamoring attraction she felt. It could be no more than a convoluted need for Patrick's presence. "You seem nice, but so did Ian."

The golden eyes lost all their warmth. "I suppose it's perfectly natural for you to chastise yourself. But please refrain from inflicting your insecurities on me. I did not murder your sister. I loved her."

Maren looked down, away from his hurt. But she couldn't apologize. Much as she wanted to believe him, she dared not trust her own judgment.

She decided to change the subject. Tossing her straight hair out of her eyes, she shook her head. "We were like the hare and the tortoise," she said blithely, ignoring their previous exchange. "My father used to do treasure hunts for us. Rachael always won. My brain was too scattered. I think in spurts. My sister always put together a chain of evidence. She would have made a great lawyer."

"She was a superior academician."

"Yes. She was." Melancholy crowded her other emotions. Her brave front dissolved at the thought of her sister receiving her Ph.D. Her father had been so proud. He had died only a month later of pancreatic cancer. And soon after that, everything had gone wrong with Rachael. Her mother had gone into seclusion at her father's death, so that occasion at the University of Chicago was the last happy Williams family memory she had. Suddenly she was near tears. Gripping her hands together in her lap, she fought them. If she gave in now, there would be no stopping the flood. Why had she turned into a watering pot? She hadn't cried this much in years.

This conversation was taking her nowhere but down. "What's the program for today?" she asked.

"On to the abbey and Professor Davies's dig," Anthony said, pouring himself another cup of tea. She sensed he was observing her out of the corner of his eye and succeeded in blinking back her tears.

Anthony's Welsh enthusiast was at her post when they reached the delicate golden fastness of the abbey. The drizzle had blown over, and the sun had emerged. As Maren looked at the reflection of the vaulted ruin in the fish pond, she thought that all should be well on such a morning. Maybe they would find the manuscript today.

"Has Dr. Davies arrived?" Anthony asked the woman, who had replaced her green plaid with red and black checks.

She replied in Welsh and pointed inside the ruin.

"We're to go through to the back. He's here with a small army, apparently," Anthony said.

At the rear of the abbey, the building was open to the sky. There stood a chicken-necked elderly man in a gray woolen suit crowing Welsh to a crowd of men dressed for digging. They all had shovels and circled a spot of ground carefully marked by stakes with pink plastic ribbons tied around them.

Anthony let him finish his instructions before advancing. The men took their shovels and began to scrape the soil cautiously.

"Professor Davies? I'm Dr. Jones, Christ Church, Oxford. This is Mrs. O'Neill. I understand you think there might be some relics from the monastery buried here?"

The little man turned to him with the surprise of the very deaf. "What's that?"

"The dig!" Anthony raised his voice. "How did you know to dig here?"

"Flora, my dear boy, flora. Make a study of it. Do a bit of botany, geology, archeology. Ground's been disturbed here sometime in the last several hundred years. Doesn't match the surrounding area. May be only a tip."

"A tip?" Maren asked.

"Garbage dump," Anthony told her. Then he turned back to Dr. Davies, who was adjusting his hearing aid. "I say! Frightfully exciting! Mind if we watch?"

For an hour, Maren stood by Anthony in the cool morning as a breeze blew through the ruins and swirled her skirt and shawl around her body. The enforced inactivity was driving her crazy. She wanted to get in there and dig with her bare hands. And what if they found something? What then? What chance had she of convincing Professor Davies that he must hand over his find to her?

And even if he did, what then? How would she get in touch with Ian?

It was at this point that the chief inspector arrived.

"Maren," he said, his eyes carrying their now familiar look of concern, "you need to come with me, please. I've had word that there's been an accident, and we need you to identify the body."

chapter thirty-nine

VALLE CRUCIS ABBEY
WALES

*W*hose body?" Maren demanded, confused by the solemn expression on the policeman's face.

"We think it might be the man you knew as your husband," Llewellyn explained, the forelock over his brow blowing in the breeze. He scraped at it with his fingers. "His car was found at the top of Horseshoe Pass. A body's been reported below. I suppose I shouldn't have said accident. He's been shot, I'm afraid."

"Shot?" she echoed. Her mind flew. "But Claire . . ."

"I know," the chief inspector stopped her. "Never mind, Maren. We'll find her."

But Maren was far from certain. Mutely, she followed Llewellyn and Cole to their requisitioned Mini, all interest in the dig forgotten.

"Have you heard anything from my friend Sam Reynolds at the FBI?" she asked as she crawled into the back of the little blue car, her mind spinning first one way and then the other.

"Reynolds filed a report last night at about ten o'clock. Apparently, there is still no sign of Valerie Kensington. He's investigated her flat, had it dusted for fingerprints, the entire drill. We'll know more later today."

Sergeant Cole was negotiating the bumpy dirt track with difficulty. It was leading them to the base of the precipice above the abbey. How odd that Ian would be here of all places! How had he known she was here? Who could have shot him? Where was her daughter? Acid burned in her throat.

At the bottom of the cliff, the sergeant stopped the borrowed Mini. Police cars were drawn up near them, like multicolored toys against the backdrop of the ancient cliff face, yellow crime scene tape fluttering in the breeze.

Maren's emotions were in such turmoil that she couldn't even identify them. Her brain was in overdrive, her hands damp with nerves, her stomach in rebellion at the approaching sight.

The body, dressed in all black, had landed not far from an idyllic little streamed. Odd. Ian never wore all black. He said it was overdone in the art world, suited only for gangsters, vampires, and teenaged Goths. The hair was also wrong. It was black, too.

She began to feel peculiar, as though she might be sick. This wasn't Ian. The man with the stain darkening the front of the black silk shirt looked like the "Greek" who had sat next to her on the plane.

"I don't know what's going on," she said, shaking her dizzy head. "This isn't Ian. But I've seen him before. He sat next to me in the plane coming from Chicago." She had never felt so clueless in her entire life. Turning to the chief inspector, she said, "What in the world is *he* doing here?"

"You're certain?" the chief inspector inquired, clearly surprised.

"Yes. I remember the gold chain around his neck. And the rings and bracelet. What does this mean?"

Sergeant Cole spoke up. "I'll tell you what it looks like. This

unlucky devil was following the BMW up the pass. I'd say he probably couldn't keep up. Hubbard, or whatever his name is, had a chance
to get out of the car and ambush him. Probably took his car after giving him the push. Knew someone was on to him."

"But . . ." Maren broke off. The corpse wasn't a pretty sight. She
ran over to the bushes and vomited. Shaking from head to foot, she
realized slowly that the charming Ian was now a murderer in fact. As
well as a thief, a drug smuggler, and a kidnapper. He was thoroughly
rotten. And he must have been following her. But what about the
"Greek?" Why had he been after Ian, if the sergeant's theory was true?
And why, oh why, had he sat next to her on the plane?

The chief inspector came up behind her and handed her a hand-
kerchief. She used it to mop the perspiration that was pouring down
her face and then to wipe her lips. It was lousy to feel this weak.
Especially when she had so many questions.

"We found Griffith last night, Maren," Llewellyn said.

"Rachael's murderer?" Her mind reeled back to that earlier crime.
The one that had started this whole, puzzling mess.

"He denies it. But you'll never guess who he is."

"I'm fed up with riddles," she told him shortly.

"Your Professor David Morgan from the Randolph. He's been
tailing us and reporting back to Hubbard."

"Dr. Morgan?" she asked, dismayed. "But I liked him! He helped
me when I was attacked!"

"I know. It's certainly confusing. He claims to know nothing
about the kidnapping or the attack. Says he only knew Hubbard as a
crooked antiques dealer."

"Does he know where Ian is?"

"He gave us his mobile number. We've been trying it since last
night. It's turned off." The chief inspector sighed. "Well, since this

isn't your . . . er, Hubbard, I guess we'll have to set about trying to identify him."

"He spoke with a thick accent," she told him. "I thought he was Greek."

"Any reason?"

She gave a half grin. "Just my imagination. He looked wealthy and Mediterranean. I thought he was a shipping magnate or something. I'm not good with accents."

"You picked up my 'lilt' fast enough." He smiled at her gently.

"Only because I'd heard it so often in Wales." She recognized that the chief inspector was trying to put her at ease. "Do you realize this man must have been following me when I was on that plane? The only person who knew my seat assignment was Valerie. Ian's girl-friend. She made my reservation, remember. And she saw my state-ment. And she's missing."

"It's a conundrum all right," the chief inspector said.

"A falling out," Detective Sergeant Cole pronounced. "Your Valerie must have alerted the cartel that you were on to Ian. They're trying to get you, and they're trying to get him. Just what did you say in that statement?"

"Do you mind if I sit down?" Maren asked, stumbling back towards the car. There was something very wrong, something that didn't make sense here. Not at all.

The chief inspector grasped her elbow. "Mind how you go here. You're a bit unsteady."

When they got to the car, she allowed the sergeant to open the door for her. Climbing in, she sat in the little bubble of warmth cre-ated by the sun on the window glass. "Don't you see?" she said. "If Ian and Valerie have had a falling out, who's got Claire?"

Both policemen stared at her for a moment, clearly unable to answer. The sun had risen high in the sky, and they stood silhouetted against its brightness. She put up a hand against the glare. Something teased her brain. A vital fact. Something she had told herself she would check. Ian Southcott aka James Hubbard. Yes! That was it!

"Mrs. Hubbard," she said. "Ian's other wife. The one in London. She must have Claire."

"I'll check into it immediately," the chief inspector said, climbing into the front seat next to the sergeant. "And if our 'Greek' friend is a member of the drug cartel, perhaps Interpol will have a record of him."

The sergeant stretched like a cat. "When things are especially muddy, it only means they've loosened up a bit. This may actually be the break we need to get things sorted out."

"We'll take you back to the dig," Llewellyn suggested. "Then we'll go into town and begin inquiries."

The dig. The manuscript. Rachael's murder. For half an hour it had completely left her mind.

chapter forty

The man calling himself William Dunstan swam in the heated swimming pool, trying to formulate his plans. The BMW could be traced to Shamus O'Leary, but fortunately he'd had a spare passport made up long ago. He had one alias left. He mustn't squander it.

Oh, Maren! Acute desire for his American wife stabbed him unexpectedly. It really wasn't any good trying to silence her now. They were on to him, obviously. His only hope was the manuscript. With the money that would bring he could disappear, buy a hacienda in Paraguay, perhaps, and live out his life in comfort.

But he couldn't trust Griffith any longer. Murder would have put James Hubbard beyond the pale. The little professor wouldn't stand for it. No, he couldn't contact Griffith.

Claire was Maren's weak spot. She would do anything for Claire. Even give up the manuscript. He would see to it.

Pulling himself out of the swimming pool, he admired his slim, strong physique. His hacienda absolutely must have a swimming pool.

chapter forty-one

POLICE STATION
LLANGOLLEN, WALES

holding his mobile phone to his ear, Chief Inspector Hugh Llewellyn watched his sergeant scan the murder victim's fingerprints into the computer. Cole was good. There was no doubt about it. He had summed up the events that must have occurred last night on Horseshoe Pass in an instant. He wouldn't be a sergeant long. People of his class never were. He only hoped Cole wouldn't be his superior someday.

"Llewellyn?" It was the detective superintendent at long last. "You wanted me?"

"Yes, Detective Superintendent. It's about that kidnapping." He explained Maren's thinking about Susan Hubbard.

"All right, I'll see to it. Now, there's another matter that's come up. You have Chief Commissioner Braden himself on his way up there."

"Braden?" Llewellyn was stunned. Braden was MI-5. He worked only on matters of national security.

"There's a plot. Against Prince Charles. You're to give him every

171

assistance. I told him you were up there on this other case. He's expecting your help. His case obviously takes priority."

"A plot to kill Prince Charles? In Llangollen?"

"It's that Eisteddfod. I've always thought no good could come of it. Encourages the Welsh to think they're superior."

Mystified, Llewellyn stared at his suddenly dead mobile.

chapter forty-two

VALLE CRUCIS ABBEY
WALES

The diggers were still at it when Maren walked to the back of the abbey, after being dropped off by Llewellyn and Cole.

"Nothing yet?" she asked Anthony, who had rolled up his brown shirtsleeves and taken up a shovel.

He looked up, anxious eyes going swiftly to hers. What he saw there must have bothered him, for he stopped shoveling and walked over to meet her. Wiping a tanned forearm across his forehead, he said, "Nothing. Whose was the body then?"

Sighing, she told him, "It's all getting to be a mess. They thought it was Ian, but instead it was this man who sat next to me on the plane coming over here." She shook her head, trying to rid herself of the vision of the broken, blood-stained body. "I'm still trying to take it all in. Ian apparently murdered him. His car was found at the top of the pass."

"And so they thought the dead man might be him? That must have been gruesome for you."

"Yeah. It was. They don't know who the guy is yet, but they're working on it."

Anthony leaned on his shovel, stroking his beard with one hand. "It sounds like we've got two story lines going here," he said. "I don't like it. Ian is obviously a dangerous man. He wants the manuscript. But someone wants him." He turned his eyes to her again. "Have you any idea why? I think I'm missing part of the picture here."

The men about them had broken into song, as the Welsh were wont to do at the slightest provocation. Harmonizing perfectly, they sang lustily in their native tongue. The skinny Professor Davies beat time with his finger in the air.

Maren seated herself on the ground, her peasant skirt billowing about her. Anthony joined her, stretching his long, gray-trousered legs before him, crossing them at the ankles. "You're missing lots, actually. The fact that Ian is mixed up with an international drug ring, first of all. Then there was the attempt on my life . . ."

"Wait!" He held up a hand. "Drug ring? Attempt on your life! Maren, what have you gotten yourself into? I thought this was just about a lost manuscript."

"Well, I thought Ian was trying to kill me because he wanted to beat me to the manuscript, or because I knew he had ordered my sister's murder, but now with this man's murder, I wonder if it didn't have something to do with the drug thing . . ."

"But Rachael's murder can't have anything to do with drugs. This all must have something to do with the other story line . . ."

At that moment, they were hailed by a new arrival. "Hullo! Mind if I join you?" It was Professor Morgan from Birmingham aka Griffith.

Maren stared at him, incredulous and instantly angry. "Why aren't you locked up?"

The stocky man gave her a troubled look. "It hasn't come to that yet. I say, I'm terribly sorry about your daughter."

"What are you doing here?"

"I came to see what all the bother was about. Digging for something?"

"You know we are," she said bitterly, all her frustration coming to the surface. "You're working for Ian or James or whatever his name is. Does it interest you at all to know that he's a murderer?"

The man's face whitened. "Who's dead?"

"Nobody knows yet. But Ian shot someone and dumped him off the Horseshoe Pass last night."

"I say!" David Morgan's eyes were large with alarm, whether real or feigned was impossible to decipher.

At that moment, a shout came from one of the workers. It was in Welsh. Maren turned to Anthony for interpretation, but Professor Morgan said, "He's found something!"

The ginger-haired man moved forward quickly, and Maren followed Anthony to the edge of the pit. Several workers were down inside the hole, digging around the sides of what appeared to be a metal box of ancient date.

Chapter Forty-Three

A HILL ABOVE VALLE CRUCIS ABBEY
WALES

They had found something! Maren's bigamous husband, now calling himself William Dunstan, looked down from the hill at the scene below. Griffith's presence displeased him greatly. Thought he could go it alone, did he? That man with Maren must be the one his unwilling partner had mentioned. Then there was the aging article in the gray suit. Not to mention a score of men armed with shovels. He trusted his SIG-Sauer but not to that extent. Luck had certainly seemed to favor him, though. He had made it down from Ruthin in the nick of time to follow up Griffith's remarks about the abbey. He had only had what the Americans called a hunch, but perhaps it was going to pay off, after all.

The gray-suited article was supervising the lifting of what appeared to be a small metal chest out of the ground onto the surrounding green lawn. Maren had moved around behind him, while Griffith and her friend stood to the right and left of her.

He clutched his pistol. Perhaps a hostage might work? He'd love to take his lively wife hostage.

chapter forty-four

LLANGOLLEN, WALES

C hief Commissioner Braden was glad Llewellyn was here. A look-alive sort of chap. Good at following through. With any sort of luck he could wind this up this afternoon and leave it to Llewellyn to sort out the details.

They were on their way to the last known address of Owen Powell aka Owain Glyndwr. It was a flat above a tobacconist's shop. "Fellow's living on his pension from the Falklands War. He was first officer on *HMS Invincible*," he told Llewellyn. "Rather a sad show, actually."

"And he's threatened Prince Charles? He's a Welsh nationalist of some sort?"

"Yes. It's all to do with some silly ideas about King Arthur."

Llewellyn was obviously startled. "King Arthur, sir?"

"Does that ring bells, or something, Llewellyn?" Braden glanced at his companion.

"Just coincidence, I imagine. The case I'm working on is also some rather silly business about King Arthur. Glyndwr is concerned as well, though only obliquely. But it involves at least one murder, a female professor, so someone is taking it seriously. What else do you know about this chap?"

"He belonged to that Glyndwr protest group in the eighties that burned English holiday homes in Wales. That's how Evans found him. He was Her Majesty's guest at Borstal for two years. There's a tidy file on him."

"So you have his fingerprints, then?"

"Yes, but none on the threatening letter, worse luck. Why?" The chief inspector was looking at him with eagerness.

"We've got an unknown quantity in this case, sir. I'm not altogether satisfied with either of my suspects in the murder. It was committed in order for someone to get his hands on an ancient document that will supposedly prove the identity of King Arthur. As a matter of fact, they're searching for it at this moment at Valle Crucis Abbey."

Braden experienced one of those flashes of intuition that he wished profoundly he wouldn't have at this late stage of his career. Such a manuscript would be a valuable token in the hands of a Welsh nationalist. Especially one who was unbalanced. What had Inspector Wolff deduced from the handwriting? *Accustomed to command. Frustrated. Dangerous. Definitely delusional.*

They had pulled up in front of the tobacconist's shop. It was a shabby place—paint peeling on black shutters, fly-blown windows, front steps littered with cigarette stubs. A weathered green door to the right of the entrance had a small buzzer with the name *Glyndwr* printed carefully on a card taped above it. Chief Commissioner Braden rang the buzzer. There was no answer.

With a disgusted sigh, he turned to the entrance of the shop. "Suppose we see what we can find out."

The shop was tended by an ancient crone who wore a black

cardigan with sagging pockets over her dress of faded pink cotton. She was engaged in knitting something in a repulsive shade of neon green. A cigarette dangled from her lips.

When the bell jangled over the shop door, she looked up out of tired eyes with yellowed whites. "What can I do for you, ducks?"

"Is your tenant around?" Braden pointed above his head.

"His Nibs, you mean? He's off mucking about with the lads, I imagine. Is most days." She gave a smoker's cough.

"The lads?" Braden queried.

"You'd think he'd have more sense at his age, wouldn't you? Always up to something."

He weighed the advisability of showing his identification and decided against it. More than likely the old woman would clam up completely.

"I'm rather anxious to get in touch with him," he said. "Have you any idea when he'll return?"

For the first time, she looked faintly suspicious. "You seem a bit of a lord to me. Not after his usual type. English, too. What did you say your name was?"

"I didn't. It's Braden, actually. Hal Braden. I've heard about his singing, you see. We're looking for a good tenor to sing the anthem at a rugger match up in Ruthin."

She narrowed her eyes now. "Happen they have a fair share of tenors in Ruthin, I've heard. The Men's Choir is that famous. You'd better take yourself off. If he's in trouble, the lads will stand up for him. You can be sure of that." She returned to her knitting.

Realizing that further interrogation would be fruitless, Braden signaled to Llewellyn, and they took their leave.

"And I thought this was going to be simple," he grumbled. "I actually expected to find him sitting blubbering on a stool, raving mad."

"It sounds as though we had better organize a watch, sir," Llewellyn said.

"I'll have the locals see to it. It won't be as alarming. What do you suppose he's mixed up in?"

"It could be anything from drug smuggling to a plot to kill Prince Charles, from the sound of it."

"He'd be living higher if it were drugs," Braden grumbled. He didn't like the look of this a single bit.

CHAPTER FORTY-FIVE

VALLE CRUCIS ABBEY
WALES

The sun went behind a cloud, darkening the little scene on the lawn outside the abbey. Maren shivered. Would they never get the box open?

Professor Davies was maddeningly slow as he toyed with the ancient lock, trying to open it without damaging it. Griffith, too, was impatient. "Just bash the thing, man!" he exploded finally.

The old man in the gray suit turned around and looked over his shoulder. "And who are you, sir? I don't recall inviting you to this dig."

"Sorry. Professor David Morgan. Anthropologist. University of Birmingham."

"I don't believe it," Dr. Davies said, returning to his study of the lock. "An anthropologist would know these things can't be rushed. Once in a lifetime find, this could be."

"You don't know the half of it, mate," Anthony whispered in her ear. He stirred with subtle impatience. She felt herself relax a bit. It was good that she was not alone.

She caught herself. Anthony Jones could have murdered for this moment. Or Griffith, for that matter. In fact, she reminded herself severely, she was probably standing in the presence of a murderer. Her scalp prickled, and she stepped away from Anthony towards the frail Dr. Davies. Where was Chief Inspector Llewellyn?

One of the workers spoke softly in Welsh to the old professor. He answered in kind. They both nodded, and the worker went back through the abbey.

"He's a locksmith," the professor said. "He's gone to get his tools. Why don't we all relax a bit? I've brought a picnic for the lads. There's enough for everyone."

There was a perceptible easing of tension. Everyone walked away, towards the baskets that were set out on the lawn next to the abbey. Maren stayed where she was. She felt uneasy leaving the chest for some reason.

Her eye caught a movement atop the hill close by. Anxiously, she looked up. Had she imagined it? There was no one there. At least no one she could see.

Anthony brought her a hard roll encasing a slab of ham. "Only lager to drink, I'm afraid. Would you like some?"

"I don't think so, thanks. And I couldn't eat anything."

"Tell me about this attempt on your life," he said, studying her. His long black lashes were like a silk fringe. How could she have thought his likeness to Patrick so great? Her husband had resembled a salty sea captain. Anthony's face was unweathered, and moods flickered over it with the subtlety of ripples on a pond. She forgot to be cautious, and under his solicitous scrutiny she felt caressed, comforted.

The sun came out again, and it was like a curtain going up. She realized she had been standing, mesmerized, staring into Anthony

Jones's eyes for an inappropriate period of time. Shifting her glance to the box, she told him about the incident in the Randolph.

"How did you get away from him?"

She grinned at his astonishment. "Mousse."

"I beg your pardon?"

"I don't know what you call it over here. The spray stuff you put on your hair to give it volume. I sprayed it in his eyes. He let go, and I kicked him." She looked up at the hill. There was another movement. She was sure of it.

"There's someone up there. Watching us," she told Anthony.

He narrowed his eyes and stared in the direction she indicated. "I can't tell if those bushes are moving, or if it's only the wind."

"I wish the chief inspector were here," she said uneasily. "And I don't like the fact that Griffith has turned up."

"Who?"

"That man who calls himself Professor Morgan. He's Ian's henchman. He could have murdered Rachael. He wants the manuscript."

"And the police don't have him locked up?"

"Not enough evidence, I guess. But I heard Ian on the phone with him. That's the conversation that sent me flying over here without a stitch of clothing except what I was wearing. Ian threatened Claire."

Anthony stared at Griffith. "He speaks Welsh rather well."

"I liked him before I knew who he was. He helped me when I was attacked at the Randolph."

"I really don't think he is a professor."

"He's got the patter down."

"Does he?"

"Absolutely. He's either a very good actor or a very clever criminal. Possibly sociopathic."

He looked at her in amazement. "You're so matter-of-fact about all of this. Aren't you frightened at all?"

"I'm frightened for Claire. More than I can say. But I think I can take care of myself."

The sympathetic glance returned at her words about Claire, coloring his eyes a darker hue. "You think it's all up to you, don't you? But, believe me, there comes a time when we all have to rely a bit on grace. Even someone as capable as you are."

"Grace?" His intensity touched her with the gentleness of a butterfly landing on a flower. He was like some priest or doctor or some compassionate soul looking down at a severely wounded creature, trying to decide what to do.

This man was no murderer. His words summoned trust she thought had disappeared long ago with the child who loved to wake up at dawn and go into the garden, where she would sit on the swing among her father's roses, inhaling the beauty and watching as the sun brought color to her happy world.

"We go as far as we can go, do as much as we can do, and then we leave the rest to God," Anthony told her softly. "As Arthur reputedly said, 'Right makes might.'"

Maren looked away from the gaze that held her. How could Rachael not have loved this man? "I'm not very good at leaving things to God. But what choice do I have?"

At that moment, a movement distracted them. Surprised, Maren looked up. Someone wearing a motorcycle helmet was crashing down the hill, a gun in his hand. "Away from there, you two!" he commanded. Before they could recover from the shock, the intruder had shot the lock off the chest. Maren felt a flying piece of metal puncture her bare leg. Worse, she recognized Ian's voice.

CHAPTER FORTY-SIX

VALLE CRUCIS ABBEY
WALES

Anthony threw himself in front of Maren. "Who the devil are you?" he demanded.

"Ian! Where's Claire? What have you done with her?" Maren cried.

But the man wasn't listening. The lunch crowd had heard the shot and were running towards them. Dr. Davies, limping, was exclaiming, "I say! Who are you? What do you think you're doing?"

By now, Ian had the chest wrenched open. Maren looked inside. Far from containing a manuscript, it was filled with gold coins.

Running footsteps echoed off the stone floors of the abbey, and she heard Llewellyn's voice, "Was that a gunshot?"

Ian, with a last glance at the heavy, gold-laden chest, shook off Anthony's restraining arm and raced up the hill.

"Where's Claire?" Maren yelled after him. Then she began running. The chief inspector caught up with her and held her back.

"He has a gun, Maren."

"That was Ian! He shot the lock off the chest."

Llewellyn began to sprint.

But Anthony was already climbing the hillside. By this time, even the deaf Professor Davies knew something was amiss. "I say," he said, tripping over to where they sheltered in an archway of the abbey. The diggers were already upon them, demanding to know what was going on. Davies spoke to them in rapid Welsh, and they made a rough formation around the small chest. Maren's heart was still tripping as she watched Anthony go over the top of the hill. Llewellyn followed him. Cole had gone in the other direction, saying, "I'll get the car."

Maren stood, surrounded by dirty, sweaty men, clenching her fists at her side. Then she heard the distant sound of a motorcycle. Ian was getting away!

The old man, oblivious, looked at the coins, and a slow grin spread over his face. "This will be worth a tidy bit."

The diggers were speaking to one another, excitedly surging forward. Davies fairly barked at them.

Anthony came pounding down the hill. "Motorbike!" he said succinctly. "Looks like there's an old sheep path back there."

"Sergeant Cole's gone for the car," Maren told him.

Davies turned to Maren and Anthony, trumpeting, "Those coins are counterfeit, or I miss my guess."

"What?" Anthony asked. Maren realized she was shaking. She moved away from the crowd and hugged the cold, rough upright of the archway. *Would Cole catch him?*

"You see, there was an abbot here, Robert of Salisbury, who was convicted in 1542 for minting counterfeit coins . . ."

If it hadn't been for that gun, they would have had him. Maren clenched her fists in frustration.

Anthony came up beside her, a bit out of breath from his chase. She looked at him accusingly. "He got away!"

"He had a gun, Maren. And he was fast. The man reminded me

of an eel in that black motorcycle gear. I'm amazed he didn't shoot anyone! Cole's got the Range Rover. It's four-wheel drive." He looked down at her, his face grave.

"Actually, this should be worth millions," the old professor was touting with satisfaction. "But of course it will go to the museum." The gunman on the hill hadn't fazed him. "It will probably be worth more than the real thing."

Chief Inspector Llewellyn came down the hillside, panting and more rumpled than Maren had ever seen him, brushing the forelock from his forehead. "Was anyone hurt?"

"Chief Inspector," Maren called to him, "did you see where he went?"

"Off the path down to the stream. Did Cole go for the car?"

"Yes."

At that moment, they saw the Range Rover rounding the abbey, heading in the direction of the stream.

"Brains, that fellow's got," Llewellyn observed. "He'll catch him if anyone can."

But he didn't. Ian's motorbike left Detective Sergeant Cole in the dust as he climbed another hill, abandoning the path completely.

"You're bleeding!" Llewellyn said, looking at Maren's ankle. For the first time, she saw rivulets of blood running into her shoe from the stinging wound on her leg.

"Don't like guns," the professor remarked. "Never have. Thought they were illegal these days. Pity about that lock."

chapter forty-seven

CHICAGO

Sam Reynolds cursed in Spanish as he reviewed the reports of his agents. No trace of Valerie Kensington. There must be *something* he had overlooked in her apartment. Scratching his full head of blond hair, he studied the pile of photos the crime scene crew had taken, trying to infuse them with the strange sense of desolation he had felt in the apartment.

He couldn't really account for that feeling. For the most part, her place had been immaculate. She had obviously been a regular Martha Stewart, his wife would have said with some envy. Pale blue walls, yellow carpet, red throw pillows on the navy couch. Magazines neatly stacked on a natural oak coffee table. Not a thing out of place.

Except the yogurt. That had struck him as weird at the time, so now he focused on it. She had been eating yogurt out of a carton, while she watched TV, apparently. An oak armoire containing her television was open, though the set was off. The half-eaten carton of raspberry non-fat yogurt, with a spoon sticking out of it, was sitting on an end table. The refrigerator contained many such cartons and very little else except carrots and sugar-free chocolate almond ice cream in the freezer.

The bedroom had been neat—a queen-sized bed with a yellow peasant-looking print used as a duvet for her feather quilt. Containing a rail of suits in sober hues, the closet had been remarkable only for a pair of red sweats hung on a hook. A tiny desk in the kitchen had yielded an appointment book.

Shaking it from its plastic bag, he now turned the pages. He had already checked all the appointments for the days before the kidnapping. Hairdresser where she had had a dye job. Yoga class. Dinner with a friend from work. No one had had anything of use to tell him. What was on for today? There was the name "Rita" and a telephone number. He dialed.

"Bahama Spa. This is Olivia."

"Olivia, has Valerie been in today?" he asked, keeping his rich baritone casual.

"No, as a matter of fact, and Rita is breathing fire. She could have sold her time ten times over. Valerie knows that. The least she could have done is call. She's usually very good about that. Who did you say you were?"

"Sam Reynolds. I'm a friend. I knew Valerie was supposed to show up there this morning, and I thought I'd try to catch her."

"Well, if you do, tell her she can find another manicurist!" Olivia hung up.

Sam had one of those eerie feelings that accompanied a hunch. He dialed a number he knew way too well.

"Cook County Morgue."

"This is Agent Reynolds, Hank. Do you have any Jane Does that have turned up over the past couple of days?"

"Three. Wanna see 'em?"

"Could you just give me a description?"

"Sure enough." The voice was smooth and slow. Sam pictured Hank, the morgue technician, with his black skin and white hair worn in dreadlocks. "First, a tattoo lady, Hispanic, about twenty, I'd say. Lots of needle marks."

"Check. Go on."

"A homeless woman. Kinda weird. She was shaved bald. No needle marks or nothin' to show how she died."

"How do you know she was homeless?"

"Found down by the shelter."

"Okay. Go on."

"Next is an old woman, must be close on seventy or so, run down on the South Side by a hit and run. No one in the neighborhood knew her, and she didn't have any ID."

"All right, Hank. Back to the homeless woman. Did you have a look at her hands?"

"Yeah, as a matter of fact, and that was weird, too. Looks like she had them phony nails on. Real long."

"Thanks, Hank. I'll be around to see you. May be able to ID that one for you."

Rita proved to be a bit of a diva, and it took his badge and some stern language about obstructing justice to get her to accompany him to the morgue. But the Junoesque redhead identified the corpse as Valerie Kensington immediately.

"It's got to be murder," she said. "She never would have killed herself with her nails in that bad a shape."

190

CHAPTER FORTY-EIGHT

SQUIRRELS GUEST HOUSE
LLANGOLLEN, WALES

e was way off road," Cole told Maren. "And, of course, with the helmet, I couldn't get a description."

Llewellyn wondered how in the world he was going to break the next bit of news. He glanced at Cole, who was lounging on his tailbone, legs stretched out in front of him. Lazy bounder. He looked elegant even in that position.

"I know it was Ian," she said. Maren was sitting on the sofa like a little girl, her bandaged leg tucked up under her, her hair in a ponytail. "Have you checked guest registrations?"

"Yes. Cole has been working on it."

"No one named O'Leary anywhere for miles around," the sergeant pronounced in a bored voice.

"Sorry the search has come to nothing," Llewellyn said. "What will you do now?"

Maren sighed. She had clearly lost her taste for this treasure hunt, and he couldn't blame her. He supposed she was consumed by thoughts of her daughter. "Dr. Jones has gone out with Dr. Davies to pick his brain. He seems to know quite a bit about North Wales."

"And you didn't want to go?" he asked, trying to keep the note of interest from his voice. Perhaps he didn't have a chance with the woman himself, but losing out to an Oxford type would be almost as bad as losing out to Cole.

"They were speaking Welsh, and anyway, I was waiting for you. You have something else to tell me, don't you? You're fidgety."

He nodded somberly. What was he thinking? Of course the woman had no thought of romance while her daughter was missing. He must concentrate on that. "I heard from the Yard. They paid Mrs. Hubbard a visit with a warrant to search her flat. I'm afraid your daughter wasn't there. She says she hasn't seen her husband since last June. She's filed for divorce, actually."

Maren looked away from him, and he knew that she was trying desperately to hide her disappointment. She looked so vulnerable with her child's hairdo and her chin in her hand. If it weren't for Cole, he would throw professionalism to the winds and go to her, holding her protectively while he told her the next bit.

Clearing his throat, he said, "I'm afraid that's not all. Your friend Reynolds from the States gave the Yard a ring about half an hour ago. It seems Valerie Kensington was found murdered outside a homeless shelter in Chicago. They just identified her this afternoon."

"What?" Maren's eyes went round with shock. "Murdered! But when? And why a homeless shelter?"

Llewellyn had never felt more helpless. Wishing he could go to the States to track down Claire himself, he gazed at her mutely.

"Her head was shaved," Cole told her abruptly. "Obviously they wanted to delay identification as long as possible."

"Reynolds talked to the people at the shelter, Maren. She was found around midnight, the same night you left the States."

"Ian!" she exclaimed, thinking rapidly, as though she were standing on her feet in the courtroom. "He must have found out she double-crossed him!" Then, she stared, and he could see the thoughts flashing through her mind mirrored in her eyes. Recognition, click. Dawning horror, click. All at once, she buried her face in her hands. "Claire," she choked. "That psychopath must have her!"

With an acute stab in his chest, her alarm jarred him. Psychopath? What psychopath? "Who are you talking about, Maren?" She was such a game little thing. No higher than his shoulder, but as his granny would have said, "Pluck to the backbone." It hurt deep down in a place he couldn't even name to see her suffer so.

"There was a man at the airport in Chicago. I thought he was after me. A definite psychopath. But it could be my imagination. I can't even begin to imagine what someone like that would do if he got his hands on Claire. I'd rather she were dead." Her voice was so flat and hopeless, he knew he had to do something.

"Look here," he said bracingly. "There's actually some good news. We've another candidate for your sister's murderer."

That brought her head up. "Who?"

"Chap who goes by the name of Owain Glyndwr. It's just a theory, but I've had the chief commissioner of MI-5 up here today to check out a threat on the Prince's life. It seems someone calling himself Owain Glyndwr is threatening revolution under the banner of Arthur. I think this manuscript would be right up his street."

"Glyndwr?" she asked, her face blank with astonishment. Tears still stood in her wide, round eyes. "But . . . oh," she fumbled in the pocket of her skirt. "My mind's not working. I was going to show you this, this morning." She handed him a folded piece of white notepaper. "I found that on the floor of my room when I came back from my run."

He flushed with discomfort as he read the lines. They made him feel slightly ill.

"Fellow seems to fancy himself a sort of Dylan Thomas," he said dully.

"A stalker!" Cole pronounced. He had risen from his comfortable chair and come to look over his superior's shoulder. "This Glyndwr must be a mad stalker!"

Maren shivered. "Do you really think he could have killed my sister?"

"We're keeping a watch on his flat," he told her. "He seems to have disappeared."

CHAPTER FORTY-NINE

SQUIRRELS GUEST HOUSE
LLANGOLLEN, WALES

Maren was trying to move past the stage where she wished there were a drug strong enough to obliterate her pain. As she paced, her mind indulged in images of Claire asleep in her bed, her hand under one cheek, of Claire on Patrick's shoulders in front of the gorilla cage at the zoo, of Claire, her tongue sticking out of the corner of her mouth as she glued glitter on a matchbox she was making into a gift for her grandmother. Then she had relived the moment when the man from her worst nightmare had stared into her eyes at O'Hare airport. Did he have Claire? Where was God, if there was a God?

Then suddenly, as she made this plea, there were Anthony's eyes, soul-deep with honeyed empathy. He had been talking about grace. But what about free will? What about all the people in the world who chose to be evil?

She sat on the bed. God must weep. Was it possible that at times he looked just as Anthony had done? Her ache was so deep inside, she couldn't do anything but wish both she and Claire were dead.

Then she raised her head and shook it. This wasn't doing anyone any good. She must try to think like the lawyer she was. As Anthony had told her, it was up to her to do as much as she possibly could. Right now, that meant *think*.

Valerie. She had read Maren's statement, realized Ian was in imminent danger of being exposed, and phoned her contact in the cartel. The "Greek"? Yes, that made sense, because she had then made him a reservation on the same flight in the seat next to hers. He had probably been the one who attacked her at the Randolph! *The bracelet!* That's what she had felt digging into her windpipe. Then they had presumably lost her. How had they gotten onto Ian?

Had someone been following him since he left Chicago? Or perhaps Griffith was Ian's traitor. Yes. That worked. Griffith must be part of the cartel. While keeping Ian informed of her movements, he was also keeping them informed of Ian's movements.

But how had Ian found out so soon about Valerie's double cross? And most important, how had he arranged Claire's kidnapping? Where in the world was she? Surely if he knew he was compromised, he wouldn't have had the cartel take her. Claire had disappeared after Valerie's death, after his revenge. That was an important point. The psychopath, ostensibly part of the cartel, probably wasn't involved.

Relieved in part but still deeply uneasy, she realized she had been staring unseeingly out the window. Now she saw that the light from the moon on the Abbey Road leached the vitality from the cheerful street as though taking the marrow from its bones. There was another Wales, it seemed to be telling her. A dark place that had been dying of poverty before tourism rescued it. A fiercely independent place where once battles had raged and blood had run "fetlock deep." A passionate place that bred the Arthurian legend into its babies' bones and gave rise to bards and poets. And lunatics, apparently. In addition to everything else, was there a stalker out there, watching this very window? Was he the same one who was crazy enough to want to kill the Prince of Wales? Crazy enough to have strangled poor Rachael? Crazy enough to send her love poetry?

A knock at the door made her jump.

"Maren, it's Anthony. I've got something important to tell you."

Rising, she went over and opened the door.

"Anthony." His eyes were alight, and he was smiling. "I've found out where the *Castell cadarn a'i safle grymus ar ben y graig* is!"

With difficulty, she pulled herself out of her preoccupation and tried to enter into his enthusiasm. "How?"

"I put it to Davies. He says that's the Welsh name for Harlech Castle!"

"Harlech! I've been to Harlech. On my honeymoon." She opened the door wider. "You'd better come in."

"Davies is keen to join us." Anthony strode to the window seat and perched there. Maren realized she had been sitting in the dark. Switching on the bedside lamp, she went over to the armchair.

"Anthony, did you tell him about Claire? About why we wanted the manuscript?"

She watched the elation evaporate from his countenance. "You've been crying," he said. "What's happened?"

"A bunch of things," she told him, looking down at her knotted hands. "I've only just figured out that Claire couldn't have been taken by the psychopath at the airport, but before that I was in absolute hell. Valerie's been murdered, you see."

Leaning forward, he pushed away a strand of hair that had come loose from her pony tail. "Tell me about it, Maren."

She recounted her chain of reasoning. Then she said, "It's more important than ever that we get that manuscript for Ian. I don't think there's a hope of recovering Claire without it. I haven't any idea what he's done with her. I can't begin to imagine."

"This chap with the FBI. What does he think?"

"I haven't talked to him. He left a report with Scotland Yard."

"I think you need to talk to him further. He should interview your brother-in-law again, for starters."

Anger flashed through her and without thinking she unleashed all her pent-up frustration. "You just don't want to give up that manuscript! You, with all your talk of grace and God . . ."

He raised a hand. "Maren, you're wrong. I'll give it up in a minute if we can get Claire back. But I think we ought to be pursuing other avenues. I don't want to alarm you, but kidnappers are not the most honorable of men."

She felt herself grow cold. "You don't think she's dead, do you?"

"What is Ian like? Tell me about him, Maren."

That was not an easy task, she realized. "You have to understand one thing first. When I married him, I wasn't myself. My husband, Patrick, had been pursuing this drug business for years. He had finally gotten his witnesses in order and was ready to bring it down. It was all very secret. Only Sam Reynolds, our friend in the FBI, knew what was going on. Even he didn't know the kingpin. Patrick wouldn't tell me. He didn't want me in danger." She paused, unable to get to the point, unable to tell Anthony how silly she'd been.

"How does this connect with Ian?" he said, his voice gentle, coaxing.

"Well, after Patrick was murdered—"

"He was murdered, too?" She looked up and read patent astonishment in Anthony's eyes.

"Yes. I thought you knew. I thought Rachael would have . . ."

"She never once mentioned him," he said flatly.

"Oh. Well. It was technically a hit-and-run. He normally didn't go anywhere without his FBI bodyguard, but we'd had a fight, and he had this motorcycle . . ."

"Spare yourself, Maren. We're talking about Ian."

She drew breath into her tight chest. "You have to understand that everything went numb in me after Patrick's death. I wasn't even a proper mother to Claire. I gave up my law practice and have spent most of my time the past year and a half working with Sam to try to reconstruct Patrick's case. You see, all of his witnesses disappeared. There was never any trial. The name of the kingpin died with Patrick."

"And then you met Ian," Anthony guessed.

"Yes. At a party my brother-in-law gave last June." She bent her head again. "He was Valerie's date, apparently, but I think he must have set out purposely to intrigue me. He didn't come on to me or anything that obvious. He was just smooth and charming and completely removed from the world I was in." She squinted her eyes. "Looking back, I guess it was like a British comedy—light relief. He seemed well-off, and I thought he could provide for Claire. I was sick and tired of darkness. Of carrying everything myself." She sighed. "I drew kind of a veil over all the stuff down inside and decided to settle for an amicable, civilized marriage. There would never be another Patrick, you see."

After a quiet moment, Anthony said, "You didn't need to tell me all of this, Maren. I'm not here to judge you. All I asked is what Ian was like."

She felt foolish, as though she had performed a striptease before an indifferent audience. "But that's just it. I don't really know. It was all hollow, every part of it. I found out he was crooked in the weeks before Rachael died. I had realized he was using me for access to steal from my friends' homes and decided to divorce him. But I never thought he was dangerous." Her voice began to rise. "I *never* had a clue he was involved with drugs. And now I find out our marriage wasn't even legal! Everything was a sham, *every last bit of it*. I even thought he was fond of Claire. I never dreamed he could do her any harm." She thought she had cried all her tears, but they began flowing freely, accompanied by sobs. "It's all my stupid fault!"

Anthony knelt by the side of her chair. Gentle, firm fingers tilted up her chin so she was looking into those bottomless, glowing eyes. "You feel as though you have betrayed Patrick as well as Claire."

"Yes," she whispered. "It's stupid, but I can't get rid of it."

"How much of this background does the chief inspector know?"

"I haven't confided in him. I've never confided in anyone."

He stood and went back to the window seat. She felt bereft and looked away, ashamed of her admission.

"I'm honored that you'd trust me, Maren," he said with a return to formality. "Do you still think Ian may have had a hand in Rachael's murder?"

She tried to pull herself together. This man had loved Rachael. She was only the little sister, and she had just shown herself in the worst possible light. "Actually, the chief inspector has come up with another candidate." She told him about the visit from MI-5.

"Glyndwr? Good heavens!" He stood and began pacing the room, clearly agitated. "Of course, he'd want that manuscript. It's imperative that we get hold of it as soon as we can! You should have seen this country in 2000!"

"What happened in 2000?"

"It was the six hundredth anniversary of Glyndwr's uprising. Wales went positively wild with nationalistic excess. And the devil of it is . . ." He appeared to be doing calculations in his head. "It was in September! In mid-September. It must be coming up any day now. Don't you see? He needs that manuscript as a token. The Welsh are very mystical where Arthur is concerned. And Glyndwr. This man is clearly plotting to rally the Celts, as Arthur did, and destroy the House of Windsor!"

"You seriously see him as more than the average nut?" She was amazed at the degree of his alarm.

"I'm Welsh. I'm a Celt. I relate."

"You hate the House of Windsor?"

"I think they're a passel of stuffed shirts. Literally. There's nothing underneath, Maren. They're as cold-hearted a bunch as you could ever hope to meet. All the soul has been bred out of them. And the Welsh are fiery, passionate. Did you ever see Richard Burton act?"

Maren nodded, dumbly. The actor's skill had been so un-British, so unreserved.

"And Dylan Thomas? Have you ever read his poetry?"

This time she shuddered. "As a matter of fact, I have. I'm sorry to say, he gives me the creeps."

He stopped suddenly in the middle of the carpet and looked at her as though trying to focus. "What do you mean?"

She shrugged, reluctant now to take him into her confidence. This was a different Anthony.

She felt as though someone were suffocating her. "Do you know much Thomas?"

"I have reams of it memorized. Rachael loved him, too. He touches a chord no one else can reach."

"Yes, well, I'm very tired, Anthony. I think you'd better go."

At once he was contrite. "Your life's a misery right now, *cariad*. Take my advice and tell Llewellyn the whole story. Start to finish. And tomorrow we'll leave for Harlech."

He kissed her on the cheek and left her.

Chapter Fifty

West Gate of Ruthin Castle
Ruthin, Wales

Owain Glyndwr was happy to meet at last with the core of his band. The night air was damp, and it was uncomfortable in the dense shrubbery that shrouded the gate to the ruin. But it was important that they meet here. This was where it had all begun, six hundred years ago. The uprising against de Grey.

"He's still going to Caernarfon, as planned, despite the threat," the man he called ap Gruffyd confided. "I think he is trying to reestablish himself with the Welsh by staging that pageant commemorating his investiture. And Sunday's still on at Bangor Cathedral. I'll have the weapon in place. Oh, and the Duchess is definitely coming with him."

"Yes," Glyndwr said. "The cathedral is a stroke of magical luck. It is a fitting symbol. I burned it to the ground when the English defended it against me, but it is Welsh down to its very foundations. Did you know it is the oldest cathedral in the United Kingdom?"

"I thought you just said you burnt it to the ground!" ap Dafydd objected.

"Some of the original stones remain," Glyndwr replied. "And think of the grand speech I can make there as I present the world with King Arthur's omen. You have access to all the security details?" he questioned ap Gruffyd.

"I'm on duty myself," the man assured him.

Owain Glyndwr paced the dry moat of Ruthin Castle long after his comrades had left him.

> *Incendiary dread on silent streets*
> *Where strangers lie before the feet*
> *Of him who comes with vengeful steel*
> *To strike and break until all grief*
> *Will nevermore by peace be healed.*
> *The darkling rain will never cease*
> *'Til thundered wrath flies through the sleep*
> *Of those whose lying, fear-filled eyes*
> *Lock open as their lips deny*
> *Last judgments written on the sky.*

They were going to succeed. After so many years, so many failures, a great and final triumph.

But he had a debt to settle first with a certain son of the Saxons who was causing his goddess great grief.

CHAPTER FIFTY-ONE

LLANGOLLEN, WALES

Chief Commissioner Braden read Maren O'Neill's strange note from Glyndwr.

"It sounds as though he's entranced by her. Well-read chap. Now who does that remind me of?"

"I believe it's in the style of Dylan Thomas, sir," Llewellyn said.

"Well. Well."

"But how would this Glyndwr chap over the tobacconist's even *know* of Maren?" Llewellyn asked.

"If he murdered her sister, he may have been keeping watch on her since she began this quest for the manuscript, hoping she'd lead him to it." The puzzle was becoming more intriguing by the hour. It had been too long since he'd done any fieldwork, he realized. He only prayed that desk work hadn't slowed his wits.

"I don't like the sound of that. Sergeant Cole thinks he's a stalker."

"He's crazy enough. I'm sticking by you, I think. Wherever she is, I think we'll find this Glyndwr person. My sergeant will stay here to keep an eye on the flat. Good lass by the name of Wincombe." He thought of his chrysanthemums without regret.

"Well, I breakfasted with Maren and Jones this morning. Seems we're off to Harlech to find a monastery."

"Any news on that other murder you're investigating? The one by the abbey?" Really, this case had more tentacles than an octopus, and he had the feeling he didn't know the half of it.

"Fingerprints were identified as Santiago Serveza. Colombian. Member of the Don Benito cartel. Has ties to the UK and the States. I called Maren O'Neill's FBI chap. The Don Benito cartel is the one her husband was investigating."

"Well, well. And his wife married right into it," Braden mused. "Have you told her yet?"

"This morning. She didn't take it well."

"Hysterics?" Braden inquired sympathetically.

"Fury!" Llewellyn replied with a smile. "Like a rocket on Guy Fawkes night. Of course, it was followed by remorse. She blames herself terribly for that marriage and what's happened to her daughter."

Braden ruminated. "She doesn't sound like a comfortable sort of person."

Llewellyn chuckled. "No, she's not that. But she is what my gran would call plucky."

Did the chief inspector admire the troubled Mrs. O'Neill then? A notorious misogynist like him? He couldn't wait to meet the lady. "Seems to me she's the key to this whole puzzle."

"Well, let's just put it like this. Ever since she landed in Britain, things have been exceedingly chaotic. Drama surrounds her."

chapter fifty-two

aren was not pleased at the sight of Griffith strid-
ing through the door to the guest house wearing
a purposeful air. She was going through the
motions of checking out, though still reeling from the knowledge that
Ian had been part of the cartel that had slain her husband. The idea
that he had ever touched her seemed the grossest betrayal of Patrick
she could possibly imagine. She was physically ill at the thought of
it. And angry, of course. What a dupe she had been! The cartel had
used Ian to keep tabs on the progress of her investigation. No wonder
she hadn't gotten anywhere. And now here was Griffith. Another
member of Don Benito? In all probability.

"Oh!" Griffith said, startled at the sight of her. She was surprised
by the look of contrition in his gray eyes. "I made certain you'd still
be at breakfast."

"I don't know what you can possibly have to say to me," she said
coldly, careless of her personal safety. "You're working with a murderer who kidnapped my daughter. He was up to his eyeballs in the

drug business. Are you one of his toughs? I don't know why you're not in jail." She turned back to Mrs. Thomas and presented her MasterCard.

"I came to tell you that I didn't know anything about any of that." The man's gray eyes were now mournful. He was a far different being from the perky professor from Birmingham who had conversed with her so flippantly on the demise of the hero. "I'm cooperating with the police, you see. I'd no idea Hubbard had kidnapped your daughter. That was never part of the plan. I would never have gone along with it for an instant, no matter what he threatened to do."

"And just what did he threaten?"

The bearded man's gaze wavered, and he looked down. "I'd rather not say, if it's all the same to you. I would lose my job if it came out."

Maren turned her back to him and signed her credit card slip, leaving Mrs. Thomas a generous tip. "Thank you so much," she said to her hostess. "I hope to come back someday and see the Eisteddfod." In actuality, she never wanted to see Llangollen again.

The small woman beamed. "I understand you made a bit of a find out at the abbey yesterday." She laughed. "Those old abbots, now. They were never to be trusted. I'm chapel, of course."

Maren automatically smiled back and turned to face her unwanted guest. "Just what are you doing here?"

"I wanted to offer my help in finding your daughter."

That surprised her. "And how could you do that?"

"Hubbard is in touch with me. I can steer you in his direction. Help arrange his capture . . ."

Her heart took a leap. Here was hope! "You've heard from him? Where is he?"

"Somewhere nearby, I think. He wants that manuscript badly."

Maren studied him frankly. "He was on the hill yesterday with a gun. Did you tell him about the abbey?"

His face was pained and became even more pale. "Yes, I'm afraid I did. But that was before the murder, and before I knew anything about the kidnapping. Now if he rings, I'll tell you straightaway. I'll stay right with you, so you'll know."

Maren frowned. Right with her? At latest count that meant Anthony, Chief Inspector Llewellyn, Detective Sergeant Cole, and Griffith traveling to Harlech. She looked hard at the small man with the wrestler's strong build. In spite of his act of contrition, was he in fact Rachael's murderer? In his suit of brown tweed with his carefully trimmed ginger beard, he looked completely innocuous. But then, she was a lousy judge of character. She had actually seen in Anthony some kind of god, when he was actually a raving Welsh nationalist.

At that moment, the subject of her thoughts entered briskly with Professor Davies, who was muffled in a gray overcoat with a red knit scarf wound around his chicken neck. "I say!" Davies exclaimed. "This is absolutely ripping! Let us make for Cymer Abbey with no more ado!"

"Cymer Abbey?" she echoed faintly. Another addition to their entourage? Her tenuous feeling of control slipped away completely.

"Nearest monastery to Harlech," Davies informed her. "About two miles from Dolgellau."

Anthony was looking at her shocked face with a gleam of amusement. Under the circumstances, it annoyed her. "The professor likes to get things done. He puts the rest of us academics to shame."

It seemed that Anthony had once more been swept away by the idea of the treasure hunt. The professor obviously appealed to the part of him that was a member of the Oxford Arthurian Society. "So you've heard of the Brothers of whatever it's called in Welsh— Harlech Castle?"

The gray-coated man put one gnarly, ancient finger across his upper lip. "No. I must tell you frankly that I haven't. But it stands to reason that they must have been some sort of cult attached to the castle or the abbey. Perhaps they were very pro-Glyndwr and were dissolved at his defeat." His eyes glinted once more with enthusiasm. "Cymer Abbey was never completed, you know. And there is precedent for hidden treasure. In the nineteenth century, silver and gilt chalices were discovered in the nearby mountainside. It is postulated that they were hidden during the Dissolution."

"You mean during the reign of Henry VIII?" Maren asked, interested in spite of herself.

"That's it. I see you know your English history, young woman."

Maren's hopes took a dive to her toes. There was absolutely no way on earth that this man would be convinced to surrender such an important piece of British heritage as Walter's manuscript, even for the sake of Claire's life. Surely Anthony must see that. Why on earth had he arranged to bring him? Had he ever intended to give it up himself?

She felt his eyes on her. They had taken on a thoughtful look. Unable to bear the complexity of the man at the moment, she suddenly strode past everyone out of doors. This had become entirely too convoluted. Maren had no idea whom she could trust.

Then she saw the Range Rover pull up in front of the guest house. It was followed closely by an aging black Bentley, out of which emerged a middle-aged man with graying red hair worn so short she could see his scalp. He wore a black and white herringbone tweed suit and somewhat scuffed and dirty black shoes.

Llewellyn approached her, and she felt her anxiety recede a bit. *He* at least was concerned for Claire. Perhaps he *would* get hold of Ian before he demanded the manuscript.

"This is Chief Commissioner Braden, Maren, of MI-5. Chief Commissioner, this is Maren O'Neill."

She shook a thick and callused hand. MI-5. On a murder case.

Then it dawned on her that he must be here because of the Glyndwr plot.

"The chief inspector has been telling me about your daughter's kidnapping, Mrs. O'Neill. I must say, I'm terribly sorry to hear about it."

Sighing deeply, she said, "There are just too many people after this manuscript. I suppose you are coming to Harlech, too?"

"There's a plot against the Prince, you see. Llewellyn showed me that bit of poetry you received from the man calling himself Glyndwr."

"Poetry? Glyndwr? What's this?" Anthony had come up behind them, Professor Davies in tow. His voice was sharply inquisitive.

No one answered him. Braden continued, "We think this chap will stick close to you. No telling what he might try. Actually, I think the more people you have around you, the safer you'll be."

Anthony put a hand on her arm. She could feel its warmth through the sleeve of Rachael's sweater. "You mean the one who's tried to kill her?"

Braden's bushy red eyebrows went up. "Now, then. No one's told me about this. Someone's tried to kill you?"

The chief inspector intervened. "My fault. I should have told you, Chief Commissioner. Someone tried to strangle her in her suite at the Randolph."

"I had thought the man posing as my husband was responsible for the attack, but now, for a number of reasons, I don't think that's likely," Maren told him. "I suppose you heard about my sister's murder?"

"See here now, Llewellyn," Braden said, turning to his junior officer. "Just what *is* going on?"

Llewellyn actually flushed. "It doesn't have anything to do with the plot against the Prince, sir. I didn't think I need bother you with it."

"Let me be the judge of that. It seems this young woman's in a rare mess. And as she's the object of this fellow, Glyndwr's, desire, I don't think we can afford to leave anything out."

"What's this Glyndwr up to? I mean . . ." Anthony interrupted. His former satisfaction with the situation seemed to have left him. He looked from one policeman to the other, confused. Again, no one answered him.

As the group stood on the pavement outside the guest house, Maren began to feel she was taking part in a farce. They needed to be getting on to Harlech, and she had no desire to ride with Anthony or Griffith or the ubiquitous Cole, who had so far stood back and surveyed them all with a gleam of humor in his eyes.

"If you're coming with us to Harlech, Chief Commissioner, why don't we ride together? I can fill you in on the way," she said, deliberately turning away from Anthony.

"I'll drive, sir, if you like," Llewellyn said. "Everyone else can go in the Range Rover with D.S. Cole."

Leaving Anthony staring after her, Maren climbed into the Bentley's rear seat with Chief Commissioner Braden, and they pulled away from the guest house.

As they crossed the River Dee and proceeded through the mountains along the River Alwen, towns were sparse, and the green of the hillsides dotted with sheep gave Maren a feeling of badly needed breathing room.

"Now, Mrs. O'Neill, start at the beginning and end at the end. I want the whole story." He wore his authority in a reassuring manner, and suddenly she wanted nothing more than to tell him everything.

"It's two stories, really," she explained. "Though they're linked by my—by the man I thought was my husband."

"The man we know as James Hubbard is part of the Don Benito cartel and likely murdered Serveza on the Horseshoe Pass," the chief inspector clarified. "We found during the course of our investigations that he was a bigamist. Maren was never legally married to him."

"Yes," she said, twining her hair meditatively around a finger. "I suppose, really, that I should go back even further than my second marriage. You see, my first husband was a United States attorney who was getting ready to indict the head of that cartel in the States. He didn't even tell me who it was. The FBI didn't know, either, because Patrick was worried about leaks. But he had his witnesses lined up." Maren closed her eyes, remembering the days before Patrick's death when he had been stretched as taut as a violin string. Always moody, he was unwontedly snappish and brooded alone in the dark, smoking his pipe on their porch, long after midnight. He had been so closed-mouthed that she really had not understood what danger they were in.

"Go on," Braden prompted.

"The day before he was going to the grand jury for indictments, he was run off the road on his motorcycle. He shouldn't even have been driving it . . . we'd had a fight . . ."

"Never mind," the chief commissioner said kindly. "I take it the case never came to trial."

"No. And the witnesses all disappeared. I felt totally responsible." Maren related her efforts to reconstruct Patrick's case while working with Sam Reynolds and the U.S. Attorney's office. "But we were coming up dry. Patrick kept his secret too well."

Braden nodded. They crossed another small river. The landscape was bare moorland with distant hilltops just visible beneath clouds carrying rain.

"Then last June I met Ian, or James Hubbard, as you call him."

"How did you meet?"

"Patrick's brother, Robert O'Neill, is a respected criminal defense attorney. He had a big party at his house on the North Shore of Chicago. Robert says that Valerie Kensington, his paralegal, brought Ian as her date. But I didn't know that until just before I came over here."

The chief commissioner ruminated on this, tapping a stubby, workmanlike finger on the leather seat between them.

"Has it ever occurred to you, Mrs. O'Neill, that Hubbard could have engineered that meeting?"

The idea shouldn't have jolted her after the revelations of that morning, but it did. Had deadly threat lay coiled like a snake in the innermost reaches of her life without her suspecting it? She had viewed her marriage as a simple act of folly. But now it was obvious that if the cartel had been behind her marriage, then Ian's ultimate mission, given her preoccupation with Patrick's case, could have been her death. She looked out at the ominous, rain-bearing clouds. The thought was deeply chilling.

Her legal mind shook off these gothic imaginings and told her that she must simply accept that however frightening, those events were in the past. What was in the present was far worse than her own danger. It was Claire's. "Now that I know what I know about Valerie, I suppose I've got to consider the possibility."

Braden asked, "And what about Valerie?"

"Well, you see, I went to my brother-in-law to leave Claire with him before I came here. When I told him I thought Ian was involved in Rachael's murder and that he was crooked, he suggested I write a statement and have Valerie notarize it before I left. He's never liked Ian, you see. And although I didn't know Ian was connected to drugs, I did know he was a thief." She remembered her reasoning at the time. She had been afraid she might die in her pursuit of Rachael's murderer. Well, she almost had died, hadn't she? But it was ironic that it was the statement and not Rachael's murderer that had been behind the attacks.

Outside, the moors took on an even greater look of desolation. "I suppose it was my knowing Ian's accomplices that went against me."

Maren reported on the whole sequence of events that she supposed must have occurred to bring Serveza into the picture. She told about Serveza being on the plane, her earlier suspicions that Valerie had been Claire's kidnapper, and Sam's discovery of Valerie's murder.

"So you think Hubbard—your Ian—murdered her before he left the States and that the person who attacked you was set in motion by Valerie?" Braden seemed undaunted by the complex puzzle of fact and supposition. It was easy to see why this unassuming man with the muddy shoes had risen to the top level of MI-5.

"I think Serveza may have been her contact. She obviously told him that I knew things about Ian I shouldn't know. That his cover as an antiques dealer was blown. He must have known who the top guy in the cartel was, or something, for them to have come after him. But how Ian discovered she double-crossed him, I have no clue." She paused a moment. "And I can't think of any reason for him to go out of his way to murder her except pique. There must be a missing piece here." Yanking a strand of hair, she continued. "I think Griffith is involved, too. I heard Ian telling him on the telephone to go after the manuscript." She pondered that morning's conversation and plugged it in to her chain of evidence. "Ian has something on him. Griffith won't tell me what. But it could be drugs. He could be hooked into the cartel without Ian knowing. How else would they have known where to find Ian?"

Braden appeared to assimilate all this. "You have been through a species of hell, it seems to me, Mrs. O'Neill. Finding this out all at once, on top of your husband's murder." He paused. "I beg your pardon if I seem overbearingly concerned with the facts, but can you tell me just when your daughter was kidnapped?"

"The second night I was in Britain. She was staying with Patrick's brother, like I said. He doesn't have children of his own and is like a second father to her. I couldn't think of a safer place." Braden's sympathy had taken her unawares. She knotted her fingers together. "I actually heard Ian threaten to hurt Claire during that phone conversation, you see. Robert said she was taken while they were out and she was with Louise, who's been with the family forever."

"How would Ian have known where she was, if Valerie didn't tell him?" Llewellyn demanded suddenly, his tone sharp.

"Oh, he would have guessed. Robert's house has been Claire's second home ever since Patrick died."

"And the ransom note?" Braden interjected.

"A computer printout. Ian could have ordered it done or done it himself. I don't know. The demand was for the manuscript, which is how that all comes together." She bit her lip. For a time she had completely put the cursed manuscript out of her mind. But, of course, that's what Braden was interested in.

"Maren," the chief inspector broke in, "tell him about Valerie's murder."

Closing her eyes, she went back to the chain of evidence she had worked out. "It must have happened the first night I was here. So Ian must have learned right away that she had double-crossed him." She stopped, wracking her brains for facts that weren't there. "As I say, I don't know how, but who else would have murdered her? And since her double cross showed that the ring was out to eliminate him, he never would have involved them in Claire's kidnapping. The thing that's driving me absolutely crazy is that I don't know what he did with her."

"All right," the chief commissioner said, with an air of finality. "We'll stir up the FBI on that one. We'll make certain your friend Sam has all the pertinent facts." Braden settled back against the seat and turned his keen eyes on her. There was a subtle change in him. He had become eagle-like, suddenly sighting his prey. "I can see how Claire must be your major concern right now, but for the nation's sake, we must move on to the manuscript. Glyndwr obviously wants it, since he is on your heels. How did he find out about it, I wonder? Think back and tell me about the telephone call you received from your sister."

Trying to shift gears from worried mother to avenging sister, Maren related what she could remember. "Ian must have heard everything. As I told you, he telephoned Griffith and told him to go after the manuscript. I ran into Griffith at the Randolph just after I'd landed."

She told the chief commissioner all about her sister's murder and her suspicions of Griffith. Llewellyn cut in with details concerning the Dylan Thomas book of poetry they had found and Professor Jones's theft from the Bodleian. After that, they related how their search had taken them first to Llanthony Priory and then to Valle Crucis Abbey.

"And this Professor Anthony has accompanied you?"

"I thought it best to keep him under my eye, sir," the chief inspector apologized.

"So," Braden said with an air of summation, "the people who know about this manuscript are Mrs. O'Neill, yourself, Cole, Hubbard, Griffith, Professor Jones, and now Professor Davies, not to mention this raving lunatic Glyndwr."

"It strikes me that there's one other, sir," Llewellyn said tenuously.

"Oh? And who is that?"

"I'm not quite sure, sir. I've a feeling that there's a factor here we still haven't grasped. Nothing fits perfectly. It might be that our paradigm is a bit flawed. But then, I may be completely wrong."

Braden grumbled, ruefully inspecting his callused hands. "All right. But look sharp, mind you. We've a madman on the loose, and the Prince is due in days."

chapter fifty-three

illiam Dunstan, hauling a lorry full of turnips, followed the bleep of the homing device he had placed on the police Range Rover that had chased him over hill and dale the preceding day and now was transporting his bigamous wife. Where were they headed?

He cursed Griffith's sensibilities, wishing he dared to contact his former colleague. From the vantage point of a roof across the street from the Squirrels Guest House, he had watched in astonishment as Griffith made up one of the party who had left together that morning. How on earth had he managed to weasel his way in?

Suddenly the heather-covered hills turned to a deep, dull gray. Depressing, this. He supposed it must be the famous Welsh slate that had once made wealthy barons of a few quarry owners. He hoped his destination was some place more propitious. He didn't have a yen for quarries or mines or anything that might entail dirtying his clothes. Which was all very ironic, as he was at this moment dressed in the filthiest of farmer's dungarees with a day's growth of beard.

217

CHAPTER FIFTY-FOUR

PORTMEIRION, WALES

O f all the horrible desecrations of his homeland, Portmeirion was surely the worst of all. Owain Glyndwr simmered in silent indignation. In the face of all that was grand and true about Wales, that dandified idiot, Clough Williams-Ellis, had insulted his heritage by building what amounted to an architectural theme park! It was supposed to represent Italy, with its elaborate facades fronting nothing. It was like that farce of a musical, *Camelot*, making serious things, life-defining legends, into candy floss fit only for the light-minded.

But they were close now. And Harlech was no site for the feeble-kneed. He had laid siege to the English forces there for six bloody months. They had fallen in his greatest victory. For four glorious years he had reigned there, as he brought Henry to heel. Wales's parliament had sounded its mighty voice from within its walls. Many a triumphant ballad had been sung. And it still stood—grim and gray and grand. Waiting. To him, the most magnificent castle in all Wales. It would be like coming home.

chapter fifty-five

HARLECH, WALES

hief Commissioner Braden had decided that the easiest way to look for accommodations for their large party was to go into the town of Harlech. After the ruins of Grosmont and Dinas Bran, Maren found Harlech Castle almost fearfully imposing. Last time she had seen it, she and Patrick had been at that rosy stage of a relationship where personal barriers were down and they were moving thrillingly within each other's reality. Words had almost been unnecessary as they roamed the grassy slopes inside the enormous reminder of ancient wars, hand in hand, conscious mostly of the nearness of each other. They had been so invulnerable then—so very, very sure that even an edifice such as Harlech Castle could never pose a threat to their love. Or their all-conquering plans for the future.

Now the enormous gray ruin was only a reminder of the pitiful frailty of humankind. Even with its massive turrets on each of its four corners and its high and mighty walls overlooking the sea, it had been vanquished many times in its history. And Patrick, of course, was dead.

Anger simmered through her. Ian. That deadly, nasty charmer might be the very man who had organized her husband's death. She was going to get him. And she was going to recover Claire. She *had* to.

Robert might know something, might remember something, might have heard something. She would call him just as soon as they reached their lodgings. And she needed to touch base with Sam.

The chief commissioner chose Byrdir House, a nineteenth-century sea captain's residence, principally because it was large enough for all of them. Unlike the other places they had stayed, its rooms were spacious and formal. Maren had a double bed to herself. Her room was cheerful and bright with a television and a triple-mirrored dressing table. After slinging her duffel onto the bed, she washed in the sink and then went downstairs to arrange her calls to the States.

She met Anthony on the staircase. So focused was she on her task that she walked right by him. Calling after her, he asked, "Maren, any news of Claire?"

Suddenly, she remembered Griffith's vow to help her. "Did Griffith take any calls on his cell phone while he was in the car with you?"

"No. Sorry." Anthony was standing still, looking down at her, a question in his eyes. Maren cursed herself for looking into them and feeling their imperative, golden pull. The wound of Patrick's death had reopened, and Ian's treachery was too fresh for her to welcome any kind of attraction. Especially to a man who clearly had other interests.

"Thanks," she said briefly and continued on her way.

"Maren . . . about this Glyndwr chap," he called after her.

Ignoring him, she went to find Mrs. Wallace, her hostess. The tall, spare woman with improbable golden hair worn in a stylish pageboy was laying the table for dinner. "Were you wanting something?" she asked.

Maren explained her need.

She made her call from Mrs. Wallace's large office, which overlooked the ocean. Tourists strode on the beach within her view, wrapped snugly against the stiff sea breeze.

Madge put her through to her boss, who answered the phone briskly. "Maren, where are you?"

"In Harlech, Robert. You know, the place with the enormous castle?"

"Ah, yes. As I recall you and Patrick sent a postcard."

"Have you heard any more from Ian?"

"Ian?"

"About the kidnapping, Robert. I'm desperate about Claire."

"The FBI found Valerie's body. But you probably know that. They seem to think he killed her. It was digitalis in her yogurt, apparently. Every carton in her refrigerator."

"That's interesting," she said. It seemed an oblique sort of way for Ian to go about killing the woman, however. "Did you know she was working with that drug cartel that Patrick was getting ready to shut down?"

"Was she, now? Who told you that?"

"Well, we deduced it, actually. You see, Ian killed a member of the cartel—Somebody Serveza—who was tailing him. We think Valerie must have realized that Ian's cover was going to be blown by me and set her boss on him before he could plea bargain or anything and tell what he knew. Do you realize that I've been living for three months with a drug smuggler who might have been involved in Patrick's death?"

There was silence on the other end of the line.

"Robert?"

"The irony doesn't escape me, Maren," he said solemnly. "I haven't heard from Ian since the ransom note. Have you any idea at all where he is?"

"If I did, don't you think I'd have put the police onto him? He was at Llangollen yesterday, but he was on a motorbike and he escaped. Now there's no sign of him. But I imagine he's staying close by so he'll know when I get the manuscript."

"Valerie must have been a mole in my office," he said finally.

"I thought you represented criminals."

"You're a lawyer. You know we bring down a lot of rackets with plea bargains."

"Oh, right. Have any of your clients disappeared since she's been working there?"

"More than a few, but I never knew why."

"Well, obviously this Don Benito thing is pretty powerful." Maren clenched the phone, thinking of the ultimate sacrifice that Patrick had made, tracing the man who would probably never be brought down.

"So, do you have a good lead on this manuscript thing?"

"Yes. But so many people are involved now that I don't know if I'm going to be able to get it. Our best hope is that the police catch Ian and get him to reveal where he has Claire."

"Do you think the police have any chance at all of catching him?"

"He really wants this manuscript, Robert. Now that he's finished with the cartel, he's probably looking at it as his only chance to secure a retirement." She watched a little boy in kneesocks, short pants, and a cap chasing an orange balloon that had escaped him. "By the way, I'm going to give Sam Reynolds a call. I'll tell him what you said about Valerie being a mole. He'll probably want to see you again. Do you think you could get together a list of the clients of yours that disappeared?"

Robert sighed audibly. "I suppose that might be possible for some of them, although there may be issues of attorney-client privilege. Of course, if they didn't pay their retainers, they're technically not my clients."

"They're probably dead," she said, shivering. "Robert . . . Robert, do you think . . . do you think *Claire* is . . . dead?"

There was a long pause. "I hate to say it, Maren. But maybe it would be better if we thought of her that way."

The little boy's balloon wafted out to sea. Tears stung her eyes and rolled down her cheeks. She softly hung up the phone, forgetting all about her call to Sam. Maren had never cried so much in her life, but the pain in her breast was so bad that she was surprised her heart could go on beating.

CHAPTER FIFTY-SIX

BYRDIR HOUSE
HARLECH, WALES

Chief Inspector Llewellyn noticed at once that Maren had been crying. As she took her place across from him at dinner, she kept her eyes down. What had vanquished her pluck? What bad news had she received?

Jones sat next to her at the round table that seated six. He was examining her face as well. She turned away from him in an action that seemed intentional.

"What is it, Maren?" the Oxford professor asked.

Standing, she wadded up her napkin and threw it down on her plate. "Robert thinks Claire is dead!" she said, furiously. Tears spilled over, and she ran out of the dining room.

Llewellyn half rose, thinking to go after her. But Jones, more confident, beat him to it. Dismayed, Llewellyn watched with no interest as a young girl in a miniskirt set a plate of tomato soup before him.

He wasn't at all sorry when Jones, obviously unsuccessful, rejoined him.

"Slammed her door in my face," the professor said with obvious surprise.

And women don't usually do that to you, do they? Llewellyn ate his soup and concentrated on Maren's problem. It was time he talked to the FBI agent himself. Between the two of them, maybe they could make some headway on discovering where Claire was hidden. And there were some specific questions he wanted answered. Something about this case was making him jolly uncomfortable. It was like the aura he saw around things after he had one of his headaches. Greenish. Off-color. Evil. Yes, that was it. Somewhere around him was someone who was very, very evil.

That night he put in an overseas call to Agent Reynolds.

chapter fifty-seven

aren could not sleep. Haunted by Claire, Rachael, and Patrick, she didn't see how one human being could endure such agony and remain conscious. It was far worse than any physical injury she had ever received. Probably close to having open-heart surgery without anesthetic. Especially in this place, where she had been so happy, where Claire had quite possibly been conceived.

Was this what she deserved for having stolen Patrick from her sister? She rose and went to the window, where she gazed at the silhouette of the massive castle.

The three of them had been working on Senator Clarke's campaign when they met. Rachael, an unself-conscious beauty, had been attracting men of every type since she was eighteen. There had been a vulnerability about her that was almost mystical when added to her natural loveliness. Men lined up to slay her dragons, but she had none. She was that rare thing among beauties, a true scholar. Rachael had spared thought only for the Celts. The sole reason she had signed on to work for Senator Clarke was that Maren had told her he was on the board of the Chicago Art Institute. Her sister had hoped that she might talk him into sponsoring the exhibit on Celtic art from the Oxford Ashmolean Museum that would shortly begin a world tour.

But Rachael had seen Patrick, and that was that. Of course, that had been that for Maren, too, but she had never thought she stood a chance against her sister. She had simply put her head down and gotten to work. Senator Clarke was a great believer in change at the grass roots. He spent time with his constituents, working with religious leaders, community youth organizations, and counselors to try to find lifestyle alternatives for youth who were involved in drugs and gangs. Himself a product of the housing projects, he knew better than anyone what lures these destructive groups held. He didn't believe in throwing money around to be wasted by self-serving administrators. He put his faith in committed volunteers. Patrick was one of the most dedicated. He spent hours playing basketball, teaching creative writing, and listening, listening, listening.

It hadn't taken long before he learned about Maren's work in the courts and with the battered women. He had called her "scrappy" and meant it as a compliment. Rachael had never even been on his radar. He had seen only Maren, a passionate co-crusader.

She had kept his ardent pursuit secret from her sister, who divulged her most private fantasies into Maren's ears. She never knew when Patrick would turn up in her courtroom with a fistful of tickets to a Cubs game, a trio or quartet of black youth in tow. Then he started going to her kickboxing lessons and driving her home . . .

Maren threw the drapes closed over the towering view. She had never told Rachael. They had been married by Patrick's favorite judge and gone off to Wales for their honeymoon. She suspected that had been the straw that broke the camel's back. Wales, Rachael's adopted country.

Right now, Maren wished she were anywhere but here in Harlech. Perhaps if she put on Rachael's shoes and ran fast enough she could switch over to some other part of her brain, some part that wasn't drenched in memories. But every part of her would still be consumed with grieving for her little angel-haired daughter. Even so, a run might give her fresh perspective, lend her a thought she had been blinded to in her pity party.

Throwing off her nightclothes, she pulled on Rachael's sweats and then her track shoes, lacing them tight. She let herself out of her room. It must be nearly midnight.

She noticed vaguely that there was a beam of light from under Anthony's door and wondered why he was still awake. Did he mourn Rachael? In some awful, convoluted way, wasn't she responsible for the fact that Rachael had never been able to love him? Wasn't everything in the universe her fault?

Maren ran down the stairs, careless of the noise, through the downstairs hall, and out into the night. There was a golf course nearby, she remembered. It would make for excellent running.

As she pounded through the night, she indulged thoughts of herself as a ruthless, selfish person who had ended up with no one at all. Who was she to deserve God's grace, assuming there was a God? She had always depended on her own wits, her own strength, her own anger against injustice to fuel her. She had never looked for a higher, gentler power who might have done things differently. Like tend to Claire's more intimate childhood needs. Kathryn had spent hours smocking dresses for her niece.

The night was almost completely black. Harlech, though home to a major tourist attraction, was actually a sleepy little town. Very, very quiet. She started to listen to the quiet until it blotted out her thoughts. It was too quiet. Too dark. Too lonely.

Stumbling into a sand trap, Maren ended up on her knees. Now that her own footfalls were silent, she could hear others. From behind her. Two sets, it sounded like.

Who else would be running at midnight in a little town like this? With a start, she remembered her stalker. The man with the poetic kink in his brain. And the crazy person who wanted to kill Prince Charles.

Maren got to her feet, but a sudden cramp in her calf crippled her. As she bent over, a shot whizzed over her head.

Throwing herself face down in the sand, she tensed for the next one. Repeated shots streaked over her, thudding into the nearby tree. Someone was running closer all the time. She could hear him.

Was this it, then? Her heart pounded blood into her ears so loudly she couldn't hear. She couldn't think of one single strategy to get her out of this mess. Was she going to die in Harlech?

Then she heard shouts. A man cursed wildly in some foreign language. More shouts. She lay, stiff with terror, aware only vaguely that her mouth was full of sand.

Then the shouting stopped abruptly, and she heard footsteps again, pounding, running right up to the edge of the sand trap.

"You can get up now, Maren," Anthony said, his voice gentle. "The chief inspector knocked him out. He's got a wicked right."

Suddenly conscious of the sand, she spat it out, wiping her mouth with the back of her hand. "How did you . . ."

"I was up with one of my headaches and heard you leave. Llewellyn was obviously awake, too. Whatever possessed you to go running alone at this hour?"

Too shaken to be anything but honest, she blurted out, "Guilt, fear, memories, all of the above."

He helped her to her feet, his hands firm and surprisingly strong. She resisted the almost overpowering urge to throw herself on his chest and stood trembling. Looking back the way that she had come, she saw an outline of a man against the scarcely lit sky. He appeared to be talking on his cell phone.

"Where's the guy with the gun?" she asked.

"Out for the count. That's Llewellyn. Calling for reinforcements, is my guess. The man's a wonder. That chap was a tough."

"How did you ever keep up with me?" she asked irrelevantly, eyeing his loafers and charcoal wool slacks. "I'm fast."

"Marathon class, I should think. But then, so am I, luckily."

She could no longer keep from looking at him. In the night, his golden eyes shone like a tiger's. They were fierce. But his face was gentle.

"I was almost killed," she said. "If it hadn't been for you and the chief inspector, I *would* have been killed."

Surprisingly, he grinned. "I told you he was gone on you. You should have seen him. I pinned the chap's arms behind him, while Llewellyn beat him into the ground."

She wanted to ask, *And you? Why did you come after me?* Maren was surprised how much the answer mattered. But she was Rachael's sister.

"Who was it?"

Anthony put an arm lightly around her shoulder. "Let's go find out, shall we?" She faced back the way the shots had come and began limping towards the policeman and her attacker. With the arm of a tiger around her, she wasn't the least afraid. Somewhere inside, she faintly berated herself. She had never been a clingy female.

chapter fifty-eight

aren was still pale, the chief inspector noted, as a sergeant fingerprinted his handcuffed, black-bearded suspect. Llewellyn suspected he was another Colombian. But why tonight? How had they known she was here? And why were they after her, anyway? Was there a leak in the FBI?

"Maren, did you call Agent Reynolds today?"

"No," she said, looking down. She almost whispered, "Not after I talked to Robert."

"Do you mind telling me why?"

She lifted tragic green eyes to his. "He said we should think of Claire as dead."

Robert O'Neill. So he knew she was here. The thought had crossed his mind; he couldn't say that it hadn't. He knew about the manuscript. But why would he want to kill Maren? Unless . . .

"Constable, I need to use your telephone to make a call to the FBI."

"Right you are, Chief Inspector. I'll just put this charmer into a cell." He shoved the handcuffed assailant in front of him. "You'd better use the phone in the sergeant's office, sir. It's through there."

Maren sat listlessly, looking down at her hands. Her lovely hair was full of sand. Llewellyn wanted to brush it out with his fingers, but he restrained himself and went down the green linoleum corridor to the sergeant's private office. Dialing the cell phone number Sam Reynolds had given him that afternoon, he reached the FBI agent almost immediately.

"Reynolds."

"Agent Reynolds, this is Llewellyn again, from the Yard."

"Yes, Chief Inspector?"

"Maren was just shot at. He missed, fortunately, but we managed to nab him. Only speaks Spanish, so we're assuming he's another Colombian. We're sending his prints to Interpol. The question is, how did he know she was here?"

"You didn't get a leak from the FBI. I haven't told a soul where she is."

"And no one was listening in on our conversation?"

"No. We were talking on a secure line from my home."

"Then that brings up only one other possibility. Robert O'Neill. She phoned him this afternoon. He gave it as his opinion that Claire was dead. Upset Maren no end. Did you question him as we discussed?"

There was a long pause. "Robert O'Neill. Well, I'll be . . . He wasn't there, Llewellyn. His secretary said he'd left on vacation. Thought I'd catch him at the house, but it was shut up. Everyone gone."

"Then Maren's put the wind up him somehow. She must have told him to expect you." He thought carefully before phrasing his next question. "Reynolds, is it possible that Claire was never kidnapped? That O'Neill had her all along?"

"She wasn't there when we went to investigate the report. But, then, neither was Mrs. O'Neill."

Llewellyn thought furiously. He had heard that Chicago winters were brutal. And if the man were wealthy . . . "A winter home, maybe?"

"You'd have to ask Maren. She'd know."

"I'll ask her immediately. Meanwhile, here's something for you to get your teeth into. Is it possible that Robert O'Neill is the American kingpin of Don Benito?"

"What on earth put that idea into your head?"

"Everything Maren attributes to Valerie Kensington could equally apply to Robert O'Neill. Something in her statement about Hubbard made him think she knew more than she did. It explains the man on the plane, the attempts on her life, the attempts on Hubbard's life. Probably thought we were close enough to nabbing Hubbard that we'd get him and Hubbard would give O'Neill away in a plea bargain. And Valerie Kensington is dead. We have come up with no feasible explanation for how Hubbard could have realized she'd double-crossed him. I think O'Neill murdered her to keep her from being questioned and saying she knew nothing."

Agent Reynolds apparently thought this through and then swore long and bitterly. "That would mean he killed his own brother. That would explain Patrick's reluctance to give us his name."

"I've heard Maren's whole story, and I think he even engineered her marriage to Hubbard. He probably saw it as a precautionary measure."

"And Claire?" Reynolds asked.

"It's just possible that he really wants Claire. He doesn't have children of his own, does he? A double motive for Maren's death."

"Find out about that winter home from Maren, Chief Inspector. I'll keep my cell phone by my bed."

Llewellyn left the squalor of the small office with its metal desk and folding chair and headed back to the even less hospitable lobby where Maren waited. She was gazing unseeingly out the window, her posture dejected, but the sand was now gone from her hair.

"Maren, I've got to ask you something. I may be jumping to conclusions. Has Robert O'Neill got another home somewhere?"

She was immediately alert. "Robert? But why?"

"He's disappeared. I think Claire is somewhere with his wife."

Maren appeared stunned. He could see the possibilities chasing themselves swiftly through her suddenly arrested mind. "Naples," she said finally. "Naples, Florida. Port Royale Estates. Number 24. I stayed there with Patrick. And Claire. She loves the ocean."

"Pardon me. I have to get back to Agent Reynolds. Hold on tight, Maren. We may have your daughter back by morning."

chapter fifty-nine

aren stared at Chief Inspector Llewellyn's back as he hastened away. *Robert had Claire? What was all that about? How could Robert, of all people, let me suffer like this? Hadn't he known I would eventually find out?*

Her exhausted body began to tremble so hard her teeth chattered. The attempts on her life. Right after she had left Claire in Robert's care. But how would Robert have had access to practiced killers? The answer wasn't long in coming, even to her exhausted brain. His criminal clients.

Running her hands through her hair, she tugged it by its roots, trying to tell herself there was a good side to this. *Claire wasn't in any danger!* Relief swamped her. If Chief Inspector Llewellyn was right—and surely they would know shortly—Claire was in the hands of the last people in the world who would hurt her.

But Maren had signed a will making Robert and Kathryn Claire's guardians, and obviously he had intended to murder her. How could

Patrick's own brother be so horribly twisted? Betrayal and anger made her shake, as fear never had.

The chief inspector came back into the room. "The FBI is alerted. They're going down from Fort Myers to the O'Neill home. Do you want to go back to the guest house? This place isn't exactly the Ritz."

He indicated the scuffed linoleum, gray metal desks, overflowing waste bins, and hard wooden chairs. The bleary-eyed lump of a constable watched them, drinking a cup of coffee, the smell of which made her nauseated.

"Do you think I care?" she said, her voice rising. "I just want my daughter." Hope was starting to warm her frozen psyche, just a bit. Icicles were forming as a slow melt began.

The fax machine sounded and began to spew a piece of paper. The constable moved towards it leisurely, glanced over the document, and then handed it wordlessly to Llewellyn.

"What's that?" Maren asked. The chief inspector had a gleam of triumph in his eye.

"The identity of your would-be assassin."

"Who was he?"

"Manuel Fernandez. A known member of the Don Benito cartel."

Maren blinked. "But why would he be after me? I thought it was Robert who was trying to kill me."

Llewellyn's blue eyes became gentle, and he laid a hand on her shoulder. "Prepare yourself for a shock, Maren."

"What are you talking about?"

Llewellyn looked her straight in the eye. "I think Robert is the leader of the drug ring. Reynolds is going to do some digging, but he's fairly certain. You see, we don't think Valerie had anything to do with anything. She was murdered to keep from telling us that."

Maren stared at him. Her tired brain deflected what he was saying, but his eyes, bright and alert flashed it back at her. Robert. Head of the drug cartel . . . Patrick's murderer. "NO!" she cried. "He can't be!"

Llewellyn was very patient. He explained his reasoning slowly. Perspiration broke out all over her body, and the room went dark.

chapter sixty

They were too late. An hour after Llewellyn had tenderly revived Maren from her faint, only the second of her life, he heard from the Fort Myers FBI agent. The O'Neill residence showed every sign of hasty departure. The Fort Myers airport reported that a private jet owned by Robert O'Neill had taken off at eleven P.M. with a flight plan for Miami.

Llewellyn put in a call to the FBI in Miami. Just as dawn was breaking over Harlech, he received a call that the jet had landed as scheduled. No further flight plans had been filed.

"He's got major connections through Don Benito," Llewellyn told the agent. "The best thing for you to do is to look for the little girl with them. Here, I'll put her mother on."

He watched as a white-faced Maren took the telephone from him. "She's just four," she said in a voice she was striving to keep steady. "She has bright red hair. Curly. She's thin, and she has deep blue eyes." Then something made her add, "She likes frozen yogurt."

The agent said, "We'll get surveillance on all the private jets."

"Check the yogurt stands in the airport," Maren urged. "Robert can't deny her anything. Oh, and for identification, she's wearing a signet ring on a chain around her neck. Gold. It belonged to her father. It has the O'Neill coat of arms on it."

When she hung up, she asked Llewellyn, "Do you pray?"

He felt an uncomfortable sensation in his chest and wondered if it could be love. After all these years. Maren was gazing at him out of trusting green eyes, the color of moss, her hair stringy around her white face. She had been sick after her faint. Hardly the most romantic of circumstances. But he yearned for her with an arid part of his heart that had never been touched.

"I don't know how," he acknowledged regretfully.

"That makes two of us," she said sadly. "But, I think, if you don't mind, I'm going to try." Getting up from the hard chair she was sitting on, she went out into the hall, obviously looking for privacy.

Dawn streaked the sky a pinkish orange in the east behind the formidable castle, and Llewellyn thought he had never seen anything so beautiful in his life. He had never known he could feel any emotion in the heart that had been so damaged by a brutal father with his stinging cane and a mother who had screamed obscenities at him like a demented witch. Once they sent his nanny away, he built frozen walls around himself, barricading himself against every feeling. Evie's going had broken all that was left of his heart, he thought, still remembering the little hunchbacked figure kissing him good-bye, tears streaming down her face. "Never forget," she had whispered hoarsely. "Never forget."

Jones strolled into the police station at that moment, looking as alert as if he hadn't lost any sleep at all. He was followed by D.S. Cole, lounging through the door in his leather jacket and yellow cashmere sweater.

"Where's Maren?" Jones inquired.

"In the back," Llewellyn said stiffly. "She's had a shock and she wanted some privacy."

"It smells as though someone's been sick in here," Cole said distastefully.

"As I said, she's had a shock. Her brother-in-law has Claire, and he's trying to flee the country. Probably to Colombia. He's the U.S. head of Don Benito."

chapter sixty-one

CREIGMOR BED AND BREAKFAST
HARLECH, WALES

ortunately, Trish and Bern, the owners of this hostelry, hadn't taken exception to his unusual attire or his lorry, once he'd shown them his roll of money. William Dunstan looked at his far-from-handsome visage in the mirror. With his two-day's growth of beard, his battered cap and filthy dungarees, he didn't think anyone would recognize him.

Now the thing to do was to discover what the devil they were doing in Harlech. If they ran true to form, he supposed they'd visit Cymer Abbey today. It was the closest monastery around. He had long since decided that what they were looking for was connected to some monastery important in the legend of Owain Glyndwr. Why this connection, he couldn't begin to imagine, but he was far from underestimating his wife's intelligence. She must know exactly what she was doing.

Taking out his pistol, he carefully cleaned and loaded it. The crowd surrounding her only seemed to grow in size. It looked more than ever as though he would have to go with his hostage idea. The contacts he had made in Chicago through his stolen antiques business were independent of Don Benito. They had to be, so the money couldn't be traced. And they, unfortunately, had reported that Claire O'Neill had disappeared from the mansion on the Lake Shore. No joy there.

chapter sixty-two

BYRDIR HOUSE
HARLECH, WALES

C hief Commissioner Braden was rudely awakened by a
telephone call from the director general of MI-5.

"Braden, they're scheduled to leave for Wales tomorrow. You still have Owain Glyndwr under surveillance?"

Braden ran a hand over his bristly, mostly gray, beard. "Well, not exactly, sir. We have his flat under surveillance, but according to my last report, he hadn't appeared."

"Your last report? You're not overseeing this personally?" The tone was incredulous.

"I think he's here in Harlech, on the track of a manuscript to do with King Arthur."

"Whatever gave you such a bizarre idea?" The director general was indignant now.

"It is rather a bizarre story, actually, sir, but we're up against an unstable mind. Remember how he invoked Arthur's name in that letter to the Prince? I believe he thinks this manuscript will give him some kind of power."

"I had no idea you were a mystic, Chief Commissioner."

"I'm not. But this Glyndwr definitely is. That's the one thing we know about him for certain."

"Well," the director general sounded resigned, "carry on."

"I intend to." Braden hung up after his superior cut the connection. He looked at his watch. It was six A.M.

chapter sixty-three

W hen Maren emerged from the sergeant's cluttered office to find Anthony and Cole, she took little notice. Her eyes went straight to Llewellyn. "Any word yet?"

The phone shrilled. "Llewellyn!" the chief inspector barked into the instrument.

His face softened into a smile, and he handed the instrument to Maren.

"Mommy?" the little voice was confident and sure.

"Claire! Oh, Claire!" Maren's knees went weak, and she collapsed into a nearby chair. "Where are you, Peanut?"

"I'm at the airport. With Uncle Robert and Aunt Kathryn. We were going on a trip, but this man came and took Uncle Robert away while we were having frozen yogurt. Aunt Kathryn is crying, and I'm in this office with somebody who has a gun under his arm."

Maren could hardly hold the phone to her ear, she was so weak with relief. "I'm coming to get you, Baby."

"I'm not a baby," her daughter objected. "I'm big."

"Yes, you are. And brave."

Chief Commissioner Braden had walked into the office. Maren watched as the chief inspector drew him into a corner. "We got to fly on an airplane," Claire was telling her, "but I didn't even get to bring my pajamas."

"We'll buy you new pajamas, Peanut. Just a minute. The policeman who helped find you wants to tell me something."

"Maren, I know you want to go to Claire," Llwellyn told her, "but, you see, it's a matter of national importance. You're the only one who can lead us to Glyndwr. Could she possibly come here? The chief commissioner has a female sergeant . . ."

"Hold on a minute, Peanut," she said, putting her hand over the telephone. "My daughter has just been through a terrifying ordeal. She's seen her uncle arrested. She doesn't understand anything that's going on . . . How can I entrust her to strangers?"

"Don't you have any relatives who could fly over here with her?"

Maren detected the anxiety in his tone. After all, she owed this man her life and the restoration of her child. And with Robert contained, the attacks would cease. "My mother could bring her, I suppose. Could this sergeant meet her in London and bring her to Harlech?"

The chief inspector hesitated. "Are you sure you want her here? There could still be danger from this Glyndwr."

"If she can't come here, I'm going there, and that's flat," Maren said, feeling her former assertiveness return.

The chief inspector breathed deeply and turned to the chief commissioner.

"The woman's made up her mind, Llewellyn," Braden said.

Maren spoke into the phone. "You stay with the man with the gun, Peanut. Grandma is going to get you and bring you over here to me. You'll like it. There's a big castle here that I visited once with your daddy."

CHAPTER SIXTY-FOUR

HARLECH, WALES

aren's conversation with her mother was not an easy one. Inclined to be dismissive of danger, her mother had not at first believed the story of the kidnapping attempt and Robert's wickedness. Once Mrs. Williams did understand, however, she wanted to take Claire all the way to Harlech herself. Maren patiently explained the difficulty of driving the winding mountain roads on the "wrong side" and tried to make her mother understand how tired she would be after her flight. At length, her mother saw reason and agreed to surrender her granddaughter to the policewoman Chief Commissioner Braden would send. She was to meet Claire in Miami with suitable clothing. Mrs. Williams ended the conversation with a prayer that no one would remember that Robert O'Neill had been Maren's brother-in-law.

Now Maren was riding back to Byrdir House with Chief Commissioner Braden. The chief inspector had stayed behind to coordinate efforts with the FBI, giving an account of all that had happened since Maren had departed the States and come under his jurisdiction. Anthony and D.S. Cole were in the front seat. The former had been strangely silent. Exhausted and aware of her dismal appearance, Maren was glad enough not to have to converse with him. Her nervous system was emitting alternate waves of relief about Claire and a disturbing, whole-body revulsion over the knowledge that Robert had killed his brother, her husband. She knew it would take her years to come to grips with that knowledge. As it was, she could scarcely believe it.

D.S. Cole was holding forth. "The anniversary of the Rebellion is on Sunday, you realize," he was saying. "I'd say if this chap who thinks he's Glyndwr were going to strike, he'd do it then. Where's the Prince going to be that day, Chief Commissioner?"

"Bangor Cathedral. We're quite aware of the danger, Sergeant. Everyone going in will be searched. But it would be far better if we could lay hands on the bloke before then. These demented chaps, you never know what they'll try. I wouldn't put a suicide bomb beyond him, frankly."

Maren, listening only vaguely, didn't even wonder what they were talking about. It was all she could do to stay awake.

When they arrived at their hostelry, the chief commissioner asked Maren if she were too tired to make the trip to Cymer Abbey that day. Every part of her wanted to say yes, but when she remembered Claire was on her way, she decided it would be best to get this other business over as soon as possible. Professor Davies thought the abbey was the most promising site yet. Surely if the manuscript were to be found, it would be there.

"Just let me take a shower, Chief Commissioner."

"I think, after all we've been through, you might just as well call me Hal."

Smiling at him, she gave him her hand. "Maren," she said. "I don't suppose the irony has escaped you?"

He grinned. "No. Glyndwr's sworn enemy—the Good Prince Hal of Wales."

"Or so Shakespeare would have it," she said. "I have a good bit of sympathy for the Welsh, remember."

Anthony followed her up the stairs. Outside her room he paused. Looking at his feet, he said, "I'm afraid I've wronged you, Maren. I want to apologize."

She needed to see his eyes. "Look at me, Anthony," she said. When he did, she knew he was deadly earnest about something. "For what?"

"I knew you had hurt Rachael. I didn't understand how, and I still don't, but I can feel your goodness. I know there must be an explanation. And I'm tremendously relieved about your daughter."

Now Maren looked away. "I'm afraid the explanation would only make you think ill of me again. Rachael was the good one. I don't think she ever would have hurt me the way I hurt her."

"Perhaps only because she didn't feel strongly enough about anything but Celts."

"She felt strongly about Patrick."

"But, then, so did you," he said, and taking her hand, he squeezed it. "Have a good, long shower. You deserve it."

Wondering at this exchange and the reasons for it, Maren went into her room and allowed herself to fall crosswise onto her bed. She would rest just a moment. There was so much to process. Principally relief. Ian was not behind Claire's kidnapping. She had nothing more to fear on that score.

As for Robert, all she could feel was tremendous revulsion. His taking Claire she could almost understand. But murdering Patrick, his own brother? His younger brother, who, in spite of their squabbles, had idolized him for his football prowess at Notre Dame, his 4.0 that had opened doors for him at Harvard Law School, his *pro bono* work for young blacks on the South Side Patrick had taken under his wing?

Slowly, anger began to rise as the sickening reality of it penetrated further.

Greed. Somewhere inside that hulking red-haired man was the fatal worm of greed. And a love of power, a disdain for the rights and weaknesses of any other human being but himself. Perhaps it was related in some way to his impotence. She didn't know; she was no psychologist. Maybe it all had to do with what Anthony called his divine void. She didn't really care to analyze it. Patrick was dead, and his own brother was responsible. It should have relieved her to know that it wasn't she who had caused her husband's death, but she was heavy and sick with her new knowledge.

Heaving herself from the bed, she stripped off her grimy sweats, pulled clean underwear out of her duffel, and went to shower. Under the hot spray, she reflected that this should be a new beginning. After all the horrors that Robert's trial was bound to bring with it, she could finally lay Patrick to rest, having found both his murderer and the leader of the cartel. And as soon as Claire arrived, she would begin to make up for the last year and a half of denial and neglect.

But, she reflected as she rubbed suds through her hair, there was one more score to settle. She had to find Rachael's murderer. She truly believed that Anthony loved her sister. He had probably set her on a pedestal, as so many men had before him. And, despite his quirky love for Dylan Thomas, she believed he was a truly *good* man. She couldn't imagine him harming her sister.

Griffith? Now there was a puzzle. How could he have been a confederate of Ian's and as ingenuous as he seemed? He truly had been concerned about the murder and the kidnapping. Horrified, actually. Scared out of his role as a friendly anthropologist. But Ian had something on him, so he wasn't completely innocent. What if he'd merely slipped into another role? What if he was just a gifted actor?

And then there was the creepy Glyndwr. But Maren thought she could safely eliminate him. Rachael would have been very careful who she let into her rooms. She did not have casual affairs. And there had been a chain lock on that door.

So where did that leave her? Griffith was her only possibility. And he was to accompany them to Cymer Abbey. She remembered his impatience at the Valle Crucis Abbey and how he had urged Professor Davies to force the lock on the box. What did the manuscript mean to him, anyway?

Dressing in Rachael's black lace-up boots, tights, and flowing black-and-white striped cotton dress, Maren grabbed an emerald green shawl and left her room to find a belated breakfast. She was starving, she realized. It had been days since she'd eaten properly.

Anthony was waiting for her in the dining room. Rising when she entered, he pulled out a chair. "I'll get your breakfast," he said, heading for the sideboard. "What do you want?"

"Everything," she told him.

He set a plate loaded with eggs, bacon, fried toast, tomatoes, and mushrooms before her. "Now," he said, "I want you to talk to me about your daughter. Is she like you?"

"I hope not!" she said, filling her overturned fork with bits of egg, bacon, and tomato. "She's much more level-headed. Do you know, I don't think she turned a hair when Robert was arrested?"

"She is probably too young to know what was going on."

"Probably. It's ironic that the one good thing in his character is what proved his downfall. He could never deny her a frozen yogurt."

"Happens in the best of tragedies," Anthony told her.

"As a matter of fact," Maren said thoughtfully, "I prefer to see it as grace."

"Grace?"

"Yes. You see I was praying rather hard at the time. For once, I knew there wasn't anything else I could do."

CHAPTER SIXTY-FIVE

ON THE ROAD TO CYMER ABBEY
WALES

William Dunstan was simmering as he drove behind the Range Rover at a discreet distance in his lorry. From across the street, he had seen the green, come-hither glance Maren threw the chap with the black beard as they joined the four others in the car. *Didn't she realize she was a married woman?*

No, of course she didn't, he reminded himself. She knew by now that that had all been a farce. Nevertheless, he wouldn't mind doing the fool in the black beard an injury. Just for old time's sake.

He patted the gun inside his jacket. Hopefully, this wasn't going to prove another wild goose chase.

chapter sixty-six

Tomorrow the "Prince" would arrive at Caernafon, Owain Glyndwr reflected. He would have that pathetic, hollow pageant commemorating his investiture. Who would attend such a gathering? No true Welshman, that was certain. As the pretender marched down the hall in his grand fur-trimmed cape and crown, only the sycophants would be there. Those who unashamedly made money off the English. Those misguided souls who thought England was their savior. Those degraded worms who had been robbed of their proper history and heritage as schools were polluted and the teaching of the Welsh language and Celtic destiny disappeared.

Oh, Arthur must return soon! Before there was nothing left to reclaim. This omen would surely summon him, Wales's greatest champion. He himself had done his best, all those years ago, but it hadn't been enough.

This time, he would not fail. This Charles was no Prince Henry, no warrior of any kind. He was a dilettante! It would be like snapping a matchstick to kill him. And as for his boys . . . Born to privilege, they had grown up to be empty-headed playboys. Their mother might have redeemed them, but she had been hounded to her death. It would be doing no favors to spare them for her sake.

The other reason he would not fail was the enchantress. She, too, was an omen. His goddess was bringing the magic to him. Perhaps even today!

> Round the wraith dark water bears
> Silent fish o'er ragged stones.
> Far beneath the placid waves
> A septic river heaves and runs.

chapter sixty-seven

CYMER ABBEY
WALES

rom her first glance at the ruined abbey, gray-stoned and tumbling down, Maren was reminded of a gothic novel. Unlike the graceful Llanthony Priory or the substantial vaulted Valle Crucis Abbey, this monastery was creepy. The guide was a man dressed in the rough clothing of a shepherd.

None of this deterred Professor Davies, who was in transports over the ruin. "This was probably the poorest of the Cistercian monasteries," he pronounced. "It was never even finished." He pointed to the remains of the tower. "See? That should have been built over the central crossing. But the east part of the chancel was never completed, and so when they decided finally to build their tower, they put it on the west end."

"Tell me," Anthony said to the guide, "have you ever heard of the Brothers of *Castell cadarn a'i safle grymus ar ben y graig?*"

Maren heard the man reply enthusiastically in Welsh, and for a moment her hopes soared. But then she saw him shake his head.

Another dead end. And she was so tired. Where would they go from here?

It had begun to drizzle a fine, Welsh mist. Winding her shawl around her head, she turned into the ruin to find what shelter she could. There was really not much to be had, except on a short staircase between two walls.

She found a boy she guessed to be about twelve sitting on the steps whittling. "Is that man your dad?" she guessed.

He nodded solemnly. "I have a little girl," she said conversationally. "She's littler than you. What are you carving?"

"Pryderi," he said shortly.

Maren wracked her memory. She knew she should know who Pryderi was. He was very important in Welsh mythology. Then she remembered. The reference was, perhaps, unfortunate. "The prince who was kidnapped when he was three nights old."

He looked up at this, his eyes a clear sky blue, surrounded by thick black lashes. "You know about Pryderi?"

"A little. My sister sometimes told stories about Rhiannon and Pwyll and how Pryderi was kidnapped and everyone thought Rhiannon did it."

"I like the old stories," he said, simply.

"I'll bet you have a good imagination, then. My daughter makes up stories about everything she sees."

"Has she ever been to Cymru?"

"Not yet. But she's on her way. She should arrive sometime tomorrow afternoon." It gave Maren immense comfort to talk to another child about Claire.

"You should take her to the mountains," he advised. "That's where the legends still live."

Settling herself a little more comfortably against the stone wall, she said, "What legends?"

"Any legend you like," he said, shrugging his shoulders. "The mountains talk to you. They tell you secrets. I go there with the sheep. Sometimes for days."

This was far more entertaining than listening to old Dr. Davies prattle on. "What kind of secrets do they tell you?"

"Every time it's something different. My great-granddad is famous for his stories. Some day I'm going to be like him."

"Oh? He's a bard, then?"

The black-haired boy nodded and exhibited his carving with some pride.

"Ah, yes," she said kindly. "I can see. You've made him part horse."

"What's your little girl's name?" he asked.

"Claire."

"That's a nice name. If she likes stories, you should take her to the Roman Steps."

"The Roman Steps? What are they?"

"No one knows. That's why you should take her there. The mountains talk to children, my great-granddad says. Maybe they'll tell her what they are."

"Have they told you anything?" she asked curiously.

"Oh, yes!" He looked up at her, black eyes glistening. "I'll tell it like great-granddad would, if you like."

"Okay." She hoped the story would not be a long one, for her seat was not very comfortable.

"In the old days," he began, "when Wales was ruled by Prince Owain—you know who he is, don't you?"

Maren perked up. "Oh, yes! He rebelled against King Henry in 1400."

"Yes, that's right. Well, in the old days, there was a grand building built over the Roman Steps. You can see all the stones around it, but

G . G . V A N D A G R I F F

it's not a ruin like this, because wicked Prince Henry destroyed it all. Not one stone left on top of another. But he couldn't destroy the Roman Steps because they were magic."

"How do you know?" she asked, intrigued by the boy's confident manner.

"There's a carving I found. It's on one of the rocks near the steps. I think it used to be part of the floor of the grand building."

"Oh? And what's on this carving?"

"The Red Dragon," he said significantly. "King Arthur's Red Dragon. Prince Owain Glyndwr's flag. And it's carrying a cross. Not an English cross. A Cymric cross."

Maren went very still. Could this be significant? Could the grand building have been a monastery?

"How far is this place from Harlech Castle?" she asked.

"Oh, the Roman Steps are the main way through the Rhinog Mountains to Harlech. It's the way the shepherds travel. My great-granddad said our family used to have a farm up there, when Owain was prince. But Henry burned it. He burned everything."

"What's your name?" she asked, her hands clenched in her lap.

"Owen," he said. "That's how the English say it. It should be Owain."

"So, you're named for him."

The boy nodded.

"Owain, I think my little girl would really like to see that place. Could you take us there, say, the day after tomorrow? I'd pay you five pounds."

The boy darted his head out to see if his father was watching. Maren turned and saw that he was occupied fully by Dr. Davies.

"Five pounds?"

"Five pounds."

"Where can we meet? I have a bicycle."

258

"Can you ride to the castle? It's a long way from here."

He laughed. "My gran can take me tomorrow in her old Mini. She's always wanting me to come stay with her. That's when I go into the mountains. She still has sheep, you see."

"Your father won't mind?"

His eyes darkened with pain. "No. He never minds."

Growing more excited at this private expedition, Maren said in a proper conspirator's voice, "We'll meet as soon as it's light, then. Day after tomorrow. By the front gate to Harlech Castle."

They shook hands.

chapter sixty-eight

CYMER ABBEY
WALES

William Dunstan sat in the cab of his lorry and watched as his bigamous wife and her cohorts climbed back into the Range Rover. From his vantage point on the small hill, he had seen Maren separate herself from the others and go to talk to a boy. He watched her go from relaxed and chatty to keenly interested. And they had struck a bargain of some sort. At least, they had shaken hands.

It could be nothing. But on the other hand, the lad might know something. It wouldn't hurt to find out.

He waited until the Rover was out of sight and then slowly, with the air of a put-upon laborer, climbed down from his lorry. He pretended to inspect what remained of the pathetic abbey. It never could have amounted to much. As ruins went, it wasn't terribly evocative. And what would a turnip farmer be doing at a place like this? Probably asking directions.

The father paid him no attention whatever, engaged as he was in counting the coins he'd been given in tips by the departing company. Approaching the boy, he asked, "Can yer help a man, lad?"

"Depends," the boy said, not taking his eyes from his whittling. To the eyes of the man calling himself William Dunstan, it looked as though the thing in his hands were some species of deformed horse.

"I'm looking fer his lor'ship," he said cryptically.

"He lives in England this time of year. Someone must be pulling your leg if you think you can off-load your lorry on him."

Pulling the cap off his head, William Dunstan slapped it against his thigh. "That's the gentry for yer—orders this lot and then up and leaves. I thought that was him here a minute since. Little old chap in the overcoat."

The boy shook his head. "You're wrong."

"Saw you talking to a pretty lady."

The whittler brightened. "She's all right. Give me five pounds, what's more."

He straightened. So! He'd been right. "Oh, and what might that be for? Yer horse?"

"No. But I might give it to her little girl. I'm taking them to . . . " He trailed off and looked up, straight into William Dunstan's eyes.

The man smiled his most disarming smile and said with a deprecating laugh, "You and the pretty lady have a secret, now?"

The boy returned to his whittling. William Dunstan took out his wallet and placed a ten-pound note beside the boy on the step. "I like secrets, too."

The boy looked from the note to the giver. "I'm no snitch."

Sighing, the erstwhile turnip farmer shed his assumed persona and straightened to his full six feet. "I see I'm going to have to take you into my confidence. I'm no farmer. I'm a businessman. Rich, I am. And that lady's my wife." Taking out his wallet again, he displayed his wedding photo. The boy examined it seriously.

"I'm having an adventure," William Dunstan confided. "She doesn't know I'm here. It's a surprise."

The boy looked him up and down, obviously giving him more attention now that he'd heard the posh accent. "You're Claire's father?"

The question startled him, but he nodded without hesitation.

"Will she be happy to see you?"

"Happy as a grig. I've a present for her."

"What is it?"

William Dunstan wracked his brain for a suitably grand present. "A pony," he said finally.

"Well, the trail's too steep for anything but a donkey," he said. "She'd probably rather have a donkey to ride. I've been sitting here worried she might not make it up to the steps."

"A donkey it is, then! Where should I take it?"

Snatching up the ten-pound note, the boy grinned. "Front gate of Harlech. At dawn. Not tomorrow, but the next day."

So. Claire was coming to Wales. And it sounded as if they were going treasure hunting. How providential that his step-daughter would be on hand. Perhaps he could interest Maren in a trade of sorts. Aided by his SIG-Sauer, he just might be able to convince her.

Chapter Sixty-Nine

Chief Commissioner Braden had not been happy when his mobile rang at one A.M. Maren had gone to bed shortly after their return from Cymer Abbey, but he had stayed up later than usual, drinking whiskey with Llewellyn, discussing the unraveling of Robert O'Neill's life. It had been a coup for the chief inspector, and he was happy for him. He'd worked hard, and he hadn't had the advantages some of his contemporaries had. This should stand him in good stead.

The call on his mobile caused Braden to shoot out of bed, dress quickly, and drive like the devil back to Llangollen. The last thing in the world he expected had happened. The would-be Glyndwr had turned up at his flat, drunk as a lord, singing "Memory" from *Cats*. Why wasn't he in Harlech, shadowing Maren on her hunt for the Arthurian manuscript?

He arrived in Llangollen before dawn and met Sergeant Wincombe, who had been keeping vigil from the window of a hair-dressing establishment across the street.

"He's stayed put," the stout, blonde policewoman informed him.

"You must be all in," Braden said sympathetically. "As soon as we've finished here, go get some sleep. I still need you to meet that airplane later this morning, though. I'd send someone else, but I promised the mother it would be someone who would be good with the girl."

"Don't worry. I had my sleep out yesterday afternoon while Constable Sewell took over the watch."

"But you have to drive all the way back to Harlech this afternoon," Braden objected. "I'm sorry for it, but the mother is understandably anxious to see her daughter." With sudden decision, he flipped open his mobile. "Tell you what. You have a kip in the rear seat with the girl, and Quinn will drive you. I'll just give him a ring."

When these arrangements were made, they walked across the street to ring "Owain Glyndwr's" bell.

A stringy, middle-aged creature with long, tangled gray hair and bloodshot eyes answered the door at last. When the chief commissioner flashed his ID, the man peered at it, held it at arm's length, and at last deciphered it.

"What do you think I've done?" he asked wearily.

"I don't know yet, frankly," Braden replied. "May we come in?"

"Place is a bit of a mess," the suspect confessed. "We'd better talk here."

This aroused suspicion in the chief commissioner's breast, but he had no warrant. "The best thing you could possibly do for yourself is to tell me without delay where you've been."

"Why on earth should I?"

"See here. I'm chief commissioner of MI-5. This is serious, mate."

Alarm flashed in the marble-like eyes. "I've got nothing to hide. I was in church. Choir contest in Westminster Abbey, as a matter of fact." The man yawned hugely without covering his mouth. "Won it, too. Got to celebrating and didn't make it home until the wee hours."

The chief commissioner stifled a sigh. The man's alibi was too easily checked for it to be false.

Nevertheless, Sergeant Wincombe asked, "When did you leave for London?"

"A week ago. Went down to see the sights. Free bus. Stayed with my auntie."

"Name? Telephone? Address?"

The man was more awake now and stared at them with patent hostility. "Gwendolyn Masefield. Married one of your lot, if you can believe it. Her husband's a copper. Getting on for retirement now." He gave an address in Putney and a telephone number.

Braden pulled out his mobile and rang the number on the spot. Gwendolyn Masefield corroborated her nephew's alibi without hesitation. "That glad I was to have him leave, too. His room looks like he's been living with pigs." She cut the connection decisively.

"I don't suppose you have plans for the next few days?" the chief commissioner inquired without much hope.

"Darts tournament. Can't miss that," the man said languidly, leaning on the doorframe, insolence radiating from him like a bad smell. Come to mention it, he did have a bad smell. Braden pressed on.

"Here in Llangollen?"

"At the pub. Next corner. The Bird and Beast."

Well, he should be easy enough to keep an eye on. But if this man wasn't the right "Glyndwr," who had left the poem in Maren's room? And who the devil was threatening the Prince of Wales?

CHAPTER SEVENTY

BYRDIR HOUSE
HARLECH, WALES

I t was a wonderful feeling to awaken to a rainy morning in a toasty, quilted bed, knowing that today Claire was safe and on her way to Harlech. Maren stretched her full length and looked at the clock. It was seven A.M. She had slept for fourteen hours straight. Rachael's cotton nightgown was not suited to the weather, however. Cozy as she was under her down comforter, she wished for her L. L. Bean flannel pajamas. Ian had hated them.

Ian. What had become of Ian? Was he still dogging their trail, on the track of that manuscript? Undoubtedly. Her sense of well-being dipped somewhat, and sighing, she sat up. Something white lay on the slate-colored carpet just this side of the door to her room. A creepy sense of déjà vu overtook her. Not again. *Glyndwr.*

From sun to sun
My heart reveres
Sweet Maren's walk.
Her hair appears
Like fire and gold.

Rich treasure hidden
In the biers
Of kings long dead
By Celtic meres
Pales as glass to angel's tears

When Maren's eyes calm all my fears.

Maren felt the hair on her bare arms rise as goose bumps spread over her entire body. This was more than creepy. It was downright scary. Such poetry might be all very well under different circumstances, but on the carpet on a cold, rainy September morning when there was a madman loose, it was petrifying.

She shook herself. The night before last she had very nearly been murdered. Her daughter had been rescued from a murdering drug lord. And she was scared of *poetry?*

Nevertheless, she must show it to Chief Commissioner Braden right away. This Glyndwr must be nearby. Here in Harlech.

After a shower, Maren put on the warmest things she could find. She layered three of Rachael's cotton sweaters over her knit skirt and pulled on tights and her knee-high boots. Then she picked up the saffron Shetland shawl and twisted it together with the sage. She looked like a patchwork quilt.

Downstairs, all the men except the one she wanted were breakfasting. Llewellyn sat by himself eating a boiled egg. Cole and Anthony shared a table and a newspaper with Griffith. Even old Dr. Davies was down, eating a full English breakfast with a napkin tucked under his chin. Everyone stood at her entrance.

"Maren," Anthony greeted her warmly. "Did you sleep well?"

Thrusting the poem behind her back, she replied, "Yes, thank you. Does anyone know where Chief Commissioner Braden is?"

The chief inspector looked at her sharply and then, abandoning his egg, walked to her side. "Braden was called away. What is it?"

Maren hesitated. "May I see you alone for a moment?" she said finally.

"Of course. Come along to the lounge."

As she exited the dining room, she caught Anthony's glance. It was puzzled. Feeling his eyes on her back, she followed the chief inspector into the lounge, where they sat on the couch in the bow window overlooking the street.

She put the sheet of poetry into the policeman's hands. "This was on my carpet this morning." As he read, she twiddled the fringe of her shawls. "It's the same handwriting as before."

"Undoubtedly," Llewellyn said, taking out his mobile phone. "This is serious." He scrolled down the little screen on his phone and pushed a button. After a moment, he said, "Chief Commissioner, Llewellyn here. We have a problem." He told the MI-5 man what she had found. "This obviously indicates that this madman is close by."

"Certainly," he said after a moment. Handing Maren the phone he told her, "He wants to talk to you."

"Maren, listen carefully," Braden's voice advised. "We think the plot to assassinate the Prince is going to come off this weekend. He's arriving at Caernafon today for a pageant. Sunday is the anniversary of Glyndwr's uprising. We've got a watch on, of course, but we think this chap's going to strike at Bangor Cathedral on Sunday." She stopped playing with her fringe and looked at the paper in Llewellyn's hands. Small, block capitals. The handwriting of a madman? "He obviously has fixated on you. I have no idea what's behind it, but I want you to be very careful. Trust no one. That includes Sergeant Cole. I don't like that fellow. He's overly well-bred.

"That leads me to something else. I'm acquainted a bit now with all these chaps who are with us, and though it's happened to me only once before, I think we may be dealing with a Jekyll-Hyde personality here."

"Multiple personality disorder?" she said, with a feeling of unease. "I've seen it in my work before. People have another personality they're not even aware of. Usually it's violent and unpredictable. I hope you're wrong, Chief Commissioner. I'd much rather deal with a straight bad guy."

"Well, it's comparatively rare, but frankly, none of those close to you fits the profile of a maniac. So we have to take it into consideration. I just want you to be on your guard."

Maren shut the phone, her feeling of well-being completely dissipated. The chief inspector took it from her. "The chief commissioner's voice is rather penetrating. I heard every word. He's right, you know. Someone is touched in his upper works."

She looked up at him. His face was, as usual, inscrutable. "How charmingly you put it," she said. "Tell me more about this plot. Can you? Since I seem to be rather involved, for some inexplicable reason."

"The Prince of Wales apparently received a threatening letter, telling him to abdicate or he would be forcibly taken down. He and his sons. It is all to do with Arthur and Glyndwr and this business about uniting the 'old Britain' under Celtic rule."

"And Sunday is the anniversary of the uprising. Hmm." Maren thoughtfully tied a knot in the fringe of her shawl. "That manuscript would be a real help to whoever it is, wouldn't it? Sort of an omen?"

"I don't begin to understand how that kind of mind works, but that probably makes sense. In spite of what the chief commissioner said, Cole would probably understand this thing better than I. Or your friend Dr. Jones." He brushed back the forelock of hair that hung over his forehead. "They're the experts on Arthur."

Maren meditated on this. Both Anthony and Cole *did* seem a bit over the top about Arthur. Gazing out at the street, she saw that the rain had given everything a grim aspect. It seemed to penetrate the little bow window where she sat with Llewellyn. She shivered. Anthony. He *seemed* so sane, so safe, so . . . comfortable. One look from those eyes saw everything in her that had ever been the least worthy or good. But there was Ian. And Robert. She had utterly failed to see the evil in either one of them. And Anthony *did* have an animus against the royal family. He *was* exceedingly proud and even superior about his Welsh heritage. He had dedicated his life to the study of Celts. And as for Arthur, well, he practically worshipped the man. And there was the Dylan Thomas book in Rachael's room and the fact that she would only have opened the door to someone she was comfortable with . . .

"I think the case against Dr. Jones is particularly damning," she told the chief inspector.

"I thought you had a soft spot for the chap," Llewellyn said, shifting his glance away from hers.

Somewhat reluctantly, she enumerated all the points against Anthony. "But I suppose you've thought of all of that."

"Yes. I must say I have. But we mustn't forget Griffith, either."

"What do we know about him, other than the fact that Ian has some sort of hold over him?"

"He's a smarmy sort of bloke. Lies without thinking about it. I believe it's truly pathological. And why is he hanging about? He's no longer a watchdog for your . . . er . . . Hubbard."

"Griffith's a Welsh name," Maren added eagerly. "So is Morgan. When I met him, he was going on rather enthusiastically about heroes. And he did say something about the royal family." She thought back to that morning that seemed so long ago, when she had been so sure of her invulnerability. They had been sitting in the dining room of the Randolph talking about sports. "Oh, I remember!

I said something about the royal family, and he said, 'They're not *my* royal family.'"

"Hmm," Llewellyn drew a finger across his smooth upper lip. "Yes, and we *do* know that he has at least one guilty secret."

"And definite identity issues," Maren added. "I wonder who he really is?"

"The Super ran a check on the fingerprints. He doesn't have a record, but there were one or two of his prints in your sister's room."

Maren perked up. The case against Griffith was growing stronger. "And did he have any explanation for that?"

"Said he searched the room after it was trashed. On Hubbard's instructions."

"You must have checked for fingerprints right after the murder."

"Yes. And in all fairness, I must say that if his fingerprints were there then, we missed them. That's the only reason the fellow's not in gaol."

Maren pulled her shawls more closely around her. The cold from outdoors was leaking through the old windows. "So. What do you know about Cole?"

The man beside her stiffened and said shortly, "Eton and Cambridge. He's an 'honorable,' if you know what that means."

"A junior member of the aristocracy, isn't it?"

"Rather like that, yes. Plenty of money. Took detecting up as a hobby. To be fair, he's rather good at it."

"Do you know, when I first met him, he reminded me of Lord Peter Wimsey. There are unplumbed depths to Cole. It could be my imagination, but I have this idea that he's sort of like one of those big cats—leopards, panthers. I wouldn't want to stand in the way of something he wanted."

"Umm," the chief inspector agreed.

G . G . V A N D A G R I F F

"I suppose he wants to be promoted pretty quickly. He probably doesn't like being a sergeant much."

"No, I'd say Cole's sights are probably set on the chief commissioner's job."

"Where are his people from?" she asked.

"Shropshire, I gather."

"Hmm, that's interesting. Bordering Wales. He could be a closet Welshman. And he's passionate about Arthur."

The chief inspector bit his lip. "I think that's all rot. I've heard him quote Nietzsche, too, but that doesn't make him an anarchist. It just means he's had a classical education. Cole's the type that is all things to all people, if you see what I mean."

"I've got an idea," Maren said suddenly. There was something about the deadpan chief inspector that brought out the mischief in her. "It's a rainy day, and I think everyone's at loose ends. Why don't we all have a chat? We could send King Arthur and the manuscript up the flagpole and see who salutes."

"You must be a fan of Hercule Poirot. I doubt anyone would be that transparent."

"We're talking about someone who's 'touched in his upper works,' remember? He might not be able to help himself."

"Don't get too clever," Llewellyn warned. "You're supposed to be careful, remember?"

CHAPTER SEVENTY-ONE

ON THE A5
LLANGOLLEN TO HARLECH, WALES

Chief Commissioner Braden here." He answered his mobile with a mind fully occupied by his worries.

"Braden, this blasted pageant is ready to begin. It's raining sheets, and I still don't know if you've got a line on that psychotic. The Duchess and the Prince are nervous as cats, and I don't blame them."

It was the Home Secretary himself, and Braden was quite aware that it was not only the royals who were nervous.

"We've got snipers all over the castle, sir. We've used metal detectors. Everyone who's inside has been searched."

"Just where are you?"

"I'm still on the track of Glyndwr. Our original lead proved to be false. But I know right where to look this time. I should have this all sewed up by Sunday. That's the anniversary of the rebellion, of course."

"The anniversary! Don't remind me! It's like offering them on a platter to this madman!"

"You can still cancel Bangor Cathedral, sir. In fact, it might be best."

The Home Secretary seemed to be thinking this over. "I doubt the Prince would care to appear a coward, but I'll have a go at convincing him. You'll have snipers there, as well?"

"It's all laid on, sir. Our men have been watching the cathedral for weeks, searching anyone who might be trying to plant weapons. And everyone who goes in on Sunday will be searched."

The chief commissioner heard a sigh. "We'll go through with it, then. It would look jolly queer if we cancelled at this late date. He's unpopular enough in Wales as it is."

"I trust all will go smoothly with the pageant, sir."

"It had better, Braden. It had better."

The chief commissioner rang off and took a deep, calming breath. Hopefully, his suspects were all snug and secure at Byrdir House under Llewellyn's eye. For some reason, the bit of poetry had shaken the chief commissioner. He wished he had a profiler with him. He would very much like to know what Glyndwr's agenda respecting Maren was. Could Davies shed any light on it? It seemed to have something to do with the Arthur legend.

chapter seventy-two

Byrdir House
Harlech, Wales

nthony glanced up sharply when Maren entered the dining room with the chief inspector. His eyes searched hers as though trying to find a clue there, and she saw disappointment mirrored in them. Standing, he offered her a chair. For some reason, she felt an air of tension in the room, as though everyone had been waiting for her.

She tried a smile, but it didn't come off. Would she ever be able to trust her instincts again? One thing was for certain, she wasn't going to take Anthony with her on the trek in the mountains tomorrow.

"Actually, why don't we go into the lounge? There's a fire there, and it's a little cozier," she suggested. Then, turning to the others, she offered, "Why don't we all go in there, as long as it's raining?"

"Jolly good," replied Professor Davies. "Haven't a clue what I'm doing in Harlech in September. These seaside places are dismal this time of year."

Sergeant Cole rose gracefully from a casual pose incorporating a newspaper, a cigarette, and a cup of coffee. He really was too elegant to be true. Griffith sat hunched over his tea, his ill humor obvious. For once, he said nothing but got up and started toward the lounge. Only Anthony remained. "Fancying yourself as some kind of Miss Marple, are you? I have an idea you think I pinched something, and you and the chief inspector are putting your heads together to entrap me."

Maren willed herself unsuccessfully not to blush. He had an almost supernatural ability to read her that made her want to hide. A fragile thread woven of empathy and shared experience stretched between them. In the part of her she no longer trusted, she knew that that thread was in danger of becoming a bond. Hadn't she sensed something the first time she saw him in the street market, saluting her with his pipe? And now, her lawyer head was telling her idiot heart that he could be a deranged monomaniac.

"You're wrong," she said evenly, coaxing him as she would a recalcitrant witness. "I don't think you've pinched a thing. Come on and join us. You've got nothing else to do, have you?"

"I thought we might look out a bookstore and find something ghoulish to read," he said. "Something twisty with spies and spyesses."

"Spyesses?" She couldn't help laughing.

"Slinky females with cigarettes and black trench coats open at the throat. Oh, and they must have vermillion lipstick. To leave stains on the cigarettes, you know."

She grinned at him. It was impossible not to. "They have cable TV here. Maybe there'll be an old Marlene Dietrich film."

"Actually I was thinking of Lauren Bacall. I don't know that she ever played a spyess, though. But one glance from those eyes, and I would have betrayed my country in a heartbeat."

Eyes. He *would* talk about eyes. She turned away and walked into the lounge. She must keep her head on straight. The Prince's life might depend upon it.

She found all the men sitting around the fire, lighting pipes and cigarettes. Except Llewellyn. He stood at the window and watched the rain. Obviously, he didn't approve of her ploy.

chapter seventy-three

BYRDIR HOUSE
HARLECH, WALES

O*h, she was game, his goddess.* Owain Glyndwr felt himself swell with pride in her. What a fitting mate she would make for him! She was the only thing that made this unbearable waiting possible. It was a pity they didn't have the omen, but her magic was strong. It empowered him all by itself. He could feel the legends stir in him, grand and daring. There was no deed he would not do for her. Slaying a straw-stuffed prince seemed far too tame.

> *The lamentation in the hills*
> *For her who left us crying*
> *Cannot atone for Celtic blood*
> *That spilt before her dying.*

CHAPTER SEVENTY-FOUR

xcept for Professor Davies, who was filling his pipe, and the chief inspector, who continued to contemplate the rain, the men in the lounge sat looking at Maren. She was reminded suddenly of the hush before a performance. Was it her imagination, or were they all as keyed up as she was, wanting to thrash out this strange situation? If so, the soundtrack would have to be a Rachmaninoff piano concerto—ominous, outwardly melodic but fraught with almost unbearable tensions. Hopefully, like the Rachmaninoff, it would end in a crashing crescendo or two.

She felt the distant threat like the rolling in of storm clouds. Which one of these people was Owain Glyndwr and planned to kill the Prince on Sunday? Which of these people was her secret stalker? Three pairs of eyes studied her—Anthony's curious green and gold, Griffith's agitated gray, and Sergeant Cole's lazy clear blue.

"Well," she said, "you know there's one thing I've really been wanting to ask you, Mr. Griffith."

"Lewis," that man said. "That's my first name. What is it?"

279

"What are your views on King Arthur?"

He stared at her, his face more blank than she'd ever seen it.

"King Arthur?" Griffith stalled. "Oh, well, I had a childhood fancy for him. I mean, who didn't? Have you seen *First Knight*? Sean Connery did a bang-up job as Arthur."

"Why are you so interested in this manuscript?" she persisted.

His right eyebrow jerked up. "Well, um, naturally I'd like to see it. I mean, who wouldn't? It's rather like discovering an Egyptian tomb."

"Like Tutankhamen, in fact?" Maren probed.

"Rather. But more meaningful for the average Brit. I mean, Arthur is one of our greatest heroes."

"So you believe he really existed?" A secondary theme entered on the piano's left hand.

"It would be rather shattering to find out for certain, don't you think?" Griffith's eyes challenged hers.

"See here, Maren, why are you grilling this chap about Arthur?" Anthony objected.

"Let's just call it a litmus test," she said, dismissively. "Detective Sergeant, do you believe he's Britain's greatest hero?"

Cole shrugged. The music slowed melodramatically. "Insofar as we could be said to have a hero. Have you read much Joseph Campbell? Every culture has its Arthur. It's the power of myth. Seems to exist even in the most savage races. I'm not certain he's not completely apocryphal."

She pounced. "The other day you said I couldn't begin to understand his mystique."

"It's true. You're an American. I would say that you're still looking for an Arthur. You haven't been around long enough to have mythic legends."

"I think the Native Americans would probably disagree with you there."

"But you haven't adopted their legends, have you? No, the closest you come to Arthur is Abraham Lincoln—the martyr to emancipation."

"Lincoln was not apocryphal."

"Arthur is idolized even in America," Anthony put in. "Rachael was chair of the American Arthurian Society. She went to conferences all over the States. She was as keen on this manuscript as anyone."

An idea occurred to Maren with the subtlety of a grace note and sent her tripping down a path she hadn't even considered. "Detective Sergeant Cole, you don't want this manuscript to be found by an American, do you?"

For the first time in her acquaintance with him, the detective sergeant squirmed uncomfortably and his gaze faltered. "If it exists, it's a British antiquity," he said flatly. The decree of generations of privilege echoed in his voice.

"Actually, it's Celtic," argued Anthony. "It should stay in Wales. Particularly if it's found here."

"It's probably time for me to come out of the closet, now," Lewis Griffith stated in a different voice from those Maren had heard him use before. The crescendo peaked. "I'm actually a professor of ancient Celtic traditions and artifacts at the University of Wales. If the manuscript belongs anywhere, it's there."

Everyone stared at him. Was he telling the truth this time?

There were four Type A personalities in this room, Maren realized. Who really had control? She felt she was fast losing it. "How did you meet James Hubbard?" she asked.

"He never knew my real identity. I was spying on him for my department. We suspected him of dealing in stolen antiquities. Celtic antiquities. Your sister alerted us."

Maren blinked, unable to take this in. "She knew you?" Of all the responses she had hoped to achieve, she had definitely not seen this one coming.

"Yes. She had seen some things in his antiques store before you ever met him, and she corresponded with me. We knew each other professionally. She wasn't certain enough to go to the authorities, but she knew I was an expert. When Hubbard came over here, I made a point of cultivating him. Even made him think I was a cocaine addict. He deals drugs, you know. Or his wife, Susan, does." He paused and squared himself in his seat. Cymbals were clashing in Maren's head. The concerto was over. Rachael had *known* Ian was crooked even before she married him? Had it been her sister's idea of revenge not to tell her?

"I don't have any intention of letting him get his filthy hands on that manuscript," Lewis Griffith continued. "It would disappear entirely. Probably into some Arab's private collection."

"Well." Maren's ears rang with the sound of his words. She forgot Glyndwr and Arthur, forgot the intricate game she was playing. "Do you have any idea why she didn't tell me?"

"She planned on telling you when you came over. That's one of the reasons she wanted you to come," Griffith said.

Anthony was looking at him oddly. "You seem to have known her fairly well. I never heard her mention you."

For the first time, the ginger-haired man grinned. "Well, she wouldn't, then, would she? Can't say she spoke to me of you, either."

At this moment, Llewellyn intervened. "This could all be another of his fairy stories, Maren. But this one's easily enough checked. They'd never heard of a Morgan at the University of Birmingham." Pulling out his mobile he asked directory assistance for the number of the University of Wales. The room remained silent while he was put through, except for the deaf Professor Davies, who, oblivious, was humming "Men of Harlech."

To Maren's distress, Lewis Griffith was exactly who he claimed to be. "Excuse me," she said, making for the door of the lounge. Her head hurt. Her heart hurt. She wanted to be alone to absorb the depth and ramifications of Rachael's betrayal. That was all she could think of now.

Anthony followed her to the door. His eyes held their dark look of compassion. "I'm sorry, Maren. This must hurt dreadfully."

She was surprised that he could sense her wound, under the circumstances. "Did you ever know there was anyone else?" she asked him quietly.

"She never gave me any kind of right. I told you the feeling was all on my side. But, I must say, this tarnishes her image somewhat."

"Don't," she said, laying her hand on his sleeve. "I hurt Rachael badly. She confided in me, you see. And Patrick and I ran off without a word. It must have been hell for her. It obviously twisted her in some way."

Maren climbed the stairs to her room. Going slowly to the window, she traced a raindrop's descent with her finger. Rachael. Gentle, Celt-obsessed Rachael. The wound cut too deep for crying. And she had let herself in for it. Hadn't she? She thought of Anthony's worship of her sister and felt what a blow this must have been to him, as well. Lewis Griffith had a natural extrovert's exuberance and charm, but for Maren, he was nonexistent next to the complex Anthony who could make love with his eyes.

Startled at the direction her thoughts were straying in, she moved away from the window and lay down on the bed. She must leave all this business with Rachael behind. Her sister hadn't deserved to be murdered. It occurred to her that Griffith could now be counted among the small ranks of those whom Rachael would have admitted to her room. And he was certainly obsessed with the manuscript. As good a candidate for Glyndwr as Anthony and certainly better than D.S. Cole, who seemed far too lazy and detached to plot to kill the Prince. But then she remembered her initial assessment of him. Beneath that laziness, she had thought he was dangerous. Had that just been her faulty intuition making up romantic mysteries again? But then there was Braden's idea of a Jekyll-Hyde personality. Was intuition really any good at all in this situation?

Thinking of her faulty intuition brought her by degrees to Ian. Somewhere out there he was still desperate to get his hands on that manuscript. How close was he? What lengths would he go to? He had that gun. She mustn't forget the gun. She would take the chief inspector with them on their dawn hike. After all, she would have Claire with her by then. She certainly didn't want an encounter with someone who carried a gun.

chapter seventy-five

C hief Commissioner Braden had called Llewellyn to the station for a conference. Hearing about the confrontation in the lounge, he nodded. "So we've got Dr. Jones and Dr. Griffith as possibles. Not only for Glyndwr but for the murder of Rachael Williams, as well. Now, let's see what we can dig up on Cole. The department should have done a fairly extensive check on him when he came on. I've had his records faxed here."

Holding up a sheaf of papers, he nodded to the chief inspector to take a seat. Together they went through the file.

"Huh! That's interesting," remarked Braden after a few moments. "Mother's name was Williams-Ellis. Wasn't that the name of the chap who designed Portmeirion, that fairy-tale Italianate place?"

"I wouldn't know, I'm afraid. He was in the other car when we drove through there. Very quiet about his family. I gather that in his class it's not considered quite the thing to talk about one's people. I do know his father's family is from Shropshire."

"Near enough to Wales," said the chief commissioner.

chapter seventy-six

*W*hen Claire, bedraggled but matter-of-fact, walked through the door with the plump police sergeant, Maren's eyes instantly filled with tears. Running to her daughter, she scooped her up into her arms and twirled around with her in the foyer of the guest house.

"Clairey! I'm so happy to see you I could eat you up!" Just holding her daughter to her infused her with a warm, relaxed peace she hadn't felt in days. Claire had always been her own private anti-anxiety pill. And she was safe! Safe! And she hadn't been molested or cut into tiny pieces. Maren's tears spilled.

Her daughter squirmed so she could see into her mother's face. "Why are you crying, Mommy? And why are you wearing those funny clothes?"

The policewoman watched the reunion with obvious complacency, though she looked dead tired. "Is the chief commissioner about?" she inquired.

"I think he's at the police station with Chief Inspector Llewellyn.

Thank you so much for meeting Claire's plane and seeing to my mother."

"We had fish and chips. Wrapped in newspaper!" Claire told her.

"Oh," Maren put Claire on her feet. "I must repay you."

"Don't worry, Mrs. O'Neill. It's on the department. Now, I'll just push off, if you don't mind."

"Thank you again!"

"Thanks, Lady Policeman!" Claire added.

It was still raining as the denizens of the lounge walked out curiously to meet the new arrival. Not waiting an instant, Maren's daughter rushed up to Anthony and threw her skinny arms around his legs. "Daddy!"

Anthony looked up, amused, and met Maren's eyes.

"He's not your daddy, Peanut," she said hastily, pulling Claire away. "That's Dr. Jones, a friend of Aunt Rachael's. And this is another policeman, Detective Sergeant Cole." The detective sergeant gave her a mock bow. "And this is another friend of your aunt's, Dr. Griffith."

"Why did she need so many doctors?" Claire wanted to know. "Was she sick?"

They spent the late afternoon getting outfitted for their "treasure hunt" the next day. As a starting point for hikes into the Snowdonia range, Harlech possessed shops that had boots small enough even for Claire. Maren also furnished them with down vests and mackintoshes, in case it proved to be another rainy day. It felt so good to be buying clothes for Claire that Maren nearly forgot the purpose behind it.

That evening, the men, including Chief Commissioner Braden, all went out of their way to charm the new addition to their numbers. Lewis Griffith surprised everyone by his familiarity with nursery rhymes. Cole and Anthony, who had both sung Gilbert and Sullivan at university, performed a duet from *HMS Pinafore*. Dr. Davies fed her peppermints from his own secret stash. And the chief commissioner showed an amazing dexterity with the harmonica he evidently carried in his pocket. Only Llewellyn refused to display a talent. But he made up for it by allowing Claire to wrestle him to the floor and treat him as a jungle gym. Never had Maren seen the chief inspector so lighthearted. It warmed her to see his taciturnity relax into a genuine smile of surprised delight.

But underneath all the gaiety, Maren knew they were waiting. Waiting to see if anyone would crack before Sunday. And despite the chief commissioner's skill with the harmonica, no one could possibly underestimate the resources of MI-5.

chapter seventy-seven

GATE TO HARLECH CASTLE
WALES

The dark morning was heavy with a translucent mist that put Maren in mind of ghosts of warriors in Arthurian armor and monks in dark brown habits. Owen was waiting for them at the gate, dressed like any shepherd boy in work pants, checked shirt, and sturdy work boots.

"We must wait," he informed them uneasily, looking into the mist.

"For what?" Maren demanded, surprised. "Oh, by the way, this is my friend Chief Inspector Llewellyn. And, of course, this is Claire." Turning to her companions, she said, "This is Owen."

The boy looked away. "I didn't know you were bringing a policeman."

"It's just for protection. There's someone out there who's a little too interested in the magic, Owen. I don't want him to hurt anyone."

Showing signs of alarm, he said, "It's never your husband?"

"What do you know about my husband?" Maren asked sharply.

"We'd better get away if you don't want to see him. He's coming with a donkey for Claire."

She didn't waste time asking him how he knew but just said, "Tell us where to go."

"Maybe we should go by car to Llanbedr. It's close to there. I'm afraid Claire won't be able to make it if we walk all the way."

As they strode away into the enveloping mist, Claire heard rapidly approaching footsteps behind them. "Hurry, Owen, we're parked behind our guest house. Just down the street."

Chief Inspector Llewellyn hoisted Claire into his arms, and they broke into a run. The footsteps behind them did, too. But they made it to the safety of the Range Rover, which Llewellyn unlocked hastily, and soon they were on their way, directed by the boy, to the little village of Llanbedr.

From this tiny village at the foot of the great Rhinog Mountains, Maren could see below them the mist that ran down to the sea.

"Pity we can't see the view," Llewellyn remarked.

"I want to ride on your back," Claire told him.

"Up you go, then." The policeman knelt so she could climb up on him and tucked her legs over the crooks in his arms.

At that point, they heard an engine and saw a diffuse light climbing through the fog.

"Can we go any further at all by car?" Maren asked.

"We could go to Cym Bychan, if this car has four-wheel drive," Owen offered.

"It does," Llewellyn said, swinging Claire back into the rear seat. "Off we go."

The roads were worse than secondary and very rocky, suitable, really, only for sheepherding. After half an hour, Owen declared that they had gone as far as they could go. Above them, out of the mist, rose an enormous sedimentary rock covered in heather.

"That's Rhinog Fawr," he told them.

Llewellyn stood as though entranced. "It's been many years since I've been in the mountains."

This was so unlike his usual impatience that Maren smiled. She had watched behind them, and no car had followed.

"Can you feel the magic, sir?" the boy asked.

"Oh, yes," he answered, tousling the boy's hair. "I can feel the magic."

They began their walk, and Maren was exceedingly glad of the policeman's company, for the going was rough. Not only was the climb steep and rocky, but the heather was long, springy, and surprisingly tough. Owen gamboled ahead of them, sure as a mountain goat.

"This is my favorite place. I think good witches live on the Rhinog Fawr."

"What do good witches do?" Claire wanted to know.

"They protect Cymru from the English. This is where Owain Glyndwr came to hide from Prince Henry's men. They never found him, you know. Some say he never died at all." Owen spat into the heather. "That's for the English."

"Your name is almost the same as his," Claire observed. "Was he very brave?"

"The bravest man since King Arthur. Some said he *was* Arthur come again."

"King Arthur's s'posed to come again," the little girl informed him.

"*You* know about Arthur?" Owen was clearly surprised.

"Oh, yes. My Aunt Rachael gave me a book. My favorite is the story of his knight Sir Kai. Did you know that he could go nine days and nine nights underwater?"

"And go nine days and nine nights without sleep!" Owen added.

291

In this manner, the youngsters entertained each other as they trudged up the mountain, scourged by rough heather, often sliding on small stones or slick sediment. As the sun rose in the sky in front of them, Maren was stunned by the arid beauty of the place. Here was a different Wales, indeed—treeless, except for tiny, twisted scrub oaks. The mountains were not green but brown and rocky. Suddenly the rising sun shone on a row of smooth, gray stone steps descending into the middle of the wilderness. Clearly ancient, they belonged to no discernible structure.

"I feel the magic, Owen," Maren told him. "Are these the Roman Steps?"

He turned to her, his face glowing. "Yes, ma'am. They must be a miracle, don't you think?"

"I do," she told him, pausing to look around her at the forbidding landscape. "Isn't there a legend about them?"

"No one knows how they came here. But I think they were part of a grand building. One that Prince Henry destroyed."

The morning air seemed to sing something from *Peer Gynt* about the dawn, and Maren saw an enormous hawk glide above them and then dart swiftly down, seize some prey, and take to the sky again. All of her concerns seemed a million miles away. She was here with Claire, safe.

"You were going to show me your special rock," she reminded Owen. "The one with the red dragon."

Llewellyn had been standing mute beside her since he let Claire down off his back. At this he said, "What's this?"

"Owen has a rock he's found. That's why we came up here to look. It's possible these steps could have been part of a ruined monastery."

She stopped, because the chief inspector wasn't listening to her. He was following the boy through the heather over some particularly large rocks that could have once been parts of walls. They stooped over a level spot, and Owen brushed away strands of thick, clingy heather. As Maren joined them, she saw the etching.

The universe went silent as a shiver crept over her body. Instead of the quiet, a haunting trumpet voluntary should be playing. This was a moment out of the ages. How long had that detailed carving lain there, forgotten, unclaimed? The image of the rampaging dragon was beautiful, delicate, clearly done by a master. The face was fierce and proud, and the eyes wide with triumph. In his forepaw he clutched a banner picturing a Celtic cross. Who had made this thing? It was certainly worn by age and weather, but it had been protected by the heather.

Claire had stolen up behind her mother and was clinging at her leg. "What a pretty dragon, Mommy. Can we take it home?"

"Let's just get this thing up and look under it," Llewellyn said, his usually temperate voice commanding.

"Here's something we can pry with," Owen said, hefting a stout stick he'd found nearby.

Maren's scalp prickled in premonition. Could this be what they were looking for? Way up here on this hill, away from everyone and everything? It was a perfect place for a monastery.

Llewellyn seized the stick from Owen and dug with it like one possessed. Claire clapped her hands. "Now we can take it home, Mommy!" Owen scraped out the black soil with his hands.

It proved surprisingly easy to pry the decorated stone from the grip of the earth. In a moment, Maren saw why. Underneath was a hollow. And in that hollow lay something.

Owen said, "It's a magic box!"

Clapping her hands again, Claire repeated, "Magic! Oh, Mommy, this is the *best* treasure hunt!"

Llewellyn had seized the box and was now struggling with the catch. Suddenly it flew open. Maren moved closer. Inside was an animal skin of some sort. "What is it?" she asked.

The chief inspector didn't answer but plunged his fingers into the box and removed the skin, unwrapping it as he did so. In his hands he held a sheaf of parchment.

chapter seventy-eight

THE ROMAN STEPS
WALES

The man who called himself William Dunstan saw the small group at the edge of the strange staircase that had appeared from nowhere. He recognized Maren and Claire. With them was the young boy from the abbey. He was holding a piece of what looked like animal skin, and a tall, dark man resembling some sort of thirties' matinee idol was unrolling a parchment.

The parchment. About time! He had begun to doubt the manuscript's existence. Standing behind a boulder, he formulated his plan as he drew the SIG-Sauer out of his jacket. Claire was doing some sort of fairy dance apart from the others, the boy was crouching over the hole, and Maren's attention was entirely upon the parchment, as was the matinee chap's.

Creeping forward, he held his gun in front of him, both hands clutching the butt, finger on the trigger. No one noticed as he neared Claire. She was singing "Ring around the Rosy." Hadn't anyone taught the child that the song was about the Black Plague?

Suddenly, the chap with the parchment looked up, straight at him. And, ready though he was to shoot, to threaten, those eyes held him with a boldness he had never seen in any human. He looked as if he were a blood-crazed beast after a fresh kill. William Dunstan stood stock-still, unable to utter a sound.

Maren flung around wide-eyed, saw him, and screamed, "Claire, get down. On the ground. Now!"

Her scream released Dunstan from his trance. Rushing forward, he aimed the gun at the beast-man.

"Halt!" the man shouted. "In the name of our sovereign, King Arthur, you will put that weapon down."

Crackers! The bloke was utterly out of his mind! Continuing to advance, Dunstan couldn't take his eyes off the man. In his peripheral vision, he saw that the lad had thrown his young body over Claire's to shield her, crying, "It's the English!"

He felt the heather scratch across his Church's shoes and automatically cursed at the ruin they were undergoing. Then, without warning, he stumbled over a rock and fell to his knees.

The beast was on him in a moment, seizing his gun and shooting.

cbapter seventy-nine

THE ROMAN STEPS
WALES

O wain Glyndwr pocketed the firearm and turned to face his goddess. Her mouth was wide, and she was staring at him round-eyed.

The fairy child had scrambled to her feet and was clinging to his goddess. The lackey went over to her, saying, "It's all right, Claire. It was only the English."

"It was Ian!" the fairy child exclaimed.

"Ian was going to kill one of us if he wasn't stopped," his goddess said, reassuringly. "The chief inspector was doing his job."

Who was the chief inspector? Well, no matter. There was no doubt this parchment was the omen. It was time to leave.

Thrusting the manuscript inside his shirt, next to his skin, he used his mammoth strength to lift his goddess off her feet, sling her over his shoulder, and start down the path through the heather. She was screaming something about Claire, but he could only see armies of men, flocking to him from the hills, the mines, the fishing boats, raising Arthur's standard. Death to the Anglo-Saxons. Pity the lackey was so young. He'd make a splendid warrior.

The magic had just begun.

chapter eighty

BYRDIR HOUSE
HARLECH, WALES

A nthony Jones looked at the bedraggled little being before him. She was trembling with cold, and her teeth were chattering. All she seemed able to do was stare at him out of those great blue eyes. Next to her stood a sullen boy in work pants.

"Where's your mum, then, Claire?"

"The p'liceman took her."

He was stunned. Almost speechless. "And left you in the mountains?"

"I took care of her, sir," the urchin said.

"He grabbed her and took her," Claire continued, tears welling in her eyes. "After he shot Ian."

"Ian? He was there, too?"

"An Englishman," the boy fairly spat. "He was after the magic, no doubt."

"The magic?" Anthony felt increasingly lost as though he had accompanied Alice down the rabbit hole and turned up in Wonderland. Only this was a species of nightmare.

"The dragon," Claire elaborated, as though this would make it all clear.

"There was an old piece of paper," her champion added. "All rolled up. It was in a box. Under the dragon rock."

Maren had found the manuscript! His heart speeded up—and then was lanced with uneasiness. Where was she?

"But I don't understand," he said gently. "Why did she leave you on the mountain?"

"She couldn't help it," Claire sobbed. "The p'liceman carried her. Over his shoulder. She was screaming, 'Claire, Claire,' but he wouldn't put her down. He just kept going!"

Llewellyn? This didn't sound like Llewellyn at all! He must speak to the chief commissioner at once.

chapter eighty-one

Chief Commissioner Braden heard the child's story with gravity. Llewellyn. He gave a deep, sad sigh. It had been Llewellyn all the time, and he had not seen it. "He's mad," he pronounced. "Thinks he's Owain Glyndwr. No doubt he sees this manuscript as an omen. A mandate to assassinate the Prince of Wales in Arthur's name at Bangor Cathedral tomorrow morning." He watched the horror dawn on Anthony Jones's face. "She didn't tell you about it, then?"

Shaking his head, the professor said, "But why did he take Maren?"

"He's fixated on her for some reason. Been sending her poetry. The man's obviously got some sort of brain disorder. Jekyll and Hyde. In his right mind, he's been after Glyndwr, same as the rest of us."

"He couldn't have been shamming it?"

"No, I don't think so. As Llewellyn, he'd never do a thing like this. Straight down the line he is. Smitten with your young lady, though."

Braden could see Anthony Jones, pacing the room in his

agitations, making an effort to think this through. "There *must* be something we can do!"

"You can help, I think," he told him. "This Glyndwr chap. He's completely over the edge now. Thinks he's some sort of legend. Myth. All that."

"All I can think of is that he probably sees Maren in the role of his enchantress," Anthony said at last. "In Celtic legend, the hero is always empowered and enchanted by a goddess who enables him to do great deeds." The man's face was deeply troubled. "Braden, he'll have Maren with him tomorrow. Is there any chance she'll come to harm?"

Deeply saddened, Braden looked from the little girl before him into Anthony Jones's tortured eyes. "Unfortunately, for the good of the nation, we can't allow him to assassinate the Prince. If he tries to use her as a shield . . ." He looked down at Claire. "Well, you see how it is."

"Yes," Anthony replied, his voice grim. "I see how it is. And I won't let anything happen to her, do what you may." Taking Claire's hand, he left the station, throwing over his shoulder, "Maren O'Neill is worth a hundred of any of those Windsors. I hope you remember that when you can't sleep. I, for one, am going to Bangor. That's where he'll have taken her."

chapter eighty-two

ERYL MOR HOTEL
BANGOR, WALES

Maren watched as the tall, magnificent stranger paced the room, talking on his mobile. She couldn't understand a word he said, because he was speaking in rapid-fire Welsh. The Welsh she knew that Chief Inspector Llewellyn had honestly and totally suppressed.

Except that one word, she recalled. At the time she hadn't attached much significance to it, but now it seemed the key to everything. *Annwn*, the Otherworld.

Did this madness all go back to his nanny, then? Had she programmed some part of his brain to be a great hero? To be Glyndwr? To fight for Arthur?

Tomorrow, Braden would have him shot dead before he could even blink. And she mustn't let that happen. In his right mind, he had saved her world. He had found Claire before she disappeared into some remote place in South America. He had avenged Patrick's murder and stymied the Don Benito drug cartel in America. And

303

today he had saved her life and Claire's from Ian's deadly gun. She shuddered. He had rid her of Ian permanently.

And, in a moment of madness, he had surely murdered her sister. Now he was preparing to murder not only the Prince but his sons, William and Harry.

Her only recourse was to try to bring him around. To try to switch off that part of his brain she didn't understand and bring him back into Chief Inspector Llewellyn's consciousness. She wished she knew more about mental illness. But he had called her his goddess, his enchantress. Possibly she could use that to good purpose. If only she knew his first name!

While his back was turned as he paced and talked into his mobile, she searched the inside pocket of his jacket, which lay thrown haphazardly across the bed. Yes! There it was. His official ID. Chief Inspector *Hugh* Llewellyn.

Oddly enough, she felt absolutely no fear for herself. He treated her with reverence, awe. And she knew, once she thought about it, that Owen was perfectly capable of seeing Claire to safety. They, of course, would put Chief Commissioner Braden on to Llewellyn. He wouldn't stand a chance.

Owain Glyndwr shut his mobile and looked at her with shining eyes. "All is in order, my love. The weapon is concealed."

"But, Hugh," she said, trying to sound reasonable, "the cathedral will have been searched for weapons!"

He grinned with a look of canny knowing. "You underestimate your hero. Don't you think I have that all arranged? It has been searched by ap Gruffyd. He is loyal to me."

For the first time, she felt doubt. Was it possible, after all, that he would succeed? Then nothing she could say or do would help him.

"Hugh, listen to me," she said, going to him and smoothing his forelock back from his head in a soothing gesture. "I am Maren

O'Neill. You are a very clever and brave police officer. A chief inspector. You have just saved my life. You uncovered a drug cartel the FBI has been working for years to penetrate. You found out who murdered my husband, Patrick. You saved Claire, my little girl, from being kidnapped. I owe you everything. You are a great man, but you are not Owain Glyndwr."

With a hand, he caressed her hair. "Smile for me, my darling. I would do anything for that smile."

"Then come with me now. We will go far away from here. We can go to the States, and I can show you a whole new world."

"Don't tempt me, my goddess. The deed I must do to earn your love is not yet accomplished. And once it is done, I must go into battle with my men. We will create a new world here in Cymru. In all of Britain!

> No word suffices for the death of love.
> Intuition speaks deceptively of hopeful dawns,
> Of reflowering hearts turning and returning.
> No greenbottle tells of dead men's dreams.

Maren recognized the poetry with a shudder. That Llewellyn could have such a complete alter ego with talents of his own was astounding. How long had he been mad like this?

She was afraid to mention the manuscript. Hugh had secreted it inside his shirt. It was with great patience that she did not ask to see it. She was afraid its words would only inflame him.

"Suppose we watch a little television, Hugh. It might make the time go faster." She hoped that seeing the world as it really was might bring him to his senses.

"I have no time for it," the man declared. "I must commune. Prepare." He sat in a chair next to the window after pulling a small leather notebook from his coat pocket and became absorbed in what she saw was the small, neat printing that had appeared on the sheets of poetry slid under her door. Maren grew increasingly anxious. Would anything bring him out of this madness? Shouldn't she call Chief Commissioner Braden and tell him where to find them?

Then she remembered Ian's gun. Hugh had it tucked into his belt, beneath his jacket, and unless she talked him back into himself, he might shoot Braden on sight. She must keep trying to reach Llewellyn.

Hugh looked up at her then with the longing of a lover in his eyes.

> *Reunion, love, hope, unrevealed desires*
> *Goshawk gliding, sun to shadow, gold to gray to black*
> *Glissade, Fouetté, Jeté, Adagio, Largo, Finale*
> *Endymion, Endow, Endeavor, Endure, Endmost, End*
> *Eneidfaddeu.*
> *Returns to ancient thrones.*

Eneidfaddeu. He said the word in reverent tones, as though it were the key to everything. She backed away from his ardor and for the first time grew frightened. There was no self-defense against this. Hugh's lifetime of submerged passions were in complete control of him now.

chapter eighty-three

hidden in the bushes, Anthony watched the doorway leading from the chancery to the cathedral. It was two A.M., and a man was on duty there, but something compelled him to remain still. The policeman might be overpowered. He seemed a careless chap, smoking cigarette after cigarette as he read a paperback novel by the light of the single bulb in the chancery porch.

All of Anthony's muscles tensed as he thought of the danger Maren must be in. At first, he had been put off by the flesh-and-bloodness of her. Previously he had been attracted to women who were on the ethereal side. But now it was that wholeness that made her so real and so dear to him. He *couldn't* lose her. He refused to let her be shot in some farcical effort to preserve Prince Charles. Pausing only long enough in Harlech to leave Claire in the dubious care of Dr. Davies, who was too deaf to understand what was going on, he had come here, reasoning that Llewellyn would show himself sometime in the dead of night. Davies had promised to put the "sprig" to bed while Anthony had "a night on the town" with her mother.

Claire's high-pitched voice was out of his hearing range, so Anthony knew he would pay no attention to anything she said. He had, with some difficulty, promised her he would bring her mother back, safe.

Could he? What was Maren experiencing? What kind of thing was this deluded being putting her through? The air was freezing cold, but now he knew a different kind of cold. Picturing Maren's open, lively face disfigured with anguish, his imagination dwelt on horrifying images. Everything inside him went still.

There! Someone was coming! He could hear steps on the cobbles. Two sets, he imagined. Then, just as he was struggling to see who was emerging from the darkness, pain crashed into his skull, and all he saw was darkness, deeper than the night.

chapter eighty-four

Glyndwr crept to the door of the chancery, where he had arranged to meet ap Gruffyd, who was guarding the door in his official capacity. His goddess followed in his wake, still calling him by that absurd name: Hugh.

"They're onto you, mate," ap Gruffyd informed him. "The place will be crawling with MI-5 come morning. And Mortimer just caught someone watching from yon bushes. You'd best get along inside." He looked at Maren. "Who the devil is this?"

"My enchantress. She must witness my great deed."

"Never knew you intended to bring a woman. Women are nothing but trouble."

Owain smiled and patted his breast. "This one has brought me my magic. I have the omen. She found it."

Ap Gruffyd's eyebrows went up. "You have the manuscript? The one about Arthur?"

Owain Glyndwr nodded. "As you said, it is time I was getting inside."

His cohort unlocked the heavy door. Owain Glyndwr entered the darkened cathedral and made his way unerringly to the bishop's private chambers. His goddess said, "Hugh! What are you doing?"

That absurd name again. Locking the door with its great key, he said, "Dressing myself for the part." Going to the old wardrobe he pulled out the red and gold satin garments.

"Hugh, think! Would your nanny really want you to kill the Prince?"

He smiled, thinking of his beloved preceptress. "Oh, yes. This was her plan, you see."

chapter eighty-five

C hief Commissioner Braden, accompanied by an insistent Lewis Griffith and a cat-got-at-the-canary Sergeant Cole, addressed Chief Inspector Evans, who stood on guard at the chancery door. "Any action last night?"

"None, sir. Quiet as a tomb. Except for yon man in the shrubbery. I've got him tied up, as you see. Didn't like to leave my post."

"What man?" Braden looked where he was pointing to a spot almost hidden by the vast porch. To his surprise, he saw a bound and gagged Professor Jones.

Going to him quickly, Braden loosed his gag. "What were you doing here, man? Did Evans knock you out?"

The professor spat out the gag. "Not him. Someone came up behind me. Worst possible moment, too. Someone was just approaching the chancery. I didn't have a chance to see who it was. Two people, I think."

Braden spun on Evans. "You didn't hit him?"

"Of course I hit him! Who else?"

"He says he was hit from behind. And that he saw someone coming."

"Well," Evans scratched his bearded chin, "you know what happens when a fellow gets a blow to the head." He tapped his temple with a finger. "Memory goes."

"I know what I saw!" Anthony insisted. "And since his name is Evans, I wouldn't trust him as far as I could toss him."

The guard stiffened. "I've been with MI-5 the past fifteen years."

The chief commissioner said, "I suppose a third of the force is Welsh, but still, I think we'd better have a look round. Has the bishop arrived yet?"

"Came in half an hour since," Evans said. "Before Mr. Beautiful over there came round."

"Well, you're relieved then. Unless you want to take part in the action."

"Wouldn't miss it for the world, Chief Commissioner."

"Then get along inside. Did you find anything in your search yesterday?"

"No, sir."

Braden brooded. "That worries me more than I can say. The Prince will be here in two hours. Can you give it another go?"

"Want me to help, sir?" Sergeant Cole asked.

"I'd like to, as well," Griffith told him.

"And now that I'm untied, I'm going in, too," Anthony Jones insisted. "Evans is lying. I intend to keep an eye on him."

The MI-5 man merely looked scornful. "Who are all these people, sir?"

Braden introduced Cole and Griffith. Then he said of Anthony, "He's been of help. Llewellyn has his young woman hostage."

Now a rueful look came over his subordinate's face. "I didn't know there were going to be any women involved, sir. Women mean trouble."

"You sound like Llewellyn before he lost his mind." Moving past Evans, he entered the cathedral, saying to the others, "You can search anywhere as long as you don't bother the bishop. That's his quarters, down the hall to the right. I'm setting myself up in the gallery above where the Prince will be sitting." Pulling a black Beretta from his pocket, he showed it to his confederates. Thank heavens in matters as dire as this one, policemen were still able to carry weapons.

Evans commenced his search, starting with the pulpit where the bishop would be delivering the sermon Braden imagined he had been preparing for months. Griffith began feeling under the pews, Cole studied the choir seats, and Anthony paced up and down the nave, keeping an eye on Evans. One by one, the sharpshooters arrived, dressed as clerics, spacing themselves throughout the cathedral.

chapter eighty-six

Owain Glyndwr, dressed in the scarlet and gold robes of a bishop, stood at the window watching the arrival of the royal entourage. The Prince was dressed in his ceremonial uniform, ever the gentleman, rigid and smart, waving at a crowd who did not cheer him. Beside him was the adulteress.

"What will happen when the real bishop turns up, Hugh?"

"He's already been disposed of."

"You *killed* the bishop?"

He smiled at her horror. "No. We didn't find that necessary. Ap Dafydd merely bound him up and took him for a long drive up into Snowdonia. He'll be set free when this is at an end. He's a loyal Welshman, I've heard. But we couldn't trust him. His Christian values might get in the way."

"But, Hugh, you say you're doing this in the name of Arthur. Arthur *was* Christian. To the core. He got all his might and strength from his virtue."

He looked at her. Somehow his goddess had missed the point

314

entirely. "And he slew the Anglo-Saxons. Just like we're going to do. Arthur was not afraid to make war. He was the greatest warrior Britain has ever known."

His goddess straightened, and two spots of color burned on cheeks that had grown paler as the night progressed. "But Arthur believed in individual integrity," she urged. "Purity of soul and body. What you're doing is cowardly, Hugh. If you must meet the Prince, you should do so in a fair battle, not kill him by treachery. Arthur never approved of treachery. Don't you remember? It was treachery that put an end to him and his ideals. He was betrayed."

Glyndwr was not unmoved by her plea. He thought of Mordred's betrayal. Guinevere's betrayal. Was what he was about to do some kind of betrayal? Deep inside, in some place he couldn't reach, couldn't reason away, a voice spoke to him. *The Prince will be unarmed.*

"I don't approve of what you're doing," his goddess told him. "You think you're doing it because it is a brave deed that will win my love. But it won't. It will only ensure that we are separated forever. This is not *my* magic." She put shaking hands on the front of his robe and looked up into his eyes, her own earnest. "The man I will always love and revere is Hugh Llewellyn. The man who saved my daughter. The man who avenged my husband. The man who saved me. That man has Arthur's heart. He is good and virtuous and mighty."

Jealousy stirred him, red and ugly. The anger of a savage beast swelled inside as he roared, "Hugh Llewellyn? Just who is this Hugh Llewellyn?" He grabbed her by the throat. He would choke the truth out of her! She was gasping, her beautiful moss green eyes not afraid but terribly, heartbreakingly sad, as though the end of the world had come. His goddess was dying at his hand.

Lightning flashed through his brain, lancing the back of his eyes with its brilliance. For a moment, he was blind. Then he stood, foreign and confused by his surroundings, looking at his hands around Maren's throat.

"He's you, Hugh, he's you," she gasped.

There was a green aura around her head. His own was pounding. He'd had another of his headaches. Another of his blackouts. What was he doing here? What was he wearing? He sank to the floor, clutching his head between his hands. The lightning had been coming so much more frequently of late. Almost every day. But it had never been this bad.

"Maren?" he asked. "Where are we?"

She stooped down beside him. There was a swift tattoo at the door. "Five more minutes, your Grace."

"Your Grace?" he echoed.

Life came into her eyes, and she put a hand to his cheek. "Oh, praise the Lord, Hugh. You've come back."

chapter eighty-seven

aren looked at Hugh anxiously. "You thought you were Owain Glyndwr, Hugh. You were getting ready to kill the Prince."

He shook his head. Maren could see he hadn't taken it on board. Time was of the essence. She had to make him understand. Quickly. "Hugh, you have a brain disorder. Sometimes you think you're someone else."

"Who?" he asked, blankly, surveying the bishop's quarters and the long, scarlet cassock he was wearing.

"You thought you were Owain Glyndwr. You were going to kill the Prince. But it's okay now. You've come back in time."

His peat brown eyes were blank as he struggled to take this in. He pulled the gold miter from his head and stared at it. "It was me? All the time? That madman was *me?*"

"I'm afraid so."

She could see his brain was processing this information, until finally he put his head in his hands. "I was posing as the bishop? Don't tell me I killed him."

"No," she whispered, stroking his hair as if he were a child. "You sent him to Snowdonia."

"But your sister? Did I kill your sister?" he asked, looking up in horror.

"I think it must have been you. I'm sorry. But I know it wasn't really you. You have a sickness. I don't really understand everything about it, but you're not going to go to prison. In fact, I'll see that you don't." She was saddened to her depths at the anguish in his eyes. How could someone as just and upright as Chief Inspector Llewellyn deal with the idea that he was a murderer? It would be impossible.

"I deserve prison," he said uncompromisingly. "Part of me did this. I'm responsible." Then he sagged, his resolution seeming to fail him. "This is the end of me. I'll lose my career, everything. I'll lose you. And Claire. I've never loved anyone before now."

There was pounding on the door now but neither of them paid any heed. "It's time, your Grace."

Maren had absolutely no experience that could compare to the pain Hugh must be feeling. *Was there only justice without mercy in this world?* she asked wildly, scanning her known universe for an answer. No one mourned Rachael's death more than Maren, unless it was Anthony.

The thought of Anthony stopped her tumultuous thoughts with a skid. What would the man say who had made Arthur his life's study? What would his values dictate? His compassion? What would Arthur himself say in such a situation? Certainly he would show mercy. Llewellyn had done his best to fill his divine void with goodness.

"You'll never lose me, Hugh. Or Claire. I owe you everything. We'll come to visit you wherever you are. We'll do everything we can to help you overcome this. King Arthur himself would forgive you for what you have done. It was a tragedy, but he would show you grace. You have been a valiant warrior."

His eyes were downcast. Emanating from him was the chill of the blackest, darkest hell. "But you see, Maren," he looked up, his eyes empty with hopelessness, "I don't believe in Arthur. He was a myth."

"Hugh, there *is* forgiveness for things we can't help." With a flash of insight she knew didn't come from her own mind, she said, "Your body is flawed. You're only mortal. We all need grace."

"No," he said. "I'm a devil."

"Devils are selfish!" she cried in desperation. "They don't care about anyone or anything. They just destroy!"

He tore at the cassock at his neck. "I've got to atone!"

"What do you mean?"

"They're waiting for me out there, aren't they?"

"If you go out there, they'll shoot you on sight," she told him, striving to steady her voice. "Stay with me. I'll get help. I'll get Anthony."

"No, Maren. Who knows what I've done? What I'm capable of doing?"

"You're capable of doing—have done—great good, Hugh. That will surely count in your favor." She kept her voice soothing, torn though she was by his anguish.

"No! Who knows what will happen next time?"

He stumbled to the door. "I'm going out there!"

Maren sprang after him, panic making her swift. She positioned herself between him and the door. But he was strong, as she had reason to know.

Wrenching the door open, he shoved her aside and strode ahead of her down the transept to the nave, where the Prince was waiting. Llewellyn shoved aside a waiting priest, who merely stared after him.

At any moment, he could be shot! Maren ran after him. "Stop, Hugh, stop! Let me go first! I'll explain!"

"No!" he called over his shoulder. "I must atone!"

She caught up with him just as he reached the nave. Feeling the stares of the congregation at this mitreless, unknown bishop, she saw the Prince, wooden-faced, sitting in the front pew. He was holding Camilla's hand.

Maren threw herself in front of Hugh, like a shield. She heard Anthony's voice. "Maren!" Even as she clung to the stalwart Hugh, Anthony tore her away and threw her to the ground, his body shielding hers.

Six separate shots exploded into Hugh's body. As she struggled to sit up, she saw a deep red stain spreading over the entire front of his cassock. In death, his face was calm.

epilogue

THE ROMAN STEPS
WALES

Maren stood on the ancient, mysterious steps and let the wind blow through her loose hair. It was a beautiful fall day, just as the day of Rachael's funeral had been. Once again, her heart was full of grief. Anthony stood beside her, holding Claire's hand.

"It's funny," he said, looking at the hole in the ground from which the manuscript had been retrieved. Ancient, fragile, worn next to Hugh Llewellyn's breast, it had been virtually destroyed by multiple gunshots and blood. Dr. Davies still had hopes of restoring it so that it might be read. "I don't really care about the manuscript anymore." Looking about him at the Rhinog Fawr and the ascent into nowhere of the Roman Steps, he added, "I've been thinking, you see. About everyone's reasons for wanting that manuscript and what havoc it caused. You can't make people believe in a higher law. They have to want to. You were right, Maren."

"A first," she said, reflecting on this sad irony.

Anthony put a comforting arm around her. "The root of the

problem is the inside of people's hearts. Unless they want to change, unless they want grace, King Arthur's ideals don't stand a chance. That's what he finally realized. Change from the inside out is the only kind of virtue that will prevail in the end. Poor Llewellyn."

Maren remembered those last few moments in the Bishop's office. "What does *Eneidfaddu* mean?"

Anthony looked at her in surprise. "It's the Druidic belief that the soul is cleansed of its sins by suffering."

"He said that word. When he was Glyndwr. How odd." She shuddered. "But he thought there was no hope for him. He thought he had to perform some act of redemption."

"Someone's already performed that redemption," Anthony said solemnly.

"What are you talking about?" asked Claire, clearly puzzled by all this grown-up talk.

"Something much better than magic," Anthony told her.

Opening the canister of ashes, Maren cast them onto the wind. "Here's hoping for mercy."

about the author

G. G. Vandagriff graduated from Stanford University and received her M.A. from George Washington University. A lover of history and an avid genealogist, she has long had a fascination with King Arthur and his idealism. Wales is her favorite country to visit, and she enjoys reading about its history, legends, and myths.

The adventure of writing this book could be called "The Case of the Forgotten Manuscript." *The Arthurian Omen* was actually begun years ago. After writing three previous books, G. G. was hospitalized with a serious illness. Part of her treatment was a procedure that caused her to lose her memory and her ability to write. In 2006, new medications were found, and she experienced a miraculous healing, but her memories were not restored. One day, her husband found on the computer an old file entitled "Arthur." Though it was written in an ancient word-processing program, he was able to restore the file and discovered the first eighty-seven pages of *The Arthurian Omen*. G. G. read the manuscript but could not remember writing it. She also discovered among her bookcases a shelf dedicated to King Arthur, the Celts, and Wales. After a great deal of research, she wrote the rest of the novel.

G. G. would love for you to visit her at arthurianomen.com